# THE SPHERE
# OF
# DESTINY

T0001167

# THE
# SPHERE OF DESTINY

*The Sphere Trilogy*
*Book one*

Nassim Odin

ODIN FANTASY WORLD
## 2021

Copyright © 2021 by Naseem Uddin
The following is a work of fiction or fantasy or wonder literature.
Any names, characters, and incidents are the product of the author's
imagination. Any resemblance or closeness to individuals, living or
dead, is absolutely coincidental.

Hardcover ISBN: 978-1-954313-11-8
ISBN ebook: 978-1-954313-00-2
ISBN Paperback: 978-1-954313-06-4

Cover Design: Naboklmuyt
Map: BMR Williams
Cover and map are protected under copyright 2021.

Publisher: Odin Fantasy World
All Rights Reserved. No part of this publications may be reproduced,
scanned, photocopied, or transmitted in any other form, digital or
printed without the written consent and permission of the author
Nassim Odin.
writer.odin@gmail.com
https://www.nassimodin.com

# Reviews

Sharp characterization boosts this leisurely paced but engrossing SF series opener. —Kirkus Review

This fresh take on the concept of an ancient Egypt inspired by aliens will draw readers in with its cultural interactions and tense action. —BookLife Review

I felt like I'm having a live experience in ancient Egypt —TheBigReads

While the marriage of science-fiction to history ... has become a well-known watering hole, Odin nonetheless refreshes the pool by establishing a wholly native point of view from which to view the action, adding a level of authenticity and care that many of its brethren fail to match. (Originality: 8 out of 10) —BookLife Critic Report

★ ★ ★ ★ ★ A nice piece of Sci-Fi novel that truly deserves 10 Stars —Mary L (Goodreads)

★ ★ ★ ★ ★ Each word turned to reality as if watching a film on a big screen —Reviewer 870256 (Net Galley)

★ ★ ★ ★ ★ You can see the depth of research put into this book —Onkangi Okari (Goodreads)

★ ★ ★ ★ Tight pacing in the unfolding of the plot —Catherine M (Goodreads)

★ ★ ★ ★ ★ Thrilling, mesmerizing, and unique work of Sci-fiction —Sarshar (Goodreads)

★ ★ ★ ★ The author has created an intriguing and inventive blend of fantasy and science-fiction —John D Reviewer (Net Galley)

★ ★ ★ ★ ★ The meticulous description incites your brain to the imagination —Nabila H Educator (Net Galley)

★ ★ ★ ★ ★ The story is packed with vivid fantasy and suspense —Charles K (Goodreads)

**Dedication**
*To all the people interested in the pyramids*

# Al-Eard Soundtrack Musical Score

Odin Fantasy World - You Tube Channel

### *The Arrival on Al-Eard*
*Music Artist: Mecheri Kheireddine (khairsound)*

### *The Misery of Space Traveler*
*Music Artist: Armen Voskanian*

### *The Revenge of Hatathor*
*Music Artist: Arkady Akhidzhanov*

⊙Ⴀ ⦂ⵀ⋈⋈⊙ ⵉ⤬⊙⼁ ⟨ⵉⵡⴷⵗⵡ⊙Ο

(As above so below)

# Prologue

I had never thought that I would write a sci-fi trilogy in 2020 and 2021. I had a feeling that I may write one when I grow old and have plenty of time. But during the spread out of the COVID pandemic, I was searching for some online books on Amazon. I found many novels showing up and I read the blurbs of some fiction books that triggered a desire to write my sci-fi fantasy.

Though I had written scientific journals and conference papers, I had no training in writing fiction, nor am I an avid novels reader. The last full novel I read was in 2016.

I would like to thank my family for their constant support, especially my wife, son, and daughter. They were the constant motivation throughout this work. Also, we engaged in long heated discussions on storyline and character flaws. I would like to thank Mr. John Truby for the software Blockbuster which I used to correct the story alignment of this novel. I would like to thank the Stellarium software makers, as this tool helped me a lot in understanding the star Vega alignment and having my own understanding of the Zodiac of Dendera.

I would like to thank Dr. Asad A. Khalid for Arabic translations of some archaic poetry and Mr. Mustapha Louzi and Mr. Anaruz for the Amazigh translations. I would like to thank Mr. Mecheri Kheireddine, Mr. Armen Voskanian and Mr. Arkady Akhidzhanov for the trilogy related musical scores which can now be listened on YouTube. I also would like to thank Anna for developmental editing of the book.

Hope all this effort materializes into an interesting and enjoyable story, which was the primary goal.

*Odin*
*2021*

# The sands of time

In the year 832 AD, during the reign of Abbasid Caliph Al-Mamun, explorers entered the Great Pyramid of Giza for the very first time. Their findings were reported by many medieval Arab historians in their numerous books many years ago; those who first entered the pyramids discovered idols, glasslike substances that could be bent without breaking, metals which did not rust, and an enormous amount of gold.

According to Arab historians Al-Masudi (d. 956 AD), Al-Hasan Al-Saffadi (d. 1317 AD), Al-Maqrizi (d. 1442 AD), and Al-Suyuti (d. 1505 AD), the Pyramids had casing stones with writings over them. The inscription language engraved on the casing stones could only be read by some local Egyptians of that era. One inscription said the Pyramids were built when the Swooping Eagle (the star Vega) was titled towards the zodiac of Cancer. This was referred to the Earth's axis, which precessed (just as a spinning top does) in a time of roughly 26,000 years.

Our planet's northern pole star—or simply, the North Pole—will differ in position from time to time. The reference to the star Vega and the constellation of

Cancer was estimated by some astronomers as roughly 36,000 to 72,000 years old, even before Jesus. In the year 1303 AD, an earthquake caused the fall of the casing stones, which were then used to construct of roads and bridges. Thus, the true facade of pyramids and the inscriptions engraved in their walls were lost in time.

This story weaves around the artifacts found by the explorers who first entered the Great Pyramid of Giza, Egypt. Al-Khidr was among those explorers who entered. And now, on to the story ...

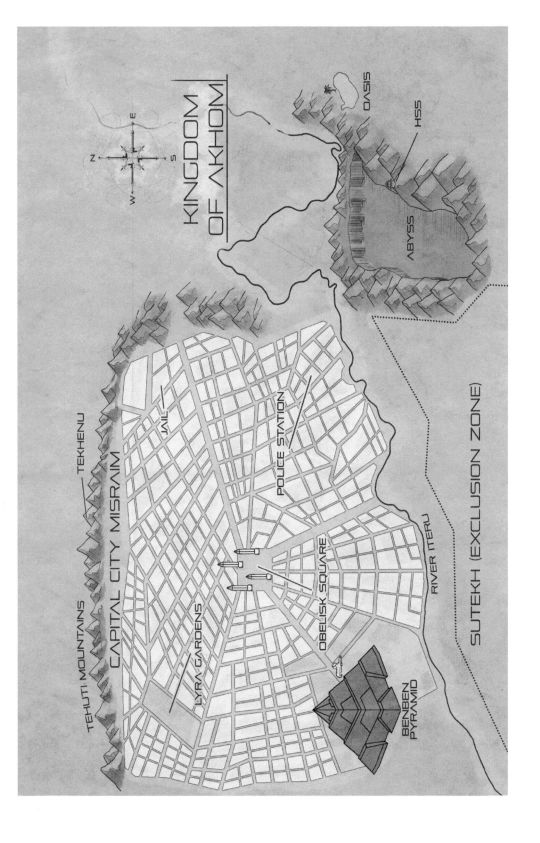

# Contents

# Chapter 1

# The House of Wisdom

*Baghdad 832 AD, two months before exploration*

IT was a marvelously pleasant evening in the glorious, mystical city of Baghdad, the capital of the Islamic Caliphate. The intimidating dark clouds were gathering gradually and merrily, and the sky was about to open up its doors for the thunderous downpour of rain. The birds and pigeons were fluttering over the courtyard located in the middle of the squared building called *Bait-al-Hikmah*—the House of Wisdom. Dancing gracefully in the middle of the courtyard was a

# Chapter 1.   The House of Wisdom

fountain that had been skillfully designed by an engineer from Asia Minor, using the water of the Tigris River. Four doors opened into the courtyard, each of them leading to a large hallway dedicated to the fields of mathematics, astronomy, philosophy, and alchemy. The recently founded city of Baghdad had acquired a reputation as a center of learning, and students from across the known world considered it a huge opportunity, as well as an honor and fortune, to travel to this magnificent city in search of knowledge.

Al-Khidr entered the ravishing hall where he hoped to listen to the lecture on alchemy. Al-Khidr was a thirty-year-old man from one of the Berber Tribes of North Africa. He had a handsome and charming face, and possessed the most gorgeous pair of bright brown eyes, along with a long and prominent nose and a chiseled, square jawline. Moreover, he sported a faint brown stubble that greatly enhanced his manly beauty, along with his carved eyebrows. He was wearing a long, cream-colored cotton robe, referred to as a *Thobe* in Arabic, and wrapped around his short hair was an emerald green turban that extended till his shoulder. He continued his walk through the massive seminar hall, which was covered with traditional silk carpets. Ancient oil lamps hung in every corner of the gargantuan hall, illuminating it with their glimmering light.

There were only a few chairs present, and those were there only for the erudite sheikhs of knowledge who had already finished their lectures for the day.

Only Master Abu Yusuf Yaqub ibn Ishaque as-Sabbah Al-Kindi could be seen inside the enormous hall. He was a renowned scholar of alchemy, and he was giving a spellbinding lecture on the subject, which was immensely popular in the entire ancient Arab world. The sight was not very different from that of a mosque, though this hall was not meant for praying, but rather used for the attainment of worldly knowledge. There were many people sitting in front of him and taking notes using ink and coal. Master Al-Kindi gave a smile of utmost delight and approval as Al-Khidr greeted him. Al-Khidr sat on the carpet in the front rows, as was his custom, and listened to his master's lecture with complete attention. Just before he finished his discourse on the treatise of Egyptian alchemy and the class was dismissed, he asked Al-Khidr to see him personally later.

***

Al-Khidr was waiting for the hall to empty, as many had gone out but a few were still were inside. He wanted to discuss with his master the reason for the meeting, and he wanted a moment of privacy. As people took their time to leave the hall, Al-Khidr decided to go out and see the changing sky. It was rare to have rain in Baghdad. He was now in the courtyard and looking at the clouds.

*It definitely must be important, as Master ordered me to stay and said I should see him once hall is mostly empty,* he thought.

# Chapter 1.   The House of Wisdom

The clouds had a different plan; they decided to shed their unending tears across the place, and it started to rain heavily. A misty gray streaked horizontally across the atmosphere, like a curtain being pulled back. The air was as steady as a drumbeat. Al-Khidr turned around and started looking at the rain, praising God for the downpour. He was mesmerized to see the billions of water droplets coming to the earth.

"Ah, what a sight, isn't it? Praise the almighty Lord for this breathtaking phenomenon." The voice sounded incredibly familiar, and made him turn out to look out of immense curiosity.

"O Suleiman, how are you, brother? Peace and blessings be on you," Al-Khidr greeted, and gave him a tight hug. "Blessings be upon you too, brother," Suleiman replied, and hugged him tightly. Suleiman was quite a handsome man as well, with a distinctly sharp face and a jagged jawline. Moreover, he possessed a pair of the most piercing eyes that anyone would get lost in, and which in turn provided him with quite a cunning look. And just like Al-Khidr, he sported a light stubble that covered his cheeks and jaw completely, although his was black. He wore a black *thobe*, along with a black turban, on his shoulder-length, curly, jet-black hair. He was a head taller than Al-Khidr and three years older than him. In addition to that, he was a heavily built man with tremendously large muscles, which gave the impression that they would tear his clothes open and be visible.

"How come I didn't see you in the master's discourse today? Perhaps I missed your presence in large hall?" Al-Khidr asked, mildly surprised. "Yes, I was occupied with some other work, so I came late. I did see you in the front row, though."

Suleiman paused and continued: "I am planning to go to Egypt, as I have heard the tragic news that my father-in-law is sick," he said with a tinge of cold-heartedness in his voice.

"I am really sorry to hear this," Al-Khidr said in a consoling tone and patted him lightly on his back.

"Anyways," Suleiman said, immediately changing the subject, "it's almost evening now. What are you doing here at this hour?" he casually inquired. "Nothing much, I am merely waiting for Master Al-Kindi to call me," Al-Khidr informed him. "And may I ask what you are doing here, O Suleiman?" Al-Khidr asked, looking at him straight in his piercing eyes.

"I too wanted to meet Master Al-Kindi before leaving for Egypt," Suleiman expressed with a surprisingly solemn face. "I understand," Al-Khidr said.

While they were deeply involved in their conversation, a man came out of the grand hall and said:

"Master Al-Kindi is about to leave, and he would like to see both of you before he leaves this place."

Al-Khidr took a quick glance at Suleiman and said: "Let's see what the master has to say to us!"

\*\*\*

They entered the hall. Several lampposts were now being erected in the middle of the courtyard, and a few men working as staff of the House of Wisdom could be seen pouring fuel into them, as the dark and dense clouds had made the light low inside the hall. The roof was high and supported by twenty pillars. The air was still thick with the smell of incense, which was now pleasantly blended with the smell of soil which had just erupted, as the heavy rain had fallen on the parched floor of Baghdad.

"Peace and blessings be upon you, Sheikh (Master)!" they chanted immediately at the sight of him.

"Peace and blessings be upon both of you, Al-Khidr and Suleiman," greeted back the master, who was delving deep into an ancient manuscript. The manuscript looked rustic brown, and it was worn out in some places. The bookshelf behind him was filled with numerous ancient manuscripts bound in leather.

"This is the Greek manuscript on plants," he said, grabbing a large book with a matte finish from one of the shelves. "Just arrived today. I have been eagerly waiting to get my hands on it since the early hours of the morning!" Master Al-Kindi exclaimed with a soft chuckle.

"That is definitely exciting, Sheikh," Al-Khidr said, staring at the large book, his eyes sparkling with immense fascination.

Al-Kindi was a bearded man with a small, fist-long grey beard, and the air he breathed carried the scent of ancient sage, as if freshened by a miswak (a twig of the *Salvadora persica* tree). He wore a long, white tunic and a brown cloak over it. His white turban gave

6

him an aura of utmost grace and grandeur. "It is very interesting indeed. The author isn't very good at the explanation, but he definitely seems to have sufficient knowledge of the plants, especially those that grew in the greater Syria," the master explained, turning the cream-colored pages of the book, which evoked the pleasantly typical essence of ancient manuscripts.

Al-Kindi looked up, and he now noticed there were two gentlemen in front of him instead of one.

"I summoned Al-Khidr, but why did you come, O Suleiman?" he inquired casually.

Suleiman glanced at Al-Khidr and said, "Master, I need your permission. I want to leave for Egypt, as my family is living there and my father-in-law is sick. They need my help urgently. I will be there only for a brief period, mostly three or four months," Suleiman requested humbly, with his head hung low.

"I am really sorry to hear this. Generally, we do not allow disciples to leave until they finish one year of the training. But in your situation, it seems like there is no alternative available.

I wish a speedy recovery to your father-in-law. May the almighty Allah grant him health! Amen," he chanted, and they repeated after him.

"You may go; but remember, Suleiman—a great number of students desperately desire to attend our lectures. And even though this hall is enormous, sometimes we feel like it is not enough to accommodate all the disciples. Some protégés even attend the discourses while standing. You know it very well," Master

# Chapter 1.   The House of Wisdom

said.

"I completely understand, Master, and I assure you, I'll be back as soon as my father-in-law recovers. Thanks to the brilliant knowledge I have gained by listening to your illuminating lectures, and the excellent training I have received in this great house of the wisdom, I can now formulate my own medicines using Egyptian plants. However, I still need to figure out what type of infliction has fallen upon him. I merely received a brief letter from my wife that he has fallen sick," Suleiman explained with a somber expression on his face.

"Yes, Suleiman, you have my permission to go, but you will not go alone," Master said with an encouraging smile on his wise, glowing face. Suleiman looked surprised, and looked at both his master and then his class fellow, Al-Khidr.

"What do you mean, master? I do not understand," Suleiman said, scratching his head.

"I have received a letter from our mighty Caliph, Al-Mamun, that he would like to visit Egypt as well," Master informed them in a mildly excited tone. "Very soon, an army will march towards Egypt. Caliph Al-Mamun would like to excavate the ancient pyramids in Al-Jeeza (Giza). A Coptic scholar, Denis of Tell Mahre, has informed the mighty Caliph that the Pyramid is actually a large cave, where Prophet Adam, peace and blessings be on him, hid treasures brought from the Paradise," the master informed further.

Al-Khidr and Suleiman were listening attentively

in silence, and a sense of unbearable inquisitiveness bubbled inside them. "Caliph would like to excavate the pyramids and perceive what lies within the triangular walls of the mystical pyramids!" Master exclaimed with immense enthusiasm. "But, Master," Al-Khidr continued slowly, as a look of confusion mixed with curiosity appeared on his handsome visage. "No living soul has entered the pyramids before. Who will guide the almighty Caliph?"

"You, my dear boy." He pointed at him with his sparse fingers and chuckled again. "You will guide him. And that is precisely the reason why I summoned you here this evening,"

"Me? But I do not have knowledge about the pyramids, Master. Besides that, I have only been to Egypt once before, when I was traveling from Al-Maghreb (Morocco) to Baghdad," Al-Khidr said in a surprised tone.

Master Al-Kindi smiled and said: "Exploration of the unknown is what you should be most excited about!" and a sense of understanding broke over Al-Khidr. "You are right, Master."

"People cannot enter the pyramids because the pyramid builders were cleverer and wiser than us. They constructed it with stones, and the previous generations failed because they didn't know where the opening door of the pyramids lay, and the way to get past the stones," master explained patiently. "O Al-Khidr, I have seen your marvelously impressive work and your deep interest in making acids," the master said further.

# CHAPTER 1.   THE HOUSE OF WISDOM

"I am proud of you, my boy, and I have complete faith in your capabilities."

"Thank you for your kind and encouraging words, master. It will be a tremendous honor to serve our mighty Caliph," Al-Khidr expressed with a heartfelt smile. "May I join this excavation, Master?" Suleiman requested hopefully, with his fingers crossed.

"I'm afraid not, Suleiman. Only one person is requested as the maker of acids who can accompany the almighty Caliph, as he has a large army to feed. I can grant you permission to go to Egypt, but I cannot guarantee your involvement in this project," the master confessed regretfully. "O Suleiman, the task is different. Your research is not on the making of the acids; rather, it is more inclined towards the distillation and extraction of the plant's essential oils," Al-Kindi informed. "Suleiman, you will leave now," the master ordered.

Suleiman gave a feeble smile to Al-Khidr, and with a respectfully deep bow to his master, he left the hall. He is definitely not happy, Al-Khidr thought worriedly, and deeply hoped that his mission would not turn out to be the cause of any sort of conflict between him and Suleiman.

When Suleiman left the hall, Master said to Al-Khidr: "Caliph is going to Egypt to control the uprising that is brewing there. Be careful while traveling, and just make sure that you remain near Fustat or Al-Aksar when Caliph arrives in Egypt. The situation may deteriorate. I hope I am clear enough," Master commanded as he dwelled deep into Al-Khidr's eyes. "Furthermore, the information on the uprising is only for your ears. Do not reveal it to any other soul," Al-Kindi warned.

"Master, you have my solemn word. I will never divulge the secrets of the Caliph to anyone," Al-Khidr asserted firmly with his chest thrown open. "But Master, do you think we will be able enter the Great Pyramid?" Al-Khidr asked doubtfully. His mind was coming up with the worst-case scenarios in which, if they managed to find a passage into the pyramids, there was a high chance of them getting lost inside.

"I mean, the pyramids seem like a gargantuan library to me, where there is a massive chance that we might not even find a proper passage inside. And even if we somehow did, we might end up losing our way inside, and may not come out of it, and may be stuck there forever...or die," he blurted out in intense exasperation.

"My dear boy, calm down," said Al-Kindi, patting his back lightly. "Do not be anxious. We have recently discovered an ancient book on the pyramids from the Coptic libraries. It says that some pyramid entrances are underground, but the largest Pyramids in Giza have an entrance on the northern side. That is why the locals call it the northern pyramid," Al-Kindi illuminated calmly.

"Once you follow the book religiously, you will be able to enter into that mystical realm with ease and guide the caliph without facing much difficulty," he proclaimed, and turned to face a large shelf that lay right in the middle. He carefully moved across the lengthy series of books, and finally, he retrieved a medium-sized book that looked extremely ancient, perhaps centuries old. It was bounded by a leather jacket covered in dust, and had ancient script on its cover page.

"It's all yours now, my dear boy. I have given it to you not just for the journey, but to keep with you forever."

Al-Khidr thanked his sagacious master greatly and began surveying the book with the intense curiosity of a cat.

"I strongly suggest that you thoroughly study the contents of this ancient book prior to starting your journey to Egypt in order to avoid any last-minute hassles while you are with the Caliph at the site of the pyramids," Al-Kindi advised him sagaciously.

"As a matter of fact, if I were you—the chosen one to accompany the great Caliph inside one of the greatest wonders of this world—I would completely swallow the contents of this textbook a week before starting my journey." Al-Kindi chuckled heartily, patting his student's shoulder and staring at him with immense pride and joy.

"Go, my boy, and fulfill your destiny as the chosen one. Trust me, there is no bigger honor and pride than what the almighty Lord of the worlds, Allah, has bestowed upon you. May he guide you on this path and protect you from all the evil and misleading devils.

God bless you and your journey."

A sense of utter relief broke over Al-Khidr as the ancient book was handed over to him. He was simply delighted on being the chosen one among the thousands of protégés of Master Al-Kindi. He threw his chest forward with pride and honor, and left the grand hall of knowledge with determination.

When he came out of the hall, the rain was still pouring. It was a delightful sight to see Baghdad rejuvenated by the heavenly rain and the gathering of a thriving community of intellectuals.

# Chapter 2

# The Great Pyramid

*Giza, Al-Misr (Egypt), March Year 832 A.D.*

A sandstorm was approaching like a red Nephilim, as if it were trying to stop Al-Mamun's army. The gusts of howling wind fluttered the clothes of those who were outside.

"It's a big sandstorm, hitting Giza!" exclaimed a man from outside.

As workers bore through the tunnel in the side of the Great Pyramid, it became darker and darker with every passing moment, as the sand that moved through the air over the Pyramids was blocking all the light coming in from the entrance. Everything went dead silent, except for the sound of the workers' tools. Slowly, all light disappeared, and it went pitch-black.

"Holy Lord! will this collapse on us?" Tariq shouted.

Everyone turned around in utter confusion as they saw a wave of dense, red sand was penetrating in from the outside and was covering the whole entrance. *"Askut Ya Hammar!"* (Shut up, donkey!), a bearded man said while adjusting his keffiyeh—the headscarf. Most of the men inside the tunnel had covered their noses and mouths using keffiyeh to protect from dust. "Brighten up the lantern. Put more oil in it!" Master Ibrahim shouted.

"No, wait for a while, they will blow out," a worker said.

The sounds of striking on the stones could be heard from one end, while at the other, the team close to the entrance of the tunnel stood in silence for several minutes, watching until the sandstorm's fury tempered down.

A man struggled to rekindle the flame of the lantern. Finally, the sound of a spark catching fire was heard, and the whole tunnel was illuminated again. The exposed parts of the men's faces were gleaming with sweat.

"What shall we do now? Is the sandstorm some kind of omen from the mummies to not to enter this pyramid?" a young man whimpered in a small voice, breaking the icy silence.

The young man gave a nervous laugh when no one responded. It was his first day, and this was definitely not what he had been expecting. He had dreamed of being the first to find the gold, and that would mean he would be given a larger wage than the others. It was exciting, and one could get lost in the thoughts of riches, but navigating through the Great Pyramid of Giza wasn't exactly a bed of roses.

Abbas decided to recite some of his favorite Arabic poetry:


"The Pyramids puzzled the minds and the genius of
the men,
And turned their ambitious dreams into
insignificance.
Pyramids! smooth and grandiose in proportion,
Arrows shot cannot pass over them.
I know not, since when the meditations fall short
before them,
And opinions are wondered around this marvel—
Whether they are graves of non-Arab monarchs,
Or wizardry of the sands or are they mother of the
mountains."


After his first two verses, others who knew of this poem started joining in. By the end of it, the whole tunnel was reverberating with the singing. "We'll get the treasure of Shaddad, the son of Ad," Ali said.

# Chapter 2. The Great Pyramid

"If God wills," a man added. One man said, "Denis of Tell Mahre said to me that the Pyramid is a cave where Adam hid treasures brought from Paradise." "Nonsense! It's certainly not a cave," another replied.

These men were among the team who were to bore a channel in the wall of the Great Pyramid of Al-Giza on the orders of Caliph Al-Mamun. It was their fifth day of working on this project, and they had already bored ten steps into the Pyramid.

Stories and myths had circulated about the Pyramids. There were fears of falling into deep depressions in the ground, and never being able to walk again; there were speculative tales about immortal snakes that would curl around you and suffocate you to death; there were tales of traps that would be triggered when you tripped across a strategically placed tripwire; and many, many more.

These legends only became more aggressive and foreboding every year to keep intruders from becoming brave enough to enter the royal sand structures. Now, these brave men had to see all these appellations in real life.

"I hope the mummies aren't alive till today," Tariq uttered.

"Shush now, baby Tariq, do you want me to ask your mother to come and collect you?" teased a man named Mubarak, whose face was embellished by a large beard. Laughter echoed all around. Everyone felt a little bit more at ease.

"Okay, listen up," said a man with broad shoulders

and a clean-shaven face as he emerged from among the group. His name was Jamal. "We're moving forward, let's go." He emphasized his words by waving his hands around. Judging by his posture, demeanor, and the confident and authoritative way he talked, it didn't take the novices long to realize who they were reporting to inside the tunnel. There were quite a few new recruits among them who had never done this before. But despite their fear of the unknown, they treaded obediently behind the man who was clearly in charge. No one fancied getting fired on the same day they were hired. The group would move further along while the team on the outside struggled against the sandstorm, trying to keep the wooden stairs at the mouth of the newly built tunnel entrance intact. By the time they would return from the exploration, the sandstorm would have passed; hopefully, the stairs would not follow. They progressed deeper into the structure until they arrived at a place where the tunnel bifurcated into two passages, one descending and the other ascending. The expedition was being carried out in two groups not only because it was safer for the workers, but also to more efficiently secure the treasure. Each team was provided with four torches. At this point, a random member of each team was made the temporary leader.

"Follow me," Al-Khidr said, and the men followed their new leader and started descending into the lower tunnel.

Al-Khidr's clothes were stained with patches of yellow and grey, caked with the smells of sweat and spices. For the last few weeks, he had concentrated all his work on making the acids. The job was easy for him, but he had travelled in Egypt to gather the salts and make new friends and also opened an apothecary to make cures for common ailments.

Al-Khidr traced his finger across the walls as he made his way through the passage, at the same time focusing on his compass, enjoying his timely intuition to align the bored tunnel with the center of the pyramid as the workers deviated a bit from the center of the pyramid. *The entire project could turn into a fiasco, but thanks to Allah, we found the real passages now*, Al-Khidr thought to himself.

Al-Khidr led his group through the small, descending passage. It was uncomfortable, as the ceiling was low, and the men had to either bend their necks or their knees. The passage was long, with nothing of interest on the walls, the ceiling, or the floor, but remarkably, it was a well-crafted piece of engineering. Al-Khidr continued through the long descending passage as it went deeper into the pyramid. The deeper the team and Al-Khidr went, the greater the risks of getting trapped; it was best to be prepared. The men were tired, but still motivated. It took them roughly twenty flips of an hourglass to carefully descend into the cobweb-filled passage. They feared that pyramid might have hidden traps.

Al-Khidr did not let his team rest. He argued that

they would find something, but in actuality, Al-Khidr wasn't sure about anything. Where they were going was the deepest this structure went, so it was the toughest place to get to. This had to be it. This had to be where they would hit the jackpot. "I am thirsty. Maybe the subterranean chamber has a pit of water?" one man from the team inquired.

"Don't drink, even if you find water here! It could be poisonous," Al-Khidr advised, and he gave his water skin to the man.

Al-Khidr proposed to his followers, "Tie up a rope around my belly, and I will go down into the passage first until I reach its bottom; and then, if all is fine, I will let you know."

The team liked this proposal, and so Al-Khidr went first into the lowest chamber of the pyramid. He found it safe and called up for his team members to come down. In the lowest chamber, they soon reached a place that appeared to be rough-hewn cavern, not as smooth as the other stones in the pyramid. The team quickly searched the cavern. One man jumped into a trench and explored the pit, but there was nothing there.

"Nothing. It's a dead end."

Al-Khidr checked around to confirm this.

"This is not a resting place. Pick up your stuff, we have to move," Al-Khidr commanded in a deep voice before anyone could say anything. The team stared at Al-Khidr, as if expecting him to say something more.

"Will you get off your asses anytime soon?"

## CHAPTER 2.  THE GREAT PYRAMID

That got everyone up. Some men, however, were suspicious. Everyone knew anyone could be dishonest and untruthful in the face of money. "Follow me. We're going to go straight up ahead and continue on to wherever this path takes us," Al-Khidr informed them, pointing toward the tunnel where they had come from.

The group started on their journey again, taking their axes, torches, ropes, food, and water. Rasheed, the person who was initially asked to lead, increased his pace and caught up with Al-Khidr. Rasheed had been made the leader of the group before they even entered the pyramid. He was the one who had been given authority, but now, Al-Khidr had taken it from him, having been made leader by the authoritative Jamal, the broad-shouldered man who was earlier coordinating with the team on the outside of the Pyramid.

"So, who sent you?" Rasheed asked, making direct eye contact. "I wasn't informed about someone else coming to lead my team." "I'm under my orders, and you should be under yours. I order you to stop questioning your superior and simply let the actual leader handle this," Al-Khidr responded. Rasheed was a rugged man from Caliph's army. He saw the pyramid as a cave of thieves in the story of Alladin. Al-Khidr, being the alchemist, was baffled by the intricate structures of the pyramid, and knew that the whole building had some different purpose. He felt an urge to take control from Rasheed. Rasheed was surprised by the sudden hostility. He gulped his anger and let Al-Khidr lead. Al-Khidr almost enjoyed his new position of power; Jamal had made a good decision of making him the leader. Al-Khidr was actually suited to power like this. It made him smile.

To the team, Al-Khidr said, "Now, I want you to explore cautiously, because these narrow corridors have higher chances of having a trap. When you go inside, I want you to pay close attention to the walls. There could be a doorway, a window, or something else."

The men nodded, picking up their stuff. Al-Khidr gave them new torches.

"No one takes a break until we complete a full search of the Pyramid. The Caliph is anxiously waiting for the fulfillment of his dream. Don't make him wait. Now, go!" Al-Khidr shouted behind the departing groups.

The men were tired, but they knew that it would be an instant jackpot if they found the bounty and presented it to the Caliph. They would be flooded with money, respect, and a good position. This kept most of them going. But even money sometimes loses its influence as a motivator. "Move in, and be aware," Al-Khidr cautioned as they went.

With slumped shoulders, the teams moved up into the darkness of the lower passage once again. Above them, they could hear the noises of the second team, who already climbed up the ascending passage earlier. Al-Khidr aggressively snatched the torch from one of his team members and ascended upwards. "Hurry up already, perhaps they found something!" he shouted.

Though they hurried, moving up in a tilted passage took more time than expected. The men again ascended, panting, and met the second team after more than half an hour.

Al-Khidr moved the torch around, trying to see what booty the second team had found. The team that had ascended the upper passage earlier said to Al-Khidr, "Come here, we have found something!"

One man was putting his ear to the wall and trying to hear something.

"Mansoor says that behind this stone there could be another passage," one excitedly claimed.

Mansoor, the man who was trying to hear from behind the stone, apparently had sharp hearing skills and was a master of excavations in Egypt. He was a short Egyptian man with a lush, black beard and crooked teeth.

"Do you see it?" Mansoor asked.

"See what?" one man exasperatedly asked.

"It's a blocked doorway. If we break through it, there might be more on the other side."

"What if there is nothing on the other side?" Rasheed chimed in.

"By God, if you don't shut up, I will smack your head against the wall. Now, help me. It's a plug stone which has blocked the entrance to the passage," Mansoor exclaimed, his voice rising.

The men behind Mansoor moved in with their equipment and bottles and some of the sturdier men started hitting nails into the stone. Once nails were hammered in to their maximum, they were jerked out. Acid and alchemical powder made by Al-Khidr were poured into the newly drilled holes, and one man started heating the stone. To fulfill the will of the Caliph Al-Mamun, all the blacksmiths of northern Al-Misr (Egypt) and the nearby regions had been summoned for this project. "Keep your mouths covered, and don't inhale the fumes," Al-Khidr advised.

As an alchemist, he had mastered the art of making the acids they now used to crack open the plug stone. The stone gave a crackling sound and started cracking and crumbling. After a while, the plug stone crumbled to the floor.

"Wallah," (By God), the men said. "It's another passage!" They jumped in excitement.

They trod forward along the newly discovered ascending passage for a couple more minutes until they arrived at an area with a ramp. It was large, appeared to be better constructed. There was a path leading to the further top of the pyramid, and in between the ramp, there was another passage. "Who can carve out such a grand, tilted tunnel?" a man named Abbas murmured as he noticed something on the tilted walls.

"Not you, that's for sure," someone interjected.

"What is this?" Abbas cried out suddenly, running his hands across the wall with strange slots.

"It's just some slots on the wall, Abbas," Rasheed, the former group leader, responded. "Keep your eyes peeled for treasure, not the slots on the wall." Abbas had more experience than Rasheed; however, even if they had previous experience, the new recruits were mistreated, and their opinions did not matter. Al-Khidr did not comment on the discussion; he simply adjusted his green keffiyeh up to his mouth, and continued on. He knew it was useless to argue with Rasheed. The slots on the walls were not warnings or directions. But they must have been made to fulfil some purpose, Al-Khidr thought to himself.

Everyone went silent when they heard someone calling out to them. Al-Khidr and his group entered the chamber close to the ramp, and the moment they stepped inside, they noticed a Mehrab, an apse, in the northern wall; the room gleamed under their torches. The men of the first team inside were in such a state of shock that they hardly could move.

"What..."

They were all stunned for a moment, as it wasn't every day that you found an emerald-colored idol that was sparkling and sending off rays of green in every direction. The idol was an eerie sight. What they had just discovered was a human-looking idol carved of malachite. On his breast, a priceless sword was attached, and on its head was engraved a precious stone as big as an egg and as brilliant as daylight.

Al-Khidr recalled hearing from Sabians of Iraq about how the Great Pyramid was the tomb of Seth, son of Adam. Is this the statue of Seth? he wondered. One man put his metallic tool and the round pounding stone aside and approached the idol. He tried to lift it, but it was too heavy; it didn't even budge. Al-

Khidr entered next, and ascended in joy through the grand, tilted passage until he reached another chamber. Though they could hear Al-Khidr and the others approaching, the four men already inside the chamber had their eyes fixed on another treasure on the floor, unable to comprehend what they saw. The men were as shocked as Al-Khidr and his group had been, maybe even more. No one moved; they just stared. Finally, Al-Khidr moved forward, commanding everyone to stay back. In this chamber, close to its southern wall, there was a large, rectangular open ark made up of a single stone. Al-Khidr went closer and inspected it. At the base of the ark was a layer of salt. He ignored this, picking up the sparkling object in the ark. It was a thin piece of what looked like glass, translucent, with a tint of orange to it. Al-Khidr tapped on it with his nails, and sure enough, it was glass. However, it was a bit too soft to be glass. The glass one can find on Earth is not normally malleable, but what the group had just found here was a glass that could be twisted and turned. Al-Khidr couldn't believe his eyes as he curled the glasslike substance and closed it on his wrist like a bangle. He raised his fist to show the group, which was in complete awe as well.

Then they saw the metals that had been there for centuries, all of them still intact. Not a single piece was rusted. There were purple, blue, and green orbs in the mix as well. Gold that was shinier than normal gold could be seen in the distance. The ark also contained a worn-out, rope-like material and a large piece of aquamarine stone. But most conspicuous was a sphere, with strange engravings over it. It looked like an amalgamation of different metals, with a rounded cavity to access the core. Al-Khidr took the ball in his hands, and was about to put his finger in the cavity, but Rasheed took it from him and put the malleable glass and sphere in the sack.

"This goes straight to the treasury, man!" Rasheed said, and smiled mischievously at Al-Khidr.

Al-Khidr gulped his annoyance and handed over the sphere. But although he had given the sphere to Rasheed physically, it maintained a magnetic effect on him, as if two attracting poles had been separated.

They found no human remains inside the chambers. Al-Khidr wondered why this northern male pyramid was so thoroughly protected, and why it had no mummy. The men were tremendously happy, as they had found something unlike any other bounty previously found. They patted Al-Khidr's back and hugged each other for good fortune. For everyone, this one expedition had made them an enormous amount of money, but among the men, there was one who was not the luckiest, despite making the most.

When the Pyramid's exploration team came out with treasures, the sandstorm was already gone. The area outside was full of spectators who were shouting in joy. Al-Khidr took the stairs and descended. He had lifted his hands like a victory obelisk and was moving toward the crowd when suddenly, an old, bearded Nubian man took hold of his hand from behind and whispered into his ear, "You'll need me; I am Dhu Al-Nun. Search for me in Akhmim." The man then disappeared into the crowd. Al-Khidr was surprised, confused, and even afraid. He looked around, but as the crowd took Al-Khidr over their shoulders, he could not locate the man who had spoken in his ear.

# Chapter 3

# The Artifacts

*Al-Askar, Al-Misr (Egypt), 832 A.D.*

Aʟ-Kʜɪᴅʀ entered the palace through the large, wooden gates reinforced with metal bars. A man in a long, white dress with a mishla (cloak) over it appeared from somewhere to the right. He nodded toward the two guards at the gate who had let Al-Khidr into the palace. "He's my responsibility now," the white-cloaked man said.

# CHAPTER 3. THE ARTIFACTS

Al-Khidr had gotten only a few moments from the Dewan of Caliph to meet him personally. Caliph bestowed the reward of personal consultation, as he was happy to subdue the recent Coptic uprising and the excavation of the Great Pyramid.

As he led Al-Khidr through the palace, the man did not talk or express any sort of emotion. Al-Khidr took advantage of this, as he wanted to collect his thoughts before being presented himself before the Caliph.

Next to Al-Khidr was a huge, white structure. It had small, golden domes on its roof and elongated windows. Normally, anyone would have been impressed by it, but Al-Khidr, who was too muddled in his own thoughts, was disinterested with the grandeur of the palace and its splendor. The expedition had stirred something inside Al-Khidr. There was something mysterious about the Pyramid and the bounty they had found there. He wanted to know more about it, but going back to the Pyramid to find answers to a mystery that may or may not even exist was not the best of moves. It was also dangerous, as he would have to go alone, and there was always a risk of getting trapped within the sand structure.

The two men strode across the soft earth and arrived at the foot of the stairs. They paused, looked at each other, and then continued up the six steps. The main gate to the palace had two round handles, one on each side. The man in the white cloak pulled both doors open, and Al-Khidr felt a chilly breeze and smelled the pleasing scent of incense from inside the palace.

When Al-Khidr entered, the man shut the door behind him. The architect hired to design the Caliph's palace was a skilled one, paid handsomely, and it was vivid all around. A lot of thought was put into the design, as the palace was the only building in the vicinity. The Caliph's palace was lavish. Engineers had spent a lot of time making the spacious rooms. The walls were simple, but the floors were covered with carpets of Persia, and the air was heavy with the smell of jasmine perfume. Abbasid caliphs liked to be surrounded by philosophers, poets, storytellers, musicians and scholars of all kind of knowledge.

The man took off his shoes, and with his feet, pushed them to the side. Al-Khidr did the same; the floor was cold under his feet. Al-Khidr and the man continued walking on white marble until they arrived at the main atrium of the building. The ceiling was extremely high there, almost thirty feet, which made their footsteps over the cold floor echo. Al-Khidr let his eyes travel to the high ceiling.

They continued walking toward the middle of the hall, which had giant columns on either side, and took three steps down to be greeted by an oak door. It wasn't the largest door in this palace, but certainly looked like the scariest one. Part of the reason for this was the fact that behind this door would be the Caliph, a very powerful man. He was a person with a firm personality and an even firmer grip. If he was in a good mood, he would sometimes even joke around, but usually, he was reserved in both demeanor and speech. He had to be; he was the Caliph. If he was too friendly, he would be taken lightly, something he could not tolerate. Something probably no one could tolerate.

The door was pushed open; Al-Khidr was nudged in, and the white-cloaked man took a few steps forward.

"Al-Khidr is here to enjoy your presence."

Without really waiting for a reply, the man walked back to the door, gave Al-Khidr a second push, and motioned for him to proceed toward the Caliph. The man then closed the doors behind him. Now, Al-Khidr was alone with the Caliph.

"Peace and blessings be upon you," Al-Khidr said.

"I can sense the nervousness in your voice, Al-Khidr." The Caliph's deep and powerful voice filled the room. "Peace and blessings upon you as well." The Caliph was sitting on an elevated throne, outfitted with a white turban and a navy-blue tunic that was sandwiched between pristine white robes. He had a lush, black beard with threads of white hair running through it, and a wide smile was smeared across his face. Al-Khidr sighed, now feeling more at ease. The Caliph is in a good mood, thank God, he thought to himself.

"Come along. Why are you acting so afraid, Al-Khidr? I am glad that Al-Kindi has given me one of his best students."

"This is the Allah's favor to me," Al-Khidr replied.

"Have you had the chance to look at the treasures from the expedition, O Caliph?"

"No, I didn't. Is that why you came here? Just to ask me this?"

"Uh...no, Ameer-ul-Muslimeen" (the Leader of Muslims).

"Then let your words flow. You have my ears."

"I came because I wanted your support on something."

"I'm a Caliph, not a welfare trust!" Al-Mamun roared.

Al-Khidr had wanted to ask the Caliph about the orb and the glass shard, but he was nervous, and did not know how to start his request. Now the Caliph was right in front of him, his ears were ready to hear why Al-Khidr wanted to see him.

Al-Khidr abruptly uttered something to start the conversation in his nervousness:

"Ya Khalift-ul-Muslimeen"—O Caliph—"I wanted to go back down into the Great Pyramid."

"Then go. Did you hear me stop you?" the Caliph remarked.

Al-Khidr continued in his nervousness: "The problem is that going alone is too risky for me. Could you get me some men that can go with me?" "So, you want me to hire and pay some men to go down into an already explored pyramid? Haven't I already paid the whole exploration team handsomely, including you?" "Yes, Ameer!" Al-Khidr agreed.

"But we have already had four more teams explore

the pyramid over the past few days to make sure we left nothing behind," the Caliph said further. Al-Khidr remained silent.

"Why would you want to go down there again, and take men with you as well?"

"It's just that I want to further explore the Pyramid," Al-Khidr said.

"Did you run out of useless things to do?" The Caliph smiled in a friendly manner. "Anyway, I'll be needing you shortly for another expedition. Until then, rest. There's no need to waste your time and my money on another expedition, especially an expedition to the same place."

With every passing moment, Al-Mamun's voice rose. There was no longer a smile on his face. He was getting annoyed.

"I think you haven't told me what you came for," he said.

Al-Khidr knew he had been dismissed. He said abruptly, "Can you let me have few artifacts for my research?" He paused. "I learned we found some non-precious stuff as well."

"You can't have the gold, but the rest you can see. Denis of Tell Mahre has separated the precious and non-precious items for me," the Caliph replied. "God bless you and reward you."

"I am quite happy with your achievements. You can keep the non-precious items as tokens of appreciation," Al-Mamun said. "Thank you very much, Ya Khalift-ul-Muslimeen. May your grace and honor increase. I will display these tokens at my apothecary, which I am planning to open soon in Baghdad," Al-Khidr said.

"Blessing of God be upon you," the Caliph said.

Al-Khidr felt relief that his request had been accepted. At least he could analyze the contents of the pyramid, if not the pyramid itself. It was surprising to him that the Caliph would allow him to have the artifacts so easily.

*If I was in his place, I would never give away something this antique and this valuable,* he declared to himself.

Al-Mamun yelled out for Abdur-Rahman, the man in the white cloak, as Al-Khidr now found out. The man had been waiting outside the door all along. "Get me those antique materials and items from the treasure room," said the Caliph.

The man nodded and, with the motioning of his fingers, asked Al-Khidr to wait. The treasure chamber was actually connected to this premier room where the men currently were.

"And not a single piece of gold should be touched!" the Caliph screeched as the man left for the treasure room.

Al-Khidr patiently waited, staring at the walls, ceiling, and everything else—everything but the Caliph. It was as if Al-Khidr feared that making eye contact might make the Caliph reconsider his decision.

Al-Khidr was running out of things to stare at. The man in the white cloak was taking ages, and that was causing quite a stir within him. Having worked under Al-Mamun for a while now, Al-Khidr knew for a fact that he was a man of his word. However, Al-Khidr did not want to reveal his excitement, so he waited quietly. It had only been a few minutes since the Caliph ordered the man to bring the artifacts, but for Al-Khidr, it felt as if eons had passed. Finally, Abdur-Rahman entered the room from the chamber with a sack containing the artifacts. Al-Khidr heard the door open, the sound of shuffling, and the sound of something being dragged against the floor.

"Al-Khidr, take these. Abdul-Rahman will show you out."

"God bless you. Salamalaikum! (blessings of God be on you!)"

Abdul-Rahman handed over the sack to Al-Khidr. The two men then crossed the main atrium and pushed out through the main gate. There was no longer a breeze. "Peace and blessings." Al-Khidr smiled, thinking that he would go be on his own from here.

But Abdul-Rahman did not reply, and continued on at the same pace. He walked Al-Khidr back to the enormous gates. There were now four guards with spears standing there. Al-Khidr said one last loud "Peace and blessings," and was happily off.

Al-Khidr was now outside on the road. He quickly slid his right hand inside the sack, and behold; he touched a sphere. A surge of joy went through his veins. He quickly searched the sack, and found three things: the sphere, the glass, and the withered rope. He untied his horse and set off for his house. His heart was pounding with delight from having received these tokens of appreciation from the Caliph. He felt fulfilled and accomplished, both as an alchemist and an archaeologist. He galloped into the darkness along the Nile with his newly gained treasure.

# Chapter 4

# The Search

IT was well after midnight, and Al-Khidr was agitated, tired, and confused. He had imagined this situation would play out in a very different way. He thought that poring over the artifacts for a couple of hours would reveal ancient languages, maybe even a map to a hidden chamber containing books on alchemical knowledge. He was least interested in metallic treasures of any kind.

Al-Khidr didn't really have a specific goal in his study of the artifacts; he was just curious about their properties. What made them so special? Why was the glass malleable, and why didn't the metal artifacts rust? All these questions had bugged him since the day he first saw them during the expedition. But now, even though he had the items in hand, he couldn't do much with them. He couldn't understand or identify anything. The longer he stared at each artifact under the light of the candle, the more hopeless he became. He looked at the orb in his hand for a long time, as if staring at it would suddenly reveal everything. He placed all the artifacts back into the sack and hid it under his bed. He then also threw a blanket over the sack, just in case. Theft was always a possibility. He blew out his candle and laid down.

*Oh God, it's so late at night. I'll miss the Morning Prayer now*, he thought to himself.

As he expected, he was unable to wake up for the prayers, sleeping all the way till noon. The first thing he did when his eyes opened was check under his bed. Thankfully, the artifacts were untouched.

Over his breakfast, which mainly included some dates and two cups of tea, Al-Khidr contemplated his next move. He had to do something about the arti-facts. An idea struck him: he could ask some of his wise and knowledgeable friends. There was Suleiman, a classmate from Baghdad; Yohannes, a Coptic Christian; and Yoshua, who was Jewish. They all had much knowledge on different topics, and he always enjoyed their company and discussion with them. Suleiman was bit disappointed that he had not been selected by

Master Al-Kindi for this exploration project. Nevertheless, after breakfast, that is what Al-Khidr set out to do.

He retrieved his dagger from his drawer, the artifacts from under his bed, and mounted his Arabian horse, Qantara. He needed the dagger because he would be in a part of the city that was far off and unsafe as he was going there to get more information on the artifacts, not lose them! The journey toward Suleiman's house would be long; it was more than an hour's ride, and the longer Al-Khidr was on the road, the higher his chances of running into bandits.

And then it happened. He was only five minutes from Suleiman's area when he realized that three horses were galloping towards him from in front of his direction. He would have thought they were just travelers like him, if all three were not tearing toward him at high speed—but they were, and instantly Al-Khidr knew something was up.

Now, Al-Khidr, though an alchemist, was a Berber from Morocco, and knew well how to deal with ruffians. He had to do something. He could now almost see the riders from the corners of his eyes. He turned around to get a full view of them, but they had covered their faces—not a good sign. Only their eyes could be seen, and Al-Khidr knew this was what bandits often did to avoid being recognized.

Two riders were now on either side of him, and one behind. As Al-Khidr had expected from the start, they were road bandits. One of them brought out a large machete. They didn't say anything; they didn't need to. It was obvious what was going on. Al-Khidr knew that he couldn't slow down, turn right or left. The only way to go was forward, which meant he would have to speed up Qantara—which was already risky for him.

A plan began to form in his head. He shouted over the sound of the four sets of hooves: "Slow down."

The three men did not hear, but he repeated twice more, and one of them nodded. The bandits started to slow down, and so did Al-Khidr. They slowed down till they were only trotting. Now, Al-Khidr reached for the strapped bag, which contained the artifacts. However, with his other hand, he simultaneously reaching for the dagger hidden in his pocket. The bandits were too focused on the sack, and did not see the dagger being unsheathed.

With a sudden motion, Al-Khidr stabbed the machete-wielding man right in the arm.

"*achkor rak kogh*," Al-Khidr shouted in Amazigh language.

The entire blade was buried in the flesh for a full second, and in the next, it was out. The man cried out in pain, losing control of his horse while the other two bandits stared in shock, as if they had expected this to be an easy one. They had let their guard down.

Blood started to spurt out from the man's arm while he tried to control the horse. But it was obvious he couldn't ride the horse at the same speed with just one arm, He couldn't, and he was forced to slow down.

Just four or five seconds after stabbing the first bandit, Al-Khidr tried to stab another one of the men, but he was unable to inflict the same amount of damage. The blade only scratched the man, forming a thin line of blood, but that was about it. Al-Khidr knew it was time for him to get away from there. He whipped at his horse and was off. The other two men sped up, tailing Al-Khidr.

Al-Khidr tried to go as fast as he could. And then he saw it—something that gave him the hope and boost he needed: the settlement of mud bricks and date-tree leaves could be seen in the distance. The bandits almost caught up to him, but soon realized they couldn't do anything, as they had now entered the town. They fell back, and Al-Khidr sighed.

"Thank the Lord," he muttered under his breath.

\*\*\*

By the time he got to Suleiman's door, Al-Khidr's heart rate and pulse had returned to normal. "Oh, noble Suleiman," he called out to his friend through the curtain. People didn't have doors in this settlement; they simply had pieces of cloth that would be hung over the doorway for whatever little privacy was possible. After a couple of seconds, a woman in a headscarf appeared. She smiled and asked who it was. "Tell him it's Al-Khidr."

She nodded and left. After two or three minutes, Suleiman pushed through his cloth door. Adorned in emerald oriental silk. "Peace and blessings."

# CHAPTER 4. THE SEARCH

"On you as well."

Suleiman beckoned Al-Khidr to follow him. He took him through his house.

"How is your father-in-law?" Al-Khidr inquired.

"Sadly, he passed away from the Jao-al-Baqr disease," Suleiman informed him.

"Very sad indeed!" Al-Khidr said.

"So, what brings you to me?" Suleiman enquired.

"I needed some help with—"

"Of course you do, you'd only come if you needed some help," Suleiman spitefully cut in.

"Can we not do this right now?"

Al-Khidr reached inside his sack and brought out each artifact carefully. The three special items were now in front of Suleiman, whose eyes twinkled. "Did you steal these?" he asked with a frown.

"No, I got them as a token of appreciation from the Caliph Al-Mamun."

"Oh, I see. Are these discovered from the Al-Ahram (the Great Pyramid)?" Suleiman looked interested. Al-Khidr nodded his head.

"And may I ask for what reason you got hold of these ancient artifacts?" he inquired.

"As you know, I was part of a pyramid exploration team," Al-Khidr said.

"They didn't pick me," Suleiman said grudgingly. "Our master, Al-Kindi, picked you instead. I guess you are his favorite student," Suleiman said sarcastically. "Master Al-Kindi selected me because of my work on acids and vinegars. Nothing more," Al-Khidr clarified.

"So, you want help for this artifact?" Suleiman asked.

Al-Khidr nodded his head and said, "Yes, it's enigmatic that it had not rusted for centuries, and I want to read the inscription over it. Maybe it contains the map of location where we might find books." He regretted saying this.

"Ah, I understand!" Suleiman's cunning eyes brightened. "Ancient Egyptians were the master alchemists. You could be right. I will try my best to solve it," Suleiman said with a spark in his eyes.

Suleiman picked up the orb and studied it for a full minute, turning it around.

"It's a cursed piece," he said abruptly. "You should throw it away."

"Never," said Al-Khidr. "I did not come here to hear this. I came so you could tell me anything you know about the origin, the nature, and everything else you can about these items."

Suleiman eyed Al-Khidr for many moments before he finally spoke.

"Fine. I'll do what I can, but you'll have to leave these with me for a week," Suleiman said. "A week? Does it looked like I have a week? You're mad."

"What's the rush?"

"I can't risk them being stolen. I want to get done with my analysis and then hide them somewhere."

"But you don't have much of a choice, because it'll take me that much time, so you'll have to wait."

"I do have a choice. There is another friend of mine, Yohannes, who is skilled in deciphering languages and uncovering the secrets of the ancient relics. Yoshua is also a friend of mine who can help."

"And...?"

"So, it's not like I don't have a choice. I came to you because I have known you longer than them."

"You'll have to give it to me and let me be alone with it so I can concentrate on it."

But Al-Khidr's gut feeling told him that no matter how much he trusted Suleiman, he couldn't leave the artifacts, because a week was a lot of time—enough for thieves to strike. Besides that, what if the orb had a map inside with information on the location of alchemy books, and Suleiman took it and hid it? "I understand. I think I'll be on my way, then."

"You're making a mistake. I can help you only if you give me some time."

"If I am unable to find sufficient information, I'll come back to you."

"I won't help you then." *Why is Suleiman acting so weirdly desperate?* Al-Khidr thought to himself.

Nonetheless, he had made his decision. A week was too much time, and he could probably get the answers he needed from someone else. Suleiman's expression soured after that. He did not ask Al-Khidr if he wanted lunch, or even tea or water. Al-Khidr was off.

\*\*\*

He rode back toward the main town, where he rested and ate at home before leaving again to meet his two other friends, Yohannes and Yoshua. This time, Al-Khidr strapped his sack of artifacts to Qantara and then placed over it a large piece of cloth so that it wasn't as visible. He set off. Yohannes, a Coptic Christian, didn't live too far, and Al-Khidr arrived at his door in only a few of minutes. Satan had made him forget that Yohannes lived nearby. It would have been better to visit him that morning, instead of going so far to meet Suleiman.

"My friend!" were the first words that left Yohannes' mouth.

"Peace and blessings."

"Onto you as well," Yohannes exclaimed in an excited tone. "It's so good to see you."

"Yes, you as well. It's been weeks since we last saw each other."

"I heard about your expedition. How did it go?" Yohannes enquired.

"Oh, it was unusually successful, thank the Lord."

"I am happy to hear that. Now, come on inside; you must be tired." When both men were seated inside, he asked: "What can I do for you?" That made Al-Khidr suddenly realize that he had forgotten the sack outside on the horse. "Help me God," he muttered as he zigzagged outside. Thankfully, the sack was still on the horse.

"Well, judging by how fast you ran to get that sack, you must have something of great value."

"True. This sack contains ancient artifacts that I am curious about, and I brought them here because you're skilled at identification and deciphering." Yohannes picked up each item and inspected them carefully. What Al-Khidr thought would have taken a mere number of minutes took half an hour. Yohannes took different books out of his library and compared the ancient scripts and the markings of the sphere. Al-Khidr was just admiring the keenness of his friend in helping him. Defeated, finally, Yohannes spoke.

"I really wish I could have helped you, but there is nothing that I can do." He paused. "You'll need to find someone who is a master at this. The markings on orb are neither truly ancient Egyptian hieroglyphs nor Coptic language."

It seemed almost as if Yohannes was sad at being unable to help. The two friends hugged, and Al-Khidr was once again on the road. This time, he was on his way towards another friend of his. Yoshua was a Jew from Alexandria who had moved to Al-Askar a few months ago and they meet in Bazaar and become friends. Yoshua lived approximately twenty minutes away from Yohannes' house, near Ben Ezra Synagogue. He was extremely happy to see Al-Khidr, because he hadn't seen him in the last three months.

"What brings you here in this old and forgotten part of town, oh noble warrior?"

"A favor. That is what has brought me here."

Al-Khidr took out the orb and the glass shard from his sack and showed them to Yoshua. For a moment, Yoshua looked at the glass shard more closely than the metallic orb.

"Where did you get these things? I hope you are

not excavating along with mummy hunters?" Yoshua laughed, and Al-Khidr followed. "No, no...I went inside the Great Pyramid!" Al-Khidr said.

"Really?" Yoshua jolted from his chair. "Did you find the Ark of the Covenant? I heard from sages that King Shishak took it from us." Yoshua was really excited. "Unfortunately, no, Yoshua. It was not there," Al-Khidr said.

"Alas," Yoshua said.

As Yoshua looked at the artifacts, Al-Khidr felt fairly sure that Yoshua would be able to help him, but when Yoshua shook his head, Al-Khidr's face fell. "Looks like I'll never find the answers to all my questions."

"You will in the afterlife!" Yoshua smiled.

Al-Khidr didn't reply. He started to put back the artifacts in the sack again.

"But I have a suggestion," Yoshua uttered. "I've heard of this man who goes by the name of Dhu Al-Nun Al-Misri. It is said that he has knowledge that most in Egypt have not even heard of. Specifically, he has the knowledge of old relics, ancient languages, *Sanat Al-Barabi* (the Craft of the Egyptian Temples) and *Khat Al-Barabi* (hieroglyphs)."

"Where can I find this man?" Al-Khidr asked, suddenly curious.

"He lives in Akhmim, the town of Hermes—but where exactly, that is unknown."

"Akhmim...Akhmim...where have I heard that word before?"

# CHAPTER 4.  THE SEARCH

"It's a well-known place, so of course you must have heard about it."

Al-Khidr had completely forgotten about the incident that had happened after the expedition; about the man who said he was from Akhmim. "Do you think it's worth a shot?"

"That is the only lead I can give you. There's no other way you will get those answers."

Al-Khidr nodded. Back on the horse, Al-Khidr knew this was his last chance. He uttered a small prayer under his breath for safety, and then rode into the distance. It was getting dark; only a quarter of the sun remained above the horizon. One man, determined and focused, rode into the sun, into the darkness, into his destiny.

# Chapter 5

# The Zawiya

Iᴛ had barely been more than half an hour since Al-Khidr started riding, but it was now completely dark. Risks of all sorts had tripled. There was no one to save Al-Khidr from bandits, because no one would see it happen—and besides, the roads were usually deserted during nighttime. There was also the risk of Al-Khidr running into something, or falling into a pit. In this darkness, and at the speed he was going, it was unlikely that he would see anything and react in time.

# Chapter 5. The Zawiya

*I should stay at an inn at the next settlement,* he told himself.

Egypt was indeed one of the hottest places to be on the planet in summers, but some nights here were considerably cold, and today was no exception. In fact, tonight was even colder than most nights. Al-Khidr wore a wool vest over his dress to cover his torso and a keffiyeh scarf over his mouth and nose to avoid the cold and dust attacking his face.

Through the darkness, a tiny light could be seen. This light was enlarging at an alarming speed. Al-Khidr figured that it was a carriage or cart coming toward him. *Do they see me?* he wondered.

If they didn't, they would run right into him. Al-Khidr slowed down and shifted his horse to the left so as to let the carriage or cart pass by. As it did, the warm glow from the lantern on the cart lit Al-Khidr's face momentarily, and as soon as the cart was out of the way, Al-Khidr resumed his journey. The more he rode, the more fear he felt inside, and the cold wasn't helping. On top of that, he started feeling sleepy. It wasn't like he had never been on a horse at night, but this time, the darkness was like a canopy covering the whole sky, and the moon seemed afraid to come out from behind its nearby clouds. He uttered a silent prayer and tightened his grip on the reins, and began looking for an inn.

Al-Khidr was so curious that he had put his life in danger just to find information about some artifacts. The only thing was, these were not just some artifacts.

They were quite special, but no one really knew yet.

*Akhmim is around forty farsakh (200 miles) from here. I require several days to reach this distance on Qantara, but he and I will surely need rest,* he thought to himself.

Near Al-Askar, there were many clusters of small towns, and he hadn't gone too far in this journey. Luckily, he found a *funduque* (an inn) in the next settlement. It was funduque Al-Hermes, a two-story house with a total of six rooms. The owner was a Coptic Christian called Aleksanaros, a short, chubby man with a long moustache. As Al-Khidr entered the lobby, Aleksanaros greeted with a wide smile. He paid forty dirhams for his stay. The Caliph had paid each of the explorer 300 dirhams, and to Al-Khidr and his acid-making team, he paid an extra 100 dirhams. He was quite content with his accomplishments, but he did not want to lose all his money in hotel fees.

"May I ask where you are going?" Aleksanaros asked. It seemed like he was bored and wanted some company. Al-Khidr was also looking for someone who could guide him on the way to Akhmim.

"I am going to Akhmim," Al-Khidr said.

"Ah, Akhmim, city of Hermes Trismegistus," Aleksanaros replied.

"Yes; one man, many names –Hoshang, Enoch, Akhnoch, Idris. But Al-Misri (Egyptian), anyway," Al-Khidr laughed.

"You don't look like an Egyptian, though," Aleksanaros said.

# Chapter 5. The Zawiya

"I am a Berber from Al-Maghreh, Amazigh speaker!" Al-Khidr said.

"Wow! Welcome, then." Aleksanaros suddenly became more interested in the conversation.

"By any chance, do you know a person called Dhu Al-Nun?" Al-Khidr asked.

"Yes, he was here last week, also heading towards Akhmim. I guess Akhmim is his hometown, but he commutes frequently from Akhmim to Fustat," Aleksanaros informed him. "I see. Anything more about him?" Al-Khidr asked, curious.

"He is generally called 'the Sufi,' but I guess he is a mystic, interested more in Hermetics. I heard he is one of the readers of the *Metut-neter* (hieroglyphs). Many Coptic Christians are among his disciples!" Aleksanaros said excitedly.

"Amazing—that is the reason I am looking for him, and I need his help in deciphering some markings and writings like Metut-neter," Al-Khidr informed him. "Can you tell me how he looks?"

Aleksanaros placed his fingers on his jaw and thought, then answered: "He is Nubian by birth, so he looks like a dark-skinned man with a curly, grey beard," "That's not very helpful," Al-Khidr thought to himself.

*** 

Al-Khidr was lying in bed and reviewing his options. He wasn't sure how much distance he had covered, or how much of his journey was left; he just wanted to get to Akhmim as fast as he could, to find Dhu Al-

Nun, and to uncover any possible clues regarding the artifacts. However, his plan was flawed in many ways. The most important flaw was that he had forgotten that he did not have Dhu Al-Nun's precise location. Another thing he had not thought through was that it was nighttime, and he had no confirmation whether Dhu Al-Nun would even want to see the objects at that time.

In a silent room, he got focused on pondering over the plan, which he now saw was not as perfect as he had previously thought it was. Things could easily go sideways for him. *What if I don't manage to find Dhu Al-Nun in the first place?* he thought. The unnecessary worries were overwhelming him.

Eventually, Al-Khidr shrugged off these thoughts and said to himself, "God will help!" He calmed himself and slept.

The next day, he started his journey anew. After an hour of riding, Al-Khidr had still not arrived at the road leading to Akhmim. He had been following his friend's directions, but now he was doubtful.

"I should have drawn a map. My mistake!" he exclaimed.

He might have missed the turn or gone in the wrong direction in the first place. Al-Khidr wanted to turn and go back, but something inside him kept him going forward—and hopefully forward was the direction of Akhmim.

"I could have taken a boat," he thought for a while, then shrugged off the thought, knowing it might delay his goal.

\*\*\*

In the end, Al-Khidr had to travel almost a week on his horse to reach Akhmim. He was aware that the journey might be long, so he had kept some extra dirhams in his pouch. He stayed at multiple inns on the hot days to avoid heatstroke or bandits, and sometimes at night, if he was too tired to carry on. Al-Khidr could see himself going lengths he had never gone before. It was almost as if he had been controlled by the artifacts since the time, he had received them; as if Al-Khidr were gaining some mysterious power from the artifacts themselves.

It was roughly an hour before sunset. Al-Khidr had traveled at a decent speed for a little over three days, including his stays at inns, when he finally saw something that uplifted his mood: the sight of a town on the east side of the Nile.

*It may be Akhmim*, he thought to himself, as Akhmim was the only town on the east side of the Nile in this region. Luckily, he was also on the east side of the Nile. Yoshua had guided him well about the distance and the direction.

Traveling for another fifteen minutes revealed more about the town in the distance, and a rush of joy surged through Al-Khidr. This journey had been a lot longer and more exhausting than most he had previously done.

This surge of happiness was short-lived, as he was

annoyed by the fact that he did not even know where to look for this random stranger. He had travelled for so long and so far; he did not want it all to be for nothing. His thoughts only continued to bug him. The smile he once had now vanished, leaving behind a creased forehead. Would people on the street know about Dhu Al-Nun? Would this man even be able to help? Had this whole endeavor been a complete waste of time and effort? He hoped not. This was the worst time for second thoughts, as the city lights were waving at him through the darkness. Al-Khidr had spent his whole week in pursuit of this place; it would be all for nothing if he backed off now. He slowed his horse to a trot as he neared the town, and asked the first person he saw on the street about where to find Dhu Al-Nun. The man looked like a village farmer.

"Salamalaikum (peace and blessings), is this Akhmim?"

"Walaikum as Salam (peace and blessings on you too), yes. It is! "

"I am looking for Dhu Al-Nun. Do you know him?"

"Dhu Al-Nun?" the man asked again with a confused expression. Al-Khidr nodded. The man thought about it for a while before he finally answered.
"No...ahhh...does Dhu Al-Nun work in the cotton fields?"

"I guess not!"

"Then I don't know."

"If you didn't know, why didn't you just tell me from the start?" Al-Khidr was annoyed.

The man walked off. This was the worst and most

demotivating start.

\*\*\*

Al-Khidr searched the street for someone else to ask. His eyes darted between people, trying to find someone who wasn't immature and would mess around with him, nor someone so old that he would have to repeat the question seven times and still not get the answer he was looking for. He found a middle-aged man in yellow clothing who was leading a goat up the street.

He seems like a person who would know, Al-Khidr thought to himself.

"Peace and blessings," he said to the man.

"Upon you as well," the man replied.

"I'm trying to find someone who goes by the name Dhu Al-Nun. Would you happen to know where this person can be found?" The man curled his long mustache, looked right and left, and asked Al-Khidr to follow him. Al-Khidr trotted behind the man and the goat for a couple hundred meters. "Here, get off your horse."

Al-Khidr obediently did as told. He tied Qantara to a nearby signboard, where Qantara found a puddle and started drinking water. Al-Khidr was happy at least Qantara had the chance to quench his thirst.

"He is awaiting your arrival inside. I will be outside." The man curled his mustache from both ends.

Al-Khidr was surprised. *If Dhu Al-Nun is waiting, he knew I was coming. How would he know when I would come*, though?

Al-Khidr decided that he would ask the man inside himself. He noticed that this house, or whatever it was, had a door. This was unusual, as people in Egypt mostly had curtains hung as doors, and not actual solid, wooden doors. This door had two locks on the outside and one on the inside. Al-Khidr didn't give it much thought, and he entered quickly.

He entered through the doorway and followed the passage. The passage was dimly lit, due to husked roof, and so was the room inside. It led to a single large room, which was not fully furnished, and a tiny connected kitchen. No one would exactly describe this place as a rundown shelter, but it was definitely shabby to some extent. One thing was sure—this didn't look like the living quarters of a knowledgeable man like Dhu Al-Nun. Al-Khidr's gut feeling told him to leave, but he didn't want to run away when he was so close.

Al-Khidr called out, but there was no reply. He sat on the battered wooden chair. He waited for a minute or two before he decided to leave. Something still didn't seem right; it was best to wait outside. He walked back through the dimly lit passage, and he saw that the door had shut. The wind should have been the obvious reason, but it was not the wind. When Al-Khidr tried to open the door, everything became clear to him. Always think positive. Always think positive,he told himself.

He tried the door, and sure enough, it was locked. *How on earth was I so foolish?* he thought. *I walked right into this one.* He didn't know what to do, but he knew he had to do something. He had been locked in here with his sack of artifacts; he would be searched, and those were the first thing they would see. The possibility was low, but if he did make it out of here, it definitely wouldn't be with his items. He knew he didn't have much time. The man with the mustache was probably on his way back with reinforcements. Al-Khidr could fight off a man or two, but there was no way of knowing how many men were coming back.

The door was a solid one. No matter how hard Al-Khidr tried to smash against it, he could not break through the lock. Al-Khidr's shoulder hurt, but the lock wasn't hurt one bit. It had been locked from the outside with a sliding lock, so that even if Al-Khidr had known how to pick locks and had a lock pick on him, the outlook would still be bleak.

With his back against the wall in the corridor next to the door, Al-Khidr slid down hopelessly. He tried to control his breath and calm down. He ran his hands through his dirt-covered hair and then over his face. How!?

Suddenly he got a sudden rush of energy and stood up. He ran back to the large room and tried to find something to help him get out, but still, he could not find anything useful to break a lock. He then heard people talking on the outside. He knew his time had run out. Then, an idea struck him. He picked up the table that was beside him, the glass and the jug that were on it smashing onto the floor. He then hit the table hard against the wall, breaking two of its legs. He knew it was a long shot, but he had to do something. He tied the sack against his stomach and then proceeded toward the door with his two table legs in either hand. The ends of the legs were sharp, but Al-Khidr was an alchemist, not a warrior. He knew that he had to play this strategically if he was to make it out of here alive and with his artifacts. He blew out the two candles that were placed in the corridor. The door was opening; he could hear the man or men outside coming in. Al-Khidr got into position to the left of the door so that when the door was pushed open, he would be hidden behind it, out of sight for the men. This meant that when the men came inside to find him, Al-Khidr could sneak out behind their backs. He kept the two table legs for self-defense, just in case things got sour. The man with the mustache was the first to enter through the door. He paused for a second, surprised by the darkness. He had a dagger in his hand, which he held out soon as he saw it was dark. Another two men followed him inside, and the door was shut. One of them had a large spear. The other, as Al-Khidr, judged, was probably the man with authority; the one would get most of whatever they got off of him.

"Light the candles and stand facing the door," the man with the mustache instructed the man with the spear." He will try to make a run for it." Al-Khidr knew that even with the candles out, the man would see him standing against the wall when he turned around, as the door was now shut and Al-Khidr was standing there unshielded. Al-Khidr knew he had to do something, and fast, or else he'd be discovered. The plan he had thought of a couple of seconds ago was now falling apart. In desperation, as he saw the guard turning toward him, he threw one of the legs spinning through the air toward the wall on the far end. All three of the men heard it and ran toward the noise. This diversion and confusion gave Al-Khidr only two or three seconds, but that was all he needed. Just one second after the noise of the table leg was heard, the door was opened. The men shifted their gazes toward the door and saw Al-Khidr running away, and all lurched towards the door after him, but once outside, Al-Khidr was quick enough to slide the locking pin into place. The door banged loudly multiple times. Al-Khidr took in a long breath of the fresh night air, checked his sack, and sprinted toward his horse. The prey had now become the predator! On his mount, Al-Khidr didn't even need to make a decision. He knew when enough was enough, and he had had enough. He now grabbed Qantara's reins and set off toward home. It was out of the question to go looking for Dhu Al-Nun anymore.

*** 

Al-Khidr was almost at the outskirts of the city when he saw a man in a long cloak up ahead in the middle of the road. Must be a hungry beggar or an old man,he thought to himself.

Al-Khidr slowed down and tried to go to the left. The man, however, moved with him and came in front of the horse without fear. Al-Khidr managed to stop Qantara only a meter away from the man.

"Are you crazy? I almost ran over you!" Al-Khidr was furious.

The man did not say anything. He looked toward Al-Khidr with his small eyes and smiled. "Oh no, it's another robber," Al-Khidr said to himself out loud.

"I am no thief," the man answered. "I am a friend."

"Care to explain why a friend would get in the way of my horse?"

"Because a friend knows what's best for you." The man removed the hood from his head. He was a middle-aged man with a medium-sized beard. "What do you want?"

"I am poor, child. Give some alms!"

"No, not when you are forcing me by getting in my way," Al-Khidr shouted.

He was annoyed and tired, and this beggar could also be part of the gang he just locked up a few minutes ago. "You are not from here; you came to seek someone."

"How do you know I am not from here?" Al-Khidr suspiciously eyed the man in the long cloak. "Are you an accomplice to those bandits?" "I am a helper."

Al-Khidr overcame his nervousness and realized that he was simply overreacting. He said, "If you can help, then just tell me where I may find Dhu Al-Nun." "Dhu Al-Nun is our Sufi master. I can take you to him."

The words hung around in the air for a moment as they sunk into Al-Khidr's mind.

"You're trying to fool me, like the other man did, and then rob me."

"If that's what you think, you're free to go back to wherever you came from, but if you want to meet Dhu Al-Nun, then follow me."

Though Al-Khidr was fairly sure this beggar was not a liar, the earlier happenings kept circulating through his head. He brought out his knife and hid it inside his sleeve so he could instantly access it if the need arose.

The beggar then took Al-Khidr to the narrow but serpentine-shaped alleyway. When they reached the end, it was a cul-de-sac, but there was a door there. "Tie your horse here." The beggar pointed toward a pole in the ground. Al-Khidr got off of Qantara. The beggar knocked at the door. An old man opened it, and Al-Khidr was stunned. The man who opened the door was the same as the one who had whispered in his ear when he came out of the Great Pyramid.

\*\*\*

The whole incident of the old man whispering in his ear outside the Great Pyramid came back to him again. The Sufi mystic wore a cream-colored cotton jalabiya, had a fist-long, curly grey and black beard, and had a disheveled, beggar-like look about him.

"By God, you are Dhu Al-Nun."

Al-Khidr followed the man into his house.

"Welcome to Khem. Sit, child." The man with Nubian face smiled warmly. Though old, he looked quite active for his age. Akhmim had two more names: Panopolis, and Khem. Al-Khidr had recently learned these names in his travels.

Al-Khidr moved his sight around the room; it had a large table with wooden chairs on either side. There was also a drawer. This place appeared to be Dhu Al-Nun's *Zawiya*, or lodge. It wasn't grand, but at the same time, it wasn't a wreck. It was a decent, well-maintained lodge, big enough to accommodate a few more people. There was only one servant present.

Dhu Al-Nun returned with a tray, and he set it down on the table.

"First, replenish your energy, and then we can talk about the reason why you're here."

Al-Khidr was extremely hungry. He took a sip from the cup. It was unsweetened, partly salty, pure camel milk. The other things on the tray were some nuts and dried fruits. Al-Khidr ate the whole plate, took a gulp of milk, and then he was done. Dhu Al-Nun smiled as he took small sips from his own cup. "Sheikh, I'm sorry for eating like an animal. I've been journeying for the last... " Al-Khidr called the Dhu Al-Nun Sheikh because he was a well-known, learned man of Hermetics and the ancient Egyptian writing system.

"No need to apologize. Food is something that one should eat in peace, and in whatever quantity they feel is healthy for them." Al-Khidr nodded.

"Child, only a man who has eaten well and rested

well can conquer the world. The body's weakness comes from illnesses, while the heart's weakness comes from sins," Dhu Al-Nun said.

"I was there in the crowd when you came out of the Great Aakhut. Many like me are interested in what you learned inside," Dhu Al-Nun continued. "Aakhut?" Al-Khidr hadn't heard this name before.

"Yes, Aakhut, the ancient name of the Pyramid in Metut Neter. Some mystics hold the view that they are ancient, very ancient, maybe even before the prophet Adam," Dhu Al-Nun said.

"Sheikh Dhu Al-Nun, I need your help. We found many interesting things in the pyramid, including the gold and the statue, but I only got the chance to get three artifacts as a souvenir for my involvement in this excavation project," Al-Khidr said.

He paused and looked at the old man, who looked interested to hear more, so Al-Khidr continued.

"I know you are interested in alchemy, and so am I. If we can open this orb, maybe we find the way to the location of the long-lost knowledge of the alchemy of ancients. I asked my friends, but none of them could open it or understand its purpose. But since I found it inside the core of the Pyramid, I am sure it must have a huge importance. That is why I am here all the way from Fustat to Akhmim, only to consult you."

"Child, the real knowledge of alchemy is long lost. It was lost in the Great Flood, when the curse of Prophet Noah, blessings be on him, was accepted by God of the Universe and He filled the Earth with the waters of the heavens. Allah destroys, and He is the one who creates. But I will try to help you the best I can, as I learned from my masters, the Metut Neter," the old man said.

Al-Khidr handed over his sack of items. Dhu Al-Nun took out each of the three artifacts and set them on the table, picked each of them up cautiously, one by one, and studied them. Al-Khidr was by now feeling extremely tired. He wanted to ask how long it would potentially take Dhu Al-Nun to give him more information on the relics, but he felt that would be rude.

Instead, he patiently waited. As the minutes went by, he started to feel sleepy. He tried to keep his eyes open, but the more he tried, the sleepier he got. Dhu Al-Nun noticed how drowsy and sleepy Al-Khidr was.

"You can rest for a while right over there, if you want." He pointed toward a straw mattress on the floor in the next room. Al-Khidr was too sleepy to say he was fine or that he would not rest till he found the answer. He got up and walked over to the next room. As soon as his body hit the mattress, an immense wave of tiredness overwhelmed him and sleep took him. He couldn't keep his eyes open. The next thing he knew, he was falling, falling into a black void.

Just as the last of his consciousness slipped away, he muttered one last sentence: "There was something in my food! God save me."

# Chapter 6

# The Sphere of Light

"Suleiman! What are you doing here?" Al-Khidr was surprised to see his friend some hundreds of miles from his house.

"I'm just here to take back a favor that Dhu Al-Nun asked for years ago." Suleiman grinned with an evil smile.

"What favor? I didn't know you knew Dhu Al-Nun," Al-Khidr inquired as he got up from the floor.

Suleiman kept quiet. Al-Khidr was completely confused. The first thing he saw was his friend standing above him in Dhu Al-Nun's house. This made little sense, as Suleiman rarely traveled such distances; in fact, he despised sitting on a horse continuously for so many hours. It couldn't have taken him less than five days and four nights to get here. What was going on?

"O Suleiman, what is going on here?"

"You'll see soon enough."

Al-Khidr didn't want to see; he wanted to know. But Suleiman was in no mood to reveal the true reason for his surprising arrival. Al-Khidr knew that Suleiman was someone who could surprise him with anything.

In the past, Suleiman had shocked Al-Khidr by giving refuge, in his own house, to a criminal with an enormous price on his head. "You have a family, Suleiman!" Al-Khidr had tried to knock some sense into his friend. "Do you understand that police can arrest you for giving that man refuge?" "I do, now shut up and walk away, or by God... "

That incident now flashed in front of Al-Khidr's eyes. There was silence for a couple of minutes. Al-Khidr didn't have to wait long for the grand reveal. The sound of heavy footsteps was heard in the distance. The footsteps stopped outside the curtain Dhu Al-Nun was behind. For a second, Al-Khidr thought he had imagined the sound. Suddenly, through the doorway came two large men. They had hefty hands, and Al-Khidr avoided thinking about all the damage they could do to someone. The large men came to a halt right behind Suleiman. It then became clear to

Al-Khidr who they worked for. "Suleiman, you better tell me what is going on here." His voice rising.

"Settle down."

"Dhu Al-Nun, give me the artifacts."

Shuffling was heard in the inside room.

"Suleiman, please..." "Al-Khidr, it would be best that you don't interfere in things that don't concern you."

"By God, what do you mean?" Al-Khidr was angered. "Those artifacts are my property."

"Not anymore." Al-Khidr couldn't believe his ears. Suleiman had let go all those years of friendship for these artifacts? Sure, Suleiman might be unpredictable, but this... Dhu Al-Nun came into view with the sack and handed it over to Suleiman.

"What are you doing? I trusted you."

"Shouldn't have trusted me so easily."

"Here, Suleiman. The key to unlocking everything is combining the artifacts together."

Al-Khidr knew he had to take a stand, or else all of this was for nothing. He raised his fist.

Suleiman smiled and patted one of the large men on the shoulder. "Just don't kill him."

"I appreciate your kindness, Suleiman!" Al-Khidr sarcastically shouted behind the departing man. "Come back here, you coward!" Suleiman was unaffected. He simply disappeared into the night outside.

"God bless you, Al-Khidr," chuckled Dhu Al-Nun, and he vanished into thin air.

Al-Khidr was so confused by his sudden disappearance that he forgot the two men who were about to beat him up. A heavy blow landed on his cheek, and Al-Khidr went flying into the wall. The two men came near, and then instead of punching him directly, they raised their fists above their heads and then brought them down on the floor.

Al-Khidr thought they had missed by mistake, but such was not the case. The earth below Al-Khidr started trembling, and then he was falling. As he fell, the only thing he saw was Dhu Al-Nun's house, suspended in the air. How was this even physically possible?

He didn't get much time to think; he was falling at a great speed. The hole from which he had fallen was getting smaller in the distance, and all around him was complete darkness. There was nothing but darkness, and it was only getting darker with every passing second. *This is not real,* he thought. *This can't be real.* Al-Khidr couldn't even see his hands right in front of him anymore; that's how dark it was. And then, somehow, the darkness was eating at him. He felt as if he was losing his skin. It didn't hurt, but he could feel it dispersing into the air around him. Slowly, he was no more. He had been shredded into tiny pieces. He didn't know if he was dead or alive.

And then his eyes opened.

***

*Am I dead?* he asked himself.

He attempted to get up, and found that he could.

But was this only his soul getting up, or was he getting up as a whole? He stumbled into the inner room, where Dhu Al-Nun was still on his chair, poring over one of the artifacts.

"You traitor!" Al-Khidr shouted. "I will murder you!"

Dhu Al-Nun threw his hands in the air, a confused expression spreading across his face.

Al-Khidr brought out his knife.

"What is going on?" Dhu Al-Nun boomed. "Are you crazy?"

"You...you gave my artifacts to Suleiman."

"First, who's Suleiman? Second, why would I give your items to someone else?"

Al-Khidr put back his knife. He apologized.

"I assume you had a very realistic dream?"

Al-Khidr nodded.

"Seek refuge in God, and none of that will transcend into real life, if God wills."

Al-Khidr dropped himself onto the chair. He ran his palms over his face.

"You got scared."

"At first I thought you had poisoned me, and then you had betrayed me."

"I wouldn't do either," Dhu Al-Nun replied. "I would do everything I can to avoid hurting a fellow brother, so you had really nothing to worry about." There was a pause.

"How long have I been out?"

"Five hours, or something like that."

# CHAPTER 6. THE SPHERE OF LIGHT

"Did you find anything about the artifacts?"

"Unfortunately, I couldn't find anything. These are truly strange markings. Maybe not from this planet."

"Not from our planet? You mean this somehow came to earth from some other planet?"

Dhu Al-Nun nodded. "It seems so."

"But what about combining all three artifacts together?"

"What?"

"In my dream, you told Suleiman to combine all three to unlock the secret."

"Al-Khidr, never mention dreams out loud. It was a bad dream, and dreams should not be discussed like this." He paused. "They can become real."

\*\*\*

"I wish I could have made your whole journey worth it."

"At least I got some rest to make it to the next town," Al-Khidr said to himself, and rubbed his eyes.

"It's almost dawn, you should pray before the sun rises."

Al-Khidr nodded. "I want to make Wudu (ablution)."

"Outside, take a left, and then the first right."

Al-Khidr made his way outside, seeing a slight tint of light blue in the sky filled with stars. It would be dawn soon.

He performed ablution and said the prayer. He remained sitting outside and beseeched God for an answer to the enigmatic orb and the glass fragment. The sun rose, and he hurried back to the room, where Dhu Al-Nun announced: "Child, it was night, so in lamp's light I couldn't see much. But now, in sunlight, I found something. I am able to decipher only one phrase written around the hole in the orb."

Al-Khidr was delighted. He hurried towards the table and sat on his knees to see what exactly was written. In the sunlight the old man noticed that on the orb there were some symbols and writings. On the periphery of the hole, some part of the symbols were like hieroglyphs.

"Only some of the markings here are similar to Metut Neter." Dhu Al-Nun placed his figure at the position, and Al-Khidr also could see the very small engraving. "Strange; I hadn't noticed it before," Al-Khidr said.

"Whatever is engraved on the orb was done with an unknown, sophisticated technology. I had never seen such precision, even in ancient Egyptian temple writings. It's engraved: '*As above, so below,*'" Dhu Al-Nun said.

"I'll be on my way, Master, thank you very much," Al-Khidr announced once he was done with feeding his horse. "You can stay for breakfast."

Al-Khidr shook his head. "It's best that I be on my way."

Dhu Al-Nun understood. Al-Khidr still had not found what he had come for.

# Chapter 6. The Sphere of Light

\*\*\*

Al-Khidr sped through clouds of sand, galloping as fast as his horse could. The more he rode, the more the curiosity brewed inside. He rode for five hours straight. The words, as above, so below, were coming back to his mind again and again. Apart from the words, the previous night's dream was also too vivid in his memories. The words from his dream, combined with the artifacts, were continuously resounding in his mind.

Close to noon, Al-Khidr arrived at a small town, where he ate, rested, and was off again. He left the town an hour after sundown, continuing his journey in complete darkness. As he rode, he started to realize that the road was bumpier this time. On his way here, he hadn't felt the road to be like this. Nonetheless, he continued on. Only when he reached the next city did he realize that he had gone in the wrong direction. He had taken a longer route.

Al-Khidr was thoroughly annoyed, but now that he had taken such a large detour, it didn't make sense to go back. Over the next several days, Al-Khidr stopped and rested at four more inns in separate small towns, which cost him some dirhams. Qantara needed the rest as well. His hooves were hot. When he was nearing another town, he realized that it was actually the town he had been to about thirteen days ago. It was the town where Kamal lived. He could ride just a bit more and arrive back at home, but he was so tired that he decided to rest for just an hour at his friend's house. Kamal had seen Al-Khidr when he was suffering from some stomach ailment. Al-Khidr treated him, and ever since, they had become fast friends.

Kamal was surprised to see Al-Khidr. He greeted him and asked him in.

"Blessings and welcome, brother," Kamal said, delighted to see Al-Khidr. "Where are you coming from?" he further asked.

"Oh, that is a long story. I am too sleepy. May I rest at your place for an hour?" Al-Khidr inquired.

"Guests are always welcome. But you are more than that my friend," Kamal said.

Kamal came closer and patted Al-Khidr on the back, something that he usually didn't do. "Come, you can rest here." He pointed toward a small room on the left. Al-Khidr followed with his sack of relics.

"Put that there."

Al-Khidr obediently placed the sack on the table, and lay down on the hay mattress in the corner of the room. "Wake me up in an hour," he told Kamal. Then he shut his eyes and drifted off.

Al-Khidr was woken at the time he had asked, ate lunch with Kamal , and then was off along with his sack of artifacts. He felt a lot better after sleeping. His house was only an hour or two away, so this journey was finally coming to an end. At least, that's what he thought. Not even in his wildest dreams did he think that this was not even the start. The actual journey would only begin a little later.

# CHAPTER 6. THE SPHERE OF LIGHT

Along the road, Al-Khidr saw other riders as well. He had departed from the town only fifteen minutes ago. He was once again lost in his thoughts about the dream. It bothered him that Suleiman was the antagonist in it. Suleiman had been true to him for years now. Yes, their friendship had gone through highs and lows, but surely Suleiman was not as evil as his dreams suggested, right?

It was almost nighttime now. The darkness had settled, but the moon was unhidden by any clouds, so there was quite a bit of light, at least enough for a rider to ride safely. Up ahead of him, he saw a man slowly trotting with his horse. He did not want to slow down his horse. This was strange, as anyone could suddenly ride up and crash into them from behind.

Al-Khidr overtook the man. Only a couple hundred meters later, he saw a carriage with horses on the side of the road. The driver was on his knees, trying to reattach a wooden wheel that had come off. Al-Khidr felt an urge to slow down to help him out, and got off his mount.

"Peace and blessings."

"Peace and blessings."

"Do you need any help?"

"If you can. My wife is pregnant; she is inside, and I hope to leave this area as soon as I can. It's not safe."

"I understand," Al-Khidr replied after glancing at the closed-off carriage. Robbers looked for targets like these, people who had a damaged wheel. Al-Khidr leaned in to inspect the wheel. It was perfectly fine; it had just come off. Al-Khidr heard another person slow down and get off their horse, but he didn't check who it was. "How come there is no damage whatsoever to the wheel? Is this a fresh one?" Al-Khidr asked, confused. "Yes. Yes, it is."

"That means there isn't a problem at all. You should be able to easily fit it on, and..." It struck him like a spear. He had been tricked again. Al-Khidr slowly straightened his back and gave one look to the man who had stopped after him. Sure enough, he stood behind Al-Khidr threateningly with a pocket knife.

"The sack," said the man who was supposedly fixing his cart's wheel, getting up from the ground. "We don't want to hurt you. Just give us whatever metallic you have."

Al-Khidr wasn't on his horse, and he was surrounded by four men. Where had they come from?

Al-Khidr quickly realized that the other two men must have been inside the carriage. There was no woman inside; that was just a lie. Al-Khidr quickly thought of what to say.

"The sack is strapped to my horse. I'll unstrap them for you." He started to move towards his horse, but in a raspy voice, one of the men said, "Stop. You think you can fool us? You will get on the horse and escape. I'll do it myself."

"But there is a lock. How will you unlock it yourself, then?"

# Chapter 6. The Sphere of Light

"Give me the key, I'll do it myself."

"No, I will do it."

"You don't have a choice. Abdullah, get the key from him," he said, commanding one of the men who came out of the carriage. The other man appeared from behind the carriage.

Al-Khidr gave the man the key to his house. By the time they realized that there was no lock, Al-Khidr had kicked to the ground the only man who was close to him, and was making his way to the other man's horse. He mounted it, and the horse started galloping. The other men tried to stab the horse, but they missed. Al-Khidr was getting away, his artifacts tied against his stomach. He knew that he could easily be robbed, so he had decided to place his objects somewhere they wouldn't expect to find them. This new horse was a lot faster than his, so he lost the robbers in no time. Al-Khidr had avoided his fate yet again. "Thank God...but we belong to God, and to Him shall we return. Alas, I lost Qantara!" he exclaimed out loud.

Al-Khidr reached home just before the sunset, as the tinge of twilight appeared on the horizon. He was right in front of his house's door, but had lost the keys to the bandits.

The lock at his door was ancient and bought from Fustat. It was made of metal, like a giant key with multiple angles and loops. It was brown, but silver in the middle. A needle had been inserted into the middle to get to the lock. He had borrowed a needle from his neighbor which was meant to be used for clamping off the tents. He used it to break the lock. After some sweat-profusing moments, he managed to break the lock.

The first thing he did as he entered his house, after breaking the lock of the door, was to bring out the three objects from his sack. He placed each of them on the table: the withered piece of rope, the glass shard, and the mysterious metallic orb. He took one look at them, and he knew exactly how he would go about it. It was as if the artifacts themselves had whispered the secret in his ears on the way back. The withered rope had almost unraveled into threads, and looked not of much use. However, the orb and malleable glass were intact.

He stared into the center indent in the orb. He blew into it, and then put his finger inside, trying to find a hinge to open up the artifact. It felt quite heavy, and it clearly weighed more than any other metal piece of the same diameter he had seen before. *It definitely holds something inside—maybe a map of the location of books on ancient Egyptian alchemical knowledge, or something else—and I will find that out*, Al-Khidr thought to himself.

As he was playing around with the orb, suddenly, something happened. The way he was holding the orb made his fingers brush against a specific, strange engraving. As they did, the sphere rotated and opened from the top. Al-Khidr was surprised. He had guessed that there was some sort of compartment inside the orb, but to see it in real life was a whole new experience.

It then occurred to him to just place the malleable glass in this empty sphere. He did so, as this was a sign from the dream, too, to combine the artifacts. He placed the glass shard into the compartment, which had some perforations. The glass looked solid for few seconds, but then it seeped through the tiny perforations and went inside like a liquid. Al-Khidr tilted and moved the orb to see if liquid glass was coming out, but nothing happened. The two artifacts were now one. Al-Khidr was holding the orb, or metallic sphere, in his hand. For a minute, nothing happened, but then the orb started to vibrate. The top of the orb started rotating slowly with the glass, which had now transformed into a strange, viscous, dark liquid, which was vibrating along with the orb. The dark liquid was darker than anything Al-Khidr had ever witnessed.

*Should I throw this liquid out?* he wondered. He was a bit confused.

*What if it's an acid?* he thought to himself.

The liquid had now started to gleam, emanating waves of blue light. Al-Khidr was frightened, and he wanted to throw away the sphere, but it was stuck to his hands and he couldn't move. He was in a trance, unable to remove his eyes from the now-blinding liquid. It was shifting its color from black to silver. Al-Khidr felt as if he was blind, because all he could see was totally unbelievable.

He now felt as if there was wind around him. "*Al-*

*Hawa* (wind)?" Al-Khidr asked aloud. "How?"

He couldn't move or see anything, apart from the blinding exotic matter, but he could tell something had changed. He felt the temperature to be a lot cooler, and he felt more wind rushing against him.

"Someone help me, please!" He tried to make a run for it, but soon realized he could not move.

Al-Khidr couldn't move, but the orb could. It started to shake violently, and then light burst out from all directions. The streams of light connected somehow, making a sphere around him. He was now inside a large, glowing sphere. The light made him want to shut his eyes, but he couldn't. Al-Khidr was paralyzed. Suddenly, he felt himself moving upward. Apparently, moving away from Earth. The large sphere he was in broke through his wooden roof, and the next moment, he was flying up, high in the sky. Looking down at broken roof of his house, he felt nauseated. He couldn't believe his eyes. He was flying upward, and in a bubble of light! As he passed them, a few birds or bats dropped dead as the heat from the sphere burned them alive.

Al-Khidr was high in the sky now, and could see the pyramids and the Nile through the blue aura of the sphere. In few more seconds, he was going through the clouds. The speed of his glowing sphere only increased by every second. Around him, things were getting darker as he was going upward toward space. And then, through the darkness, a glowing tunnel started to come into view. The glowing sphere fit through it, and now he was going through a tunnel with no control whatsoever.

There was one major, overwhelming thought going through Al-Khidr's mind:

*Am I dead, and going towards the door of the sky?*

The sudden headache made him unconscious while the orb was still stuck to his hands.

# Chapter 7

# The Arrival on Al-Eard

AL-KHIDR'S woke up. Only God knows how long he was in this state. His hands were still holding the orb. The black matter inside was boiling within it, and the reverberations were traveling to Al-Khidr's fingers. It was strange to him how it wasn't hot to the touch, despite it very clearly boiling.

"This is all a dream," he told himself out loud. "Do not believe anything you see."

# Chapter 7. The Arrival on Al-Eard

But even then, he doubted his own opinion. He didn't know how to confirm whether it was a dream. It certainly didn't feel like one, but the visuals only made sense if they were a dream. How could he possibly fly? Flying was completely out of the question.

Al-Khidr, still within the glowing sphere, continued through the tunnel for several minutes. He could see the stars. At last, he saw the end. The sphere zoomed out of the tunnel, and now he was right above a planet.

The planet was a large one, but not completely round like a ball; it had a slight depression at one side. The glowing sphere continued to levitate above the planet with Al-Khidr inside.

The boiling became very intense, and then the glowing sphere lurched toward the planet in a sudden motion. Al-Khidr fell, but the artifact orb's fluid didn't spill out as it should have. The whole time, the black exotic matter was boiling in the orb and generating a glowing, spherical aura around him. The sun, he noticed, was surrounded by a circumstellar debris disk.

Maybe it's not visible from the ground because of the clouds, he thought.

The glowing sphere was still descending. As he got closer to the planet, he had a clearer view. A shockwave formed, but inside the sphere, it wasn't hot. However, due to drag, Al-Khidr was pushed towards the wall of the energy ball.

"*Al-Eard* (the Earth), *Al-Eard!* I am not dead yet. O God, have mercy," Al-Khidr exclaimed in Arabic, his sobbing eyes wide with excitement. The glowing sphere came closer to the planet, brightened by the sun and surrounded by strange, circumstellar debris.

As he drew closer, Al-Khidr saw recognizable topography. He could tell he had seen this place before, but couldn't point out where he was. When he got closer, the realization stuck: the place looked like Egypt, yet somehow, strangely, it had taken him a while to identify it. He could see the familiar pyramids and obelisks, which were clearly visible, but lo and behold, there was something very different about them. For a moment, Al-Khidr couldn't believe his eyes. He blinked his eyes, as if that would suddenly bring the spectacle back to normal. But the dark, black pyramids looked back at him.

*How could these suddenly be a different color?* he wondered. The creepy black pyramids sent shivers down his spine.

"*Ikhan! Abouhari!* (Crazy, shit!)" he was shouting in Amazigh, his mother tongue. He was so consumed in trying to comprehend how the pyramids could have changed their colors overnight, he forgot that he was literally in a strange sphere, slowly descending towards the ground.

"How can all this be real?"

The sphere slowly came close to the river below. The water from the river was flowing towards the sphere, but was unable to penetrate it. The birds near the river dove down inside it instead of flying, as the sphere glided over river swiftly.

*"The Nile?"*

# CHAPTER 7. THE ARRIVAL ON AL-EARD

The artifact in his hands was now giving strange beeping sounds. He had never heard anything like it before. Al-Khidr wanted to move his hands away from the artifact in fear of what might happen, but the artifact didn't let him. It was firmly stuck to his hands. Then the sphere moved up to a large structure surrounded by mountains. The sphere sped up, and Al-Khidr then realized where the sphere was heading. Between two giant statues of standing Anubis-looking figures which were carved in the cliff, he saw a narrow opening with a metallic door. There were suspended clouds all around, giving the entire area a mystical appearance. The entrance was too high in cliffs and inaccessible by foot.

At first, Al-Khidr thought he would smash into the door of the opening, because it didn't open until the very last moment, gobbling up the sphere into its depths. It seemed as if the door had been waiting for the arrival of the sphere.

Al-Khidr was astonished. *There must be a person who was looking from the windows and opened the door,* Al-Khidr told himself. As soon as the sphere entered the structure and the door was shut, there was momentary darkness. The sphere was still moving forward, and the further it moved into the depths, the more visible things became. The tunnel the sphere was going through was a well-crafted one, Al-Khidr noted. After a few moments, the tunnel ended and the sphere entered a large hall.

The sphere hurled upwards and moved towards the

station at the far end of the hall. Slowly, the black matter inside the orb slowed down its agitation. After it had completely stopped boiling, the lid of the orb closed, and no signs of any black boiling liquid could be seen any longer. As soon as the orb turned inactive, Al-Khidr felt weak. It was almost as if it was the orb had been powering Al-Khidr throughout the journey. Al-Khidr felt so exhausted that he started getting dizzy; the artifact now fell from his hands. He rested with both his hands on the glass-like sphere he was in; it was a cocoon of energy around him.

Despite the orb being the obvious powering object, the glowing sphere was still intact, and the artifact was rolling like a ball at the base of the glowing sphere even after it fell. Then Al-Khidr felt some strange force move his head toward the ceiling of the sphere, and the force took control over his arms. With no energy to resist the force, his arms were forced to spread open. Now his fingers on either hand touched the glasslike material of the sphere on both sides. For a second, Al-Khidr felt as if he was levitating, as if he was suspended within the glowing sphere. He had no control over anything that was happening. It was like the energy had slowly drained from his body, and now he was clutching his last breath. Unexpectedly, a surge of electric shocks struck him and traveled throughout his body. Al-Khidr's eyes rolled to the back of his head, and his mouth opened. He was looking at the top of sphere, and could not even close his eyes. He was in a strange state which he hadn't experienced before; it was like an amalgamation of trance and consciousness, with no control over body. A wave of words, phrases, and images were going through his mind, while his saliva was pouring out.

In his last conscious moments, he felt as if he knew something that he didn't before; as if this electric shock had sent information and knowledge through his brain. Then the shocks ended, but he remained in the levitating state for some time. He eventually regained control of his body, and finally, he could shut his eyes. The glowing sphere then burst like a bubble, almost as if someone had popped it with a needle. Al-Khidr, who was suspended within it, instantly collapsed onto the hard floor. The heavy impact knocked him into the depths of unconsciousness.

*** 

*Ah, my head! Yezan! What happened to me?* Upon waking up, Al-Khidr was seriously disoriented. He was trying to identify where he was and how on earth he had gotten there, recollecting the information from his brain. It took him a couple of seconds, but it all came back to him. For a while, he lay there on his side, looking at whatever was in front of him. There were metallic clamps, metallic threads like wires, cables, and much more.

When he eventually felt well enough to get up, he did so slowly. His head and hands felt sore. He took a turn on his side, then crawled like a baby to the nearest structure and then gathered strength to stand. After some effort, he was standing and began to inspect the grand hall. "What is this place?" he asked himself.

Al-Khidr soon found himself in a house made up of metal and unusual substances. In his whole professional life as an alchemist, he had never before experienced elements like these.

He cautiously looked around and began exploring the hall. Everything was futuristic in appearance, and there were a lot of fascinating things. The metallic frames, the cables, the plastic and rubber. All was mind-boggling for Al-Khidr, as he never seen such materials before. He spent some minutes touching and smelling the materials.

As he focused on the materials, their unusual and unheard-of names were coming to his mind, as if he were remembering these things. He started trembling with an eerie feeling and moved away.

Whatever it was, he had to keep on moving, and he had to find out what he was supposed to do now. For the first time, he noticed that the orb was no longer attached to his palm. When the orb fell from his hands, he hadn't noticed it, because suddenly he had felt exhausted. The orb was now lying free on the floor, no longer glowing. It was hot, and giving off a faint plume of smoke. Strangely, it was not hot before. By the burn marks on its surface, it appeared to have burned out. With a fearful heart and trembling fingers, he traced his fingers over the artifact. He sighed and closed his eyes, then grabbed it and placed his second hand on top of it. He almost started to feel as if he was lifting off the ground. But this was only his head playing tricks on him. He was still standing on the ground. He then realized that he had not moved an inch. The orb's power had run out. He was stuck. Who knew where? A rush of anger surged through him, and he punched the metallic orb in his frustration. The orb was totally unaffected; it just rolled over a little.

*"How could the glass shard make this object so magical?"* he questioned himself.

There was no one around, and besides pyramids, he had never seen such a vast building on Earth before. He simply called for help. Maybe someone was around and could tell him where he was.

" *Saeadouni* (help me)!" he shouted in Arabic several times. But there was no one to help him. He was sure that the place was completely deserted. He recovered and got up from his position. He ran his hands over the metallic sphere once more. Punching things or getting angry wouldn't do anything; he had to think logically. He tried to think of what would be the most logical thing to do at this point. He had no idea where he was. He had more questions than answers. To Al-Khidr, it seemed like he was still somewhere on Al-Eard (Earth), but he didn't know where he was exactly. He had to find his way back home.

He first had to scout the area and find out why he was here in the first place. Why did the orb transport him here, to another city in Egypt?

As soon as Al-Khidr started to move again, he

started to feel as if his skin was falling off. He was shocked. When he looked at his legs, he realized that it wasn't his skin that was coming off, but his clothes. His clothes had worn out to the point where it almost seemed as if locusts had attacked them. He tried to walk slower than normal, as if to stop his clothes from falling off, but by the time he had arrived in the middle of the room, his clothes were completely gone. His sheephide sandals were also worn out. He hadn't noticed it before, as he was overwhelmed by the place, the electric-shocks, the materials, and so on.

Al-Khidr had only the metallic sphere now clutched in his hand. The place also looked abandoned, so it was unlikely anyone would see him like this, anyway. The room he currently was in had multiple large cabinets with orange handles.

I need some clothes, Al-Khidr said to himself. He then opened every cabinet he came across to find something to clothe himself with. It was only a waste of time, as he found nothing. He not only didn't find clothes, but he found nothing at all. It was only one of the last cabinets in the room that had something inside. When Al-Khidr found the piece of parchment within, he raised it up so he could shine more light onto the paper.

He was astonished to not encounter the usual Arabic or Coptic words one found in Egypt. The writing that he held in his hand was not any of those.

*Am I no longer in Egypt?* he thought to himself.

As he stood there inspecting the writing, he gradually felt as if he could read it. This made little sense to him, as he had never seen these writings before; how could he read them?

"This looks like *Khat-Al-Misri Al-Qadeem* (ancient Egyptian Metut Neter)," he excitedly exclaimed, shocked at his ability to read and understand the text. He was reading a language he had never spoken, never heard, and never read. That is when it struck him: it was actually that moment inside the sphere, when he got an electric shock, that gave him this knowledge. That glowing sphere had transferred to Al-Khidr the ability to read a new language. The piece of parchment with the writing on it was about the circuitry diagram of some equipment. Al-Khidr could read it, but he did not have a real understanding of the wisdom behind the circuitry diagram, so he discarded it.

*Maybe I know more than just a language.* Al-Khidr's eyes widened. *Who knows what other knowledge I have?*

He moved out of the room, and he was now in the corridor. There, he found an upturned cabinet with a broken handle. Al-Khidr wasn't tempted to open it at first, but then he decided he would. He opened the cabinet and found there was a long, green shirt and a pair of brown, baggy trousers inside. As the trousers had large pockets, he could slip the orb into one of them. He then found and put on a pair of black shoes which completely covered his feet, unlike his sandals.

\*\*\*

After many, many minutes of aimless wandering, Al-Khidr finally found some windows, and he could now see outside. What he saw was a desert with sand dunes, and monumental buildings erected from within those dunes. There were mountains all around it. He could also see an oasis at the end of the mountains. The water was shimmering and reflecting on him. He could see the sun shining above, but strangely, it looked bigger today. Al-Khadir had a sudden urge to drink water. In order to get out, he would have to smash the window, as that was the only way out; there were no doors in view. So, he took out the artifact from his pocket and used it like hammer to break the glass window. After few blows, the glass was completely broken. The window was big enough for Al-Khidr to crawl out through. He was shocked when he saw that the glass shards did not damage his skin. Glass normally would have pierced through his skin and made him bleed, but as he slithered through the opening, not a single slash was made in his skin. He dropped onto the sand below, which felt cold and foreign to his skin. He then got up and looked back at the building, which looked like a pyramid with bluish glass layers between the white stone layers. On top of them were words which looked like Metut Neter:

*Hept Sehetch Sheta—23*

Al-Khidr understood the meaning: The facility was about something related to secrets of skies and wandering stars. But he couldn't focus more, as he still felt thirsty. After some walking, he realized that sand had a kind of frozen sheath over it, as if the moisture or condensed water was frozen over it. He ran toward the oasis and drank water to his heart's content. There were also date trees there, which had teal-colored fruits that looked like dates, on which some exotic birds were nibbling. He knew birds would not devour poisonous fruits, and realized that the fruits must be edible. He picked some fallen fruits from the ground and ate them; they tasted like dates mixed with apples. The fruit's taste wasn't bad.

There were cirrus clouds, and the sky was blue, but it had pockets of violet at some spots, as if God had smeared colors on the sky. *How unusual!* Al-Khidr thought to himself. Maybe the sight will take time to adjust.

He now noticed that the weather had suddenly changed. In the morning before the journey, it was hot, but now it was much colder than expected. After he had eaten the teal-colored fruits and drank the fresh water, his entire body was flooded with a wave of exhaustion. All the fatigue from the journey and the complete experience came crashing down on him. Now the only thing he wanted to do was sleep. He fell to the white, sandy ground and was asleep in no time.

When Al-Khidr woke up, he found the sun shining over him. A chilly breeze was also coming from one direction. He slowly rubbed his eyes and turned his body to the other side to relax a few more minutes. Suddenly, he noticed a hand protruding out of the sand. It was all darkened and withered, like that of an Egyptian mummy. The creepy-looking dead hand was enough to scare him away. He was frightened. Brushing off his hair and clothes in a panic, Al-Khidr rushed away in a disoriented manner, out of that oasis. He was sometimes looking back while running, as if the creepy hand was following him, and then he hit something.

He looked at it, and he was surprised to see a hovering, metallic camel. Al-Khidr hadn't seen a camel like this before. It was made of metal, and had lights and buttons. As soon as Al-Khidr mounted it, the camel shape shifted into a round, donut-like formation. A control panel spanned all around him.

Shortly after the noise, some writings appeared in a display panel in the same strange language that was written on the pyramid. He then felt something against his thigh. He didn't even notice it at first. Then he felt it slither against his side, and his first instinct told him it was a snake. Al-Khidr brought his hand crashing down on a flat piece of rope. It was no snake; it was something completely harmless. He hadn't seen such material before, but in his mind, he knew the name of the flat rope. It was called an Antht (belt).

*"Abouhari! Abouhari!"* Al-Khidr was exclaiming in his mother tongue. He wanted to know what it was, so he focused on it. "Putchu Antht (seat belt)," he suddenly said. "Seat belt?"

But before he could recall what it was, a strap

suddenly zoomed across his belly and tightened. Al-Khidr still wasn't sure why this flat rope had tried to trap him, but whatever it was, it was related to safety.

*"How could I know this?"* Al-Khidr was again surprised. The writing on display changed, and he could understand again: To start, please place your right palm anywhere on the specified square.

Al-Khidr did as told. As soon as he placed his hand on the scanner, the camel vehicle changed into another sphere, much like the glowing sphere he had come here in. The writing on display changed again: No identification found—Beep—No identification found—beep! Unidentified life form discovered...Going to quarantine," the voice said after a pause. The vehicle now closed, and Al-Khidr couldn't get out. "Oh no, not again!" Al-Khidr exclaimed.

# Chapter 8

# The Hiding

THE vehicle picked up pace as it came out of the mountains and into a vast desert covered with sand dunes. The vehicle had no wheels, and was hovering over the sandy surface. Al-Khidr had never experienced such a ride before.

Regardless, this wasn't really a camel. It was some kind of transportation machine that could morph into a camel, and Al-Khidr had fallen prey to it. He was now trapped in this vehicle and going at a speed that was persistently increasing.

"Ah...how do I stop this crazy thing?" he exclaimed.

Al-Khidr was surprised, as this particular earthly vehicle was moving really fast—much faster than any well-bred Arabian horse. The vehicle hovered like a particle over the sand dunes, and this made Al-Khidr feel ill. "Ugh," he said out loud, "I feel sick." Suddenly, a small compartment opened to his left, and he saw a brown paper bag extend from it. He was astonished; the vehicle had listened to him. It understood that Al-Khidr was having trouble and adapted its speed, as well as provided a bag for him to get sick into. It was truly shocking to Al-Khidr, because he hadn't even planned to do it. He had simply said it out loud, in vain and in desperation. Now that the speed was only half of what it had been, he felt a lot better. He took the paper bag and laid it on his lap, just in case. Once he felt well enough, he looked out of the transparent windows. It was still a sort of a desert, but there were small hills here and there with palm and date trees.

It was also not as dry as before. There were wells and even pools of water, evenly spaced. He was surprised, as Egypt never had this sort of landscape. *What is even going on here?* he thought to himself.

"Hello, would you like updates?" a female voice beeped.

Al-Khidr almost jumped in fear. "*A djinn (hidden creature)?*" His body stiffened as he tried to determine what that sound was and where it was coming from. He then realized that it was the vehicle who was talking.

"Can you take me back to Fustat?" Al-Khidr requested.

"No data found on location 'Fustat,'" the voice erupted.

"Please enter your identification number, or you will be taken to the quarantine for unidentified life forms," the voice said again.

Al-Khidr did not have any identification number. Even so, he tried to recall one, and some number combinations started appearing in his mind. He knew what an identification number was, but what his own number was, he did not know.

Al-Khidr was now seeing monoliths and large buildings, even some pyramid-like structures here and there. Finally, he saw some people wearing strange, non-Arabic dresses, who were coming out of a building. Al-Khidr could not identify them, as he hadn't seen such culture before. The further along on the path they progressed, the more visible the people became.

Al-Khidr saw many technologies that he had never seen before. Then he saw another vehicle, coming from who knows where and heading right toward him. It seemed to be another kind of machine that moved at great speeds. For a moment, Al-Khidr thought there would be a head-on collision because of the great speed the other vehicle was coming. He even braced himself, but then he saw the other vehicle slightly move toward

CHAPTER 8. THE HIDING

the right, and the collision was avoided. The vehicle was now passing through a deserted place. There was white sand everywhere, and the vehicle was heading towards a gloomy building without windows. *Sajin (A jail)*? Al-Khidr thought to himself. He adjusted his new, large clothes and then leaned back. He felt relaxed in this crazy machine for a moment, but then suddenly, a surge of fear in his heart overtook him with a storm.

*What if the people of this territory imprison me?* he wondered. I must escape somehow.

He was truly frightened now, and wanted to run away from this land. The vehicle was moving over the sand dunes and fast approaching a large, gloomy building. "Think quickly, before it's too late!" Al-Khidr said to himself.

An idea struck him. If he jumped into the hovering vehicle or somehow tilted it, perhaps it would crash to the ground and stop. Al-Khidr started moving agitatedly, and was somehow able to get rid of the strap holding him in position on the seat. There was a beeping sound in the vehicle, and the female voice said: "For your safety, seat belts are recommended and enforced."

Al-Khidr had no intention to listen to this random flying machine. He pushed the vehicle on one side with his bare hands, trying to topple it, hoping to make it halt. The hovering vehicle tilted and started rotating as a galloping horse would when losing its speed. However, the auto-positioning system countered the tilt and restored the original orientation.

Al-Khidr realized that a much stronger force and more agitation would be required to stop this smart beast of a machine. Once again, he thrust his full body weight towards one side of the vehicle. The vehicle tilted again, but this even more. Before the machine could correct its orientation, Al-Khidr made his move, kicking the glass window with his feet. For a moment, he was horrified when the glass was undeterred, but then there was a sound of breaking glass. Luckily, one of the side windows had shattered. Meanwhile, the hovering vehicle had again restored its orientation, but now there was a broken window. The vehicle was continuously also giving multiple warnings and danger notifications, which Al-Khidr completely ignored. He now had one last chance to jump out of the vehicle before it was too late.

It would hurt, but he would rather endure a bit of pain than be made prisoner to whatever people controlled this place. Al-Khidr dove out of the vehicle, went through the gap, and landed on the sand. Luckily, the vehicle was a man's height away from the ground. He was surprised to find that he was mostly fine, even though the speed he had been going was quite fast. He had incurred a couple of cuts from the glass, which had scratched his hands and legs, but nothing beyond that. He recovered, and then just started running in whatever direction he was facing. He could hear many warnings from the hovering vehicle in the distance, which was now at least a couple hundred meters away.

In front of him, the sand and the vast expanse had merged. As he looked towards the horizon, he saw the purplish haze of twilight. He knew that the sun was about to set. "The sun will set soon. I need food, he told himself."

As he moved over a huge dune, Al-Khidr could see lights sparkling from a dwelling in the distance, which looked like the legendary city of Aad, the city of pillars. Is this the long-lost city of Shaddaad, the son of Ad? He had many questions, but no one to answer them. No matter what city it was, the important thing at the moment was his survival. He planned to go to the city and hide somewhere.

***

After walking on sand dunes for half an hour, he reached the city boundary. As Al-Khidr entered the city, it was glittering with lights of all kinds. The buildings were tall and majestic. He was still confused about how and why he was here, and what had happened to Egypt. There were many more questions going through his head, but he knew he would have to wait if he wanted any answers.

As he looked around him, Al-Khidr realized he had just entered an unknown world where there were peculiar-looking people. Some appeared to have long, colored hair, and they were wearing strange clothing.

Strange race, unfamiliar language, alien way of life, Al-Khidr said to himself.

106

*They've probably rubbed some pigment on their hair,* Al-Khidr thought, trying to make sense of what he was seeing. But why?

Almost everyone had some gadgets as their bracelet or clothing on their body that was completely new to Al-Khidr. But something strange then happened. The more Al-Khidr saw the new objects, the more familiar they felt. He understood what the objects were, and how they were used. But how could he know that? He hadn't seen, let alone used them. Then he realized that it all came back to that electric zap that had occurred in the glowing sphere, before he passed out. Probably, that was how he had learned about things and objects he had never interacted with before.

On the building ahead of him was a display screen. Al-Khidr was surprised to see such big screen, and he started looking at it. A warning message regarding gun control now appeared on the screen. Then, it showed how a person could fire and kill another person. According to the warning, such acts bore hefty fines— imprisonment, or even death.

Al-Khidr saw that near him was a man who had an object in his hand that was cylindrical, and looked similar to the gun shown on the display screen. "A gun!" Al-Khidr exclaimed. "I don't know if I should be happy or sad, with this strange power of mine. Someone could use it to kill someone." Al-Khidr held his hand to his mouth, shocked at his own words.

"It fired a beam of intense light that could pierce through human flesh."

# CHAPTER 8.   THE HIDING

"You're in hostile land!" Al-Khidr exclaimed to himself.

The things he saw were baffling. He knew their names, but not their purpose. He shifted his glance, not wanting to know any more. He rubbed his eyes and then closed them.

*Is this all a bad, yet very realistic dream?* he thought to himself.

This was all too much to take in for him. After a few moments of moving forward, he was in a more densely populated area. This was probably the metropolis. There were many wagons just like the one Al-Khidr had been in. Some were moving while touching ground, some were hovering over the earth, some were floating in air, and amazingly, there were no accidents. At the same time, he saw no creatures which people could ride.

*Are there no actual mares and camels here?* he thought to himself.

As he was thinking, he spotted a camel in the distance. It was the same camel he had seen near the oasis, which had then had turned into a machine. "That was not a camel!" he exclaimed.

He tried his best not to focus too much on any object or person, because he knew that would make him automatically tap into the information bank that he had at the back of his head from the electric surge. He took everything in, not speaking, not thinking, just watching silently. He continued walking down the road until he arrived at a huge bazaar. There were many people in the stalls, trying to buy things. Nonetheless, the familiar feeling of seeing a bazaar was enough for him. Al-Khidr was hungry, but he had no money to buy any sort of food. He walked silently for several minutes, then decided he would ask someone to give him some food as charity, or lend it to him, and he would promise to return the money as soon as he could. He walked around the area to see what he could find to eat, but apparently, the food here wasn't as appetizing to him. Still, for his own survival, he needed to eat something.

Then the idea struck him. It was unlikely that someone would give him food now and agree that he could pay later. There was only one way to go about it. It was the only thing was circling through Al-Khidr's head, and he felt that there was no other way. He would have to steal. "In the toughest times, one has to make the hardest of decisions," he said under his breath as he cautiously approached a busy area. He went close to the vendor, who was selling some fruits with red skin and green fur on it. People were calling Shaqarqabi. There was a vast crowd there, and the fruits looked exotic. It was no wonder why so many people were gathered here like bees at a hive.

Al-Khidr took the artifacts out from his pocket and took a deep breath. He acted as if he had tripped over something and fallen, almost hitting the fruit stall. His items flew into the air and landed close to the vendor. As everyone looked at the items, Al-Khidr got an opportunity to swipe a fruit and slide it into his sleeve. Some people turned and looked at him, but they suspected nothing.

The vendor overreacted and shouted in a guttural voice: "What's the matter with you? Are you insane?"

Al-Khidr quickly got up and moved away from the area, muttering, "I'm sorry."

He was surprised that he uttered words in a strange language which had never learned.

What is happening to me? Is it a dream? He said to himself.

It might have appeared that he only took what was rightfully his—the artifact. But such was not the case. Al-Khidr disappeared into the crowd, walking briskly, and took multiple turns in order to avoid being captured. He was holding the artifact in his hand and the fruit under his arm. He was happy that he had accomplished his mission, but he was astonished at how he had pulled the whole thing off.

As Al-Khidr looked at the artifact, he realized there was no information coming up in his mind, no data on it. It simply looked like a metallic ball with a hole in it. Another thing he was surprised about was his pronunciation and grammatical capabilities in this new language. He had talked like he had spoken that strange language for decades, yet it was his very first time.

"I spoke...I replied in that language!" he exclaimed, but with a puzzled look on his face. He turned into a deserted alley and leaned against a wall, now holding the fruit in his hands.

As an alchemist, Al-Khidr had a habit of sniffing

different materials to understand their nature. The smell could give an excellent sense of whether this item was edible, toxic, etc. So, before he absolutely devoured the fruit, he smelled it. Apparently, the fruit had no scent at all. But he was too hungry to carry out further tests.

Al-Khidr stuffed the fruit down his throat. He wanted all traces of his stolen item gone from existence, and he couldn't be caught with it. Not only did the fruit have no smell, but there was no taste, either.

*Hmm, is this even a fruit? And is it even edible?*he thought to himself on the first bite. But then he shrugged off such thoughts and ate the whole fruit. When he was done with the fruit, he marveled at the whole incident and his planning. He was a good thief! But then what settled in was the guilt. Different voices inside his head told him he had done wrong, while others told him there was no other option. First, hunger had eaten him from the inside, and now guilt was doing the same.

For a couple of minutes, he just stood there, trying to think if he did right or wrong by eating the fruit; but before he could decide, a wave of sleep hit him. He thought it was just tiredness, but the more he thought about it, the more it made sense.

*Survival is a must!*

After few more minutes, Al-Khidr felt increasingly strange and heavy-headed. Then he felt dizzy to the point where he fell on the ground and began seeing psychedelic images in his dreams.

## CHAPTER 8.   THE HIDING

The Shaqarqabi had already started its work.

# Chapter 9

# The Mother

Aʟ-Kʜɪᴅʀ finally regained consciousness. He was completely disoriented, and had forgotten everything from before. He looked around with his drooping, red eyes and tried to make sense of it. He stared at the walls of the alleyway he was in, trying to understand where on God's earth the sandstone had gone.

The most common building material in Egypt was sandstone, yet not even one brick of sandstone was visible to his eyes. Instead, around him was a granite that was clearly a lot stronger. He got up slowly and cautiously. He felt sick and nauseated, almost as if he was drunk. He placed his palm on the wall beside him so he could at least stand. *What even happened here?* he asked himself.

Al-Khidr tried to reach the back of his mind and retrieve his memories. He slowly felt the fog over his mind lift, and soon everything came back to him. He was in some foreign territory, he had eaten a stolen fruit called Shaqarqabi, and he still did not know how to go back.

He sat back down in distress. He tried to think of what to do now. He had to do something; he couldn't just roam around the city. Someone would eventually notice him, and he would be in great trouble. He had to get back to Egypt and inform the Caliph somehow. But how? That, he did not know.

"I need to get a horse first, and some food, and then the best would be for me to depart from this land," he said, starting to make a plan.

*But what if I don't find a horse? The worry took over him,* and then abruptly, the orb came to his mind. I have to get that orb working.

He reached into his pocket, but soon, an expression of pure horror spread over his face. The orb was not there. He smacked his forehead. While he was unconscious, someone must have stolen it from him. He stood up and punched and kicked the walls in rage. He had lost his only way back. Now what? As he continued to take out his frustration on the wall, he stepped on something hard. As he looked down, he saw the orb under the peels of the fruit. He praised God in happiness.

"Okay, now that I have this, I need to make this orb work again."

The orb wasn't damaged or anything; it was just like it had always been, so that was a good sign. He tried to think back to how it all started. He had fitted a piece of glass into the orb, and that had powered it up.

"Maybe that is how this works—using a piece of glass." Al-Khidr sighed. "How will I find any glass now?"

It became clear to Al-Khidr that he was not about to find any glass if he stayed there, lying in the alley. He had to get up and exert himself. He had to try his best. He got up and exited the ally with a new sense of motivation and determination. He now at least kind of knew what he was going to do.

*The first thing I need to do is to cover my face or head. It is best in cold regions, such as here in this land, to cover the head and face sometimes,* he thought. Al-Khidr was missing his keffiyeh.

He walked toward a residential area that he could see. The houses in the vicinity were nothing like he had seen before. He had seen tiny houses with curtains covering the doors. These houses were immense, and comprised of an unknown material. He passed through the area, keeping his head low so he would not be recognized. He occasionally looked up to try to find something; a cloth, maybe, to cover up his face. While walking, he finally found himself in front of a large building that looked a lot like an obelisk with windows. The building was all covered in display panels, on which images and writings were moving in front of his eyes. For a while, Al-Khidr couldn't believe that the writings could be so colorful. He had seen in Egypt many writings on an obelisk, but they were all static. However, the writings in this unknown land were not only moving, but they also had different colors and shades. It was a magnificent display of art and grandeur, and Al-Khidr was stunned by the visuals.

As Al-Khidr focused on the writings, he realized he could read the pictorial-writings. It was some news about the queen of the country of Akhom. Apparently, there was an upcoming address of the queen, which would happen this evening.

The advertisement board also showed the queen's picture. Al-Khidr was amazed, because the queen looked like the Egyptian goddess Hathor. She was stunningly beautiful, with long, white hair and bright black eyes, but she had strange ears. Still, she was elegant and mesmerizing by all means.

*She must be young, but she has white hair, Al-Khidr thought to himself. I should watch her address to understand their land and culture. Is this land far away from Al-Maghreb (Morocco), somewhere in Bahr Al-Atlasi (the Atlantic Ocean), or in Bahr Al-Abiyad (the Mediterranean ocean)?* Al-Khidr wondered.

*Definitely, these people are more advanced than us!*
Al-Khidr confessed. Had Master Al-Kindi been here
earlier, he would have been mesmerized! he told himself, thinking about his mentor, Abu Yusuf Yaqoub
ibn Ishaque.

It was a celebration day, and there were many food
stalls where exotic food was freely distributed. For Al-
Khidr, this was a bounty from God. He ate and filled
up his belly.

Following the directions displayed all over the city,
Al-Khidr reached the large field with huge obelisks on
his right and left. There were around thirty obelisks
on either side. There were stairs in between these
obelisks, and people could sit on them. At the end,
there was a large building with a grandly decorated
balcony. All the spectators had their faces toward the
balcony, as if eagerly waiting for the queen's arrival.
There were two screens on the sides which were showing the history of the land.

The men, women, children were all chatting and
looked happy. Slowly, the crowd began to cheer,
"Mother! Mother!"
And after waiting for around twenty minutes, the queen
was finally there. She was physically present on the
balcony, and her face was shown on the two displays,
which were installed on the sides of the balcony. She
was old, but still quite elegant. She was wearing a
crown with horns, and her white hair was down to her
sides. Al-Khidr had seen royalty before, but this was
a whole new experience.

# Chapter 9. The Mother

When the queen appeared, all the people stood in silence. There was pin-drop silence, and that just went to show how incredibly respectful these people were toward their queen. The queen spoke in a firm voice:

"In the name of the eternal God, may his Blessings be on each of you.

"Citizens of our beloved land, the Akhom, there is no place under Vega's lights which is as advanced as ours. You all know that there are no other people like us, either. We are the only people in the entire universe who have explored, recorded, and encoded information to this great of an extent. We have collected data, samples, and species that will help us improve science, technology, and medicine across the universe. I believe that our species' survival lies in knowing more about the other life forms in the universe. Before becoming your queen, as a scientist, I explored many other places. I want to assure you that there is no life better than ours on any other planets. I want to assure you that the day is approaching when you will have disease-free, longer lives, and all of you will live to see your great-grandchildren. We are constantly working to increase our lifespan, overcome the scarcity of food, and make our lovely land more hospitable to live in. Our military is advancing and progressing, and our enemies have no chance to take the Amris from us.

We have subdued our enemies from planets Honkira and Sovidos. They challenged us, we gave reply to their challenge, and they lost."

The crowd cheered and shouted: "Mother, Mother, Mother." The queen enjoyed the cheering of the crowed for some time; she raised her hand to the side of her face, showed the people the back side of her right hand, and lowered it. The crowed become quiet again, and she continued:

"I also want to tell you we will soon find a solution for the deadly disease, Mutmut, that we are struggling with. The data we have is protected and shared with my high council for further analysis. I'm assured that they will soon find the solution. Citizens of our beloved land, our society progresses and works holistically towards a single goal. So, do not give heeds to cults. I firmly believe that the lost souls in the mountains will rejoin our civilization one day."

Al-Khidr saw that the crowd enjoyed every statement uttered by the queen. They cheered and rejoiced long after the address was over. A flying vehicle then came from sky, and the queen went inside, vanishing from the public view.

Al-Khidr had learned that the people in this land were struggling with many problems, and one of them was some sort of disease. The news was disturbing for Al-Khidr.

# Chapter 9. The Mother

*It is better that I leave this land before I contract the Mutmut disease, Al-Khidr thought nervously. But how do I go back when I don't know exactly where this land lies? I have been brought here by the artifact, which needs that mysterious glass. To go back, I must find the glass first.*

Al-Khidr looked around at the crowd, trying to find someone who could help. He soon saw a young lady standing only a few feet away from him. She had pink hair, and that was what initially caught Al-Khidr's eyes. But she was also pretty, and looked approachable. Al-Khidr approached her and remarked on the weather.

"It's so hot today. What do you think?"

The girl looked at him and giggled. "Yes, quite warm!"

Al-Khidr brought out the artifact from his pocket and showed it to the girl. The pink-haired girl looked at the artifact and raised her palms to her mouth. "You took it from the museum?" She then nervously laughed.

Al-Khidr was confused and didn't know what to say. Then, before he could say anything else, the girl continued, "What is your name?"

"Al-Khidr, I am a traveler from the south."

"South? You must be joking. That's a no-man's-land." She paused. "I am Amorah. Nice to meet you."

That must be why the place was deserted, Al-Khidr thought. But at the moment, he did not want to arouse any suspicion.

"Amorah, I like the pink dye you did on your hair."

"Dye? No, it is natural. You're the one with black-dyed hair!"

"This is my natural hair as well," Al-Khidr told her.

"I have never come across a man with natural black hair before."

Al-Khidr was now even more confused, and laughed just to ease off his nervousness. "I am looking to change the color of my hair but could not find the right plants here," Al-Khidr said.

Amorah laughed. "Why would you need plants? No one uses plants to dye hair anymore." Amorah then asked Al-Khidr if he would like to have some free drinks and receive gifts from the queen. Then she took Al-Khidr to a stall where people were giving away gifts to the crowd. There were also drinks of different colors and flags and caps. Al-Khidr took one cap and put it on, and it somehow covered all his hair. But when he turned to ask her more about the disease, there was no Amorah in sight. She had vanished, but she had kept Al-Khidr good company. The other people looked not so approachable, so he discarded the idea of investigating the disease for a while.

\*\*\*

Al-Khidr hadn't seen himself in the mirror yet, but he knew he now looked slightly strange.

"If I go back home with this turban, people will laugh at me!" he exclaimed under his breath. He moved swiftly from this area, intending to explore the city further. He started walking, and soon reached the bazaar. It was huge, and was larger than he had thought. It would probably take Al-Khidr multiple hours if he wanted to buy anything in particular, as he would have to search this place thoroughly. It was already getting dark, and it was unlikely that this bazaar would be active for more than a couple of hours.

While looking at the shops, Al-Khidr's eyes caught something. It was the same glass that he saw in the Great Pyramid and the same glass that he had used with the artifact to get to this strange land. He tapped the vendor lightly on his shoulder and pointed towards the glass. The vendor told him the price, but Al-Khidr couldn't understand. The vendor shook his head, and Al-Khidr insisted through his gestures. This continued for many moments until Al-Khidr offered the cap he had gotten for free at the stall. But to Al-Khidr's dismay, the vendor rejected the offer.

Al-Khidr insisted one last time before he tried a different stall. Suddenly he thought of stealing again and running. As the vendor was speaking to one buyer, he took the malleable glass piece and started walking briskly but confidently, as if he had bought the glass.

That was almost too easy, Al-Khidr thought to himself. And that's when it happened. There was a shout from somewhere, and then there was another shout, followed by two more: "There he is!"

Al-Khidr did not need to hear anything more; he just knew that the shouts were directed toward him.

He sprinted furiously across the street, nearly missing a passing, hovering camel vehicle. Four guards in armor and uniformed attire rushed behind him. Al-Khidr actually thought that he would be able to lose those guards, but he was wrong. The guards were twice as fast as Al-Khidr, and they could literally jump so high, they could easily hop over a camel vehicle. Al-Khidr could see the problem now. There was no way. He still tried, but there was no possibility of escaping the wrath of these new kind of human beings on his human legs. In a matter of seconds, they caught up to the heavily panting Al-Khidr and surrounded him.

"You're coming with us, prisoner."

Al-Khidr now realized that was what he was to them: just another prisoner. He was in for a dreadful ride, and he could feel it. Al-Khidr helplessly let the guards place two large, metal bangles over his wrists. One guard took out the sphere from his pocket and threw it towards his team. "No, no...please. Do not take it," Al-Khidr requested.

"Shut up!" the guard said.

Another guard pressed a button on a rectangular device he had in his hands, and those two metallic rings became connected by chains of flowing energy. Al-Khidr was in some sort of advanced shackle!

He then sat down in a large vehicle and was transported somewhere. Al-Khidr couldn't see outside, but by judging the time he had been in that hovering truck-like vehicle, they were no longer in the city. The prisoner transportation vehicle stopped. The doors were opened, and the darkened sky stared back at Al-Khidr.

It was a large facility on the outskirts of the city. He was ushered inside, stripped of his existing clothing and whatever else he had in his pockets, and was given the clothes which seemed to be worn by almost all prisoners there. The fact that the metallic orb was confiscated was what really made him want to scream. He had lost his ticket just when he got it back.

# Chapter 10

# The Quest

Aʟ-Kʜɪᴅʀ was roughly dragged to a cell, and was thrown into it as if he wasn't even a person. The guards locked the door and left him in his dark solitude. Once he was all alone in the cell, he felt multiple emotions at the same time. He felt homesick, angry, dreadful, helpless, and hopeless. Tears rolled down Al-Khidr's cheeks as he sat huddled against the wall, his knees against his chest. His eyes were shut, and it was so silent that he could hear his own heartbeat. He was bundled like that for who knows how long. He soon tired of his sitting position, so he laid down. He stared at the ceiling for what he thought to be only a couple of minutes, but actually was multiple hours.

That's where the guards found him when they finally came to retrieve him. They struggled to get him up, because Al-Khidr refused to walk. They then simply took his legs and dragged him feet-first out of the cell. Although his face would get scraped up, Al-Khidr still refused to walk by himself. He simply placed his palms on his face to avoid getting hurt. He was pushed and pulled from room to room, from corridor to corridor, and then finally, the guards let his legs drop to the floor. Al-Khidr removed his hands from his face and stared around. It was a much larger room than before, but it was still another cell, just a larger one, and there were many other prisoners here.

Al-Khidr counted the number of prisoners and found there were nine other large men in the room. Some had beards; some didn't. Some had colored hair, but some didn't. There was a small compartment to the right of the cell, a toilet. To his left, there were eleven or twelve beds, and there was also a large dining table. They take care of their prisoners, Al-Khidr thought. In his own hometown, prisoners didn't get such a large area, and especially not a dining table! Al-Khidr's eyes then caught a couple of machines with moving pictures, where, some prisoners were playing some game.

"Strange prison!" he exclaimed.

Suddenly, two guards took him to the side of the room, where there was a man in a large white overcoat and with some sort of machine in his hand. The guards held up Al-Khidr's hands.

The other man pushed some buttons on the machine and got ready to do something by pulling back his sleeves. Al-Khidr's left hand was then placed in the machine. He had no clue what to expect. Then, suddenly, something was pierced into his skin and went deep into his hand. The machine left something inside and then released his hand. Al-Khidr looked into the machine and saw three large sharp needles.

"This must be administered to every prisoner admitted to this facility. We have inserted a chip into your hand," one officer said. The guards then helped Al-Khidr up. The other man applied something to Al-Khidr's wound where the needles had penetrated.

Another man in a white coat came, sprayed some chemical on the wound, and left. The pain went away at once, and the wound healed instantly. Al-Khidr was shocked. *Where is the needle mark?* Al-Khidr asked himself. He stared at his left wrist, where there were three holes which formed an upward triangle.

Another officer held his hand to check everything. He took out a small torch from his pocket and threw a blueish light on Al-Khidr's wrist. He said to him: "A code is etched on your wrist, visible only in ultraviolet light. The Ar-t-Heru  mark and number will remain on the skin, but the chip inside may be removed later if you are declared innocent. The mark will not be visible to the naked eye."

Al-Khidr had no idea what 'ultraviolet light' meant, but he was flabbergasted to see, under the bluish light, the Ar-t-Heru mark on his hand. In the middle of holes there was an eye symbol that looked like this:

Underneath the symbol, the number 10001001 was etched on his wrist in strange numerals. One guard said to him: "Ar-t-Heru is the seal of the kingdom's security. Beware, do not try to tamper with it, or else you will learn a harsh lesson," the guard said further.

Al-Khidr was astonished with the technology of this new undiscovered country, even when he should have been annoyed. He blew into holes, but nothing happened; the holes were blocked from the inside. Al-Khidr genuinely wanted to know more, but he couldn't, as the guards took him back to his cell.

\*\*\*

Al-Khidr was now with nine other men in a decent-looking cell. He looked around the room again, taking everything in. The appearance was a mixture of some ancient Egyptian temple and modernity. The writing sometimes blinked, and he was baffled to see that. "They are watching you, boy!" one old prisoner said.

Al-Khidr looked back and asked: "What is this place?"

"Your grave!" the prisoners said and laughed.

Al-Khidr was annoyed to hear that, and he left the laughingstock and continued to look at the walls.

He couldn't believe how crazy the last few days had been. He walked over to the dining table and sat down. The implant did not hurt, but he could feel it inside. It made his hand feel heavier. Looking around, he saw that the other prisoners also had the same implants on their wrists.

The rest of Al-Khidr's day was spent getting to know his fellow prisoners. Some were friendlier than others, and everyone was in prison for very different reasons. One of them, called Lapis, was captured while he was trespassing the boundaries of the forbidden zone. The area was well known for rare and precious metals, but was off-limits because of the disease called Mutmut, and excavations or even visitors were not allowed.

Al-Khidr was surprised to hear that, and asked Lapis a question. "What happens if you get the disease called Mutmut?"

Lapis replied, "I've heard that this disease is far

worse than any. Its dries you up from inside out, sucking out all the water and nutrients from your body." He paused. "Your organs get shriveled up, and a person with the disease dies in hours. It's a disturbing sight." "How did this disease start? Tell me more about it. Our Caliph can send doctors to treat you, we have some talented doctors back home," Al-Khidr said, trying to be helpful.

"Caliph? Who is that?"

"Okay, just tell me where your country is located. Is your country west of Iraq, or is it east of it?" Al-Khidr asked.

"What are you even talking about? What is Iraq?" Lapis looked at Al-Khidr from head to toe.

Hondo, a prisoner with a tattooed face who was seated among the group at the dining table during dinner time, joined in. "I guess this 'Iraq' is on planet Mahona, in the constellation of Beberu. One of my old friends visited it and told me about it."

"Never heard of it," others at the table exclaimed.

Another prisoner, Kemosri, clearly spotted that Al-Khidr seemed a bit lost. "I think I know what is going on here." He smiled as he spoke, showing oddly crooked teeth. Everyone at the table focused on Kemosri, as if what he would say next would be some very important information. "What do you know? Maybe you can share it with us," Al-Khidr retorted, his voice rising.

"This person here lives on a small rock." Al-Khidr instantly took offense to it. He stood up from his seat, but the two men on either side made him sit again. Al-Khidr had made an enemy. "No need to get offended. I am just stating the fact," Kemosri continued. "I can tell when a person—" "What are you trying to say?" Al-Khidr frowned.

"Al-Khidr, are you aware of where we are?" Kemosri inquired.

"Of course he is," two people exclaimed.

"Yes, I am," Al-Khidr replied. "Where do you think you currently are?" "I don't know exactly what place this is, but I can guess it is either Europe, Africa, or India." "Do you all see?" Kemosri laughed. "Our fellow here does not know where exactly he is. "What are you talking about? Stop trying to get inside my head!" Al-Khidr exclaimed. Kemosri's smile only got wider.

"I am an Alchemist; I know chemicals more than any other," Al-Khidr continued.

Lapis giggled. The rest of the prisoners followed. The laughter of all nine prisoners really irritated Al-Khidr, but he hid it, because he knew he shouldn't be picking fights at this point. Who knew how long he would be here, and making enemies would make everything worse?

When everyone had settled down from their laughter, Al-Khidr inquired: "Where are you all from? Are you from Europe? India? Or Africa, maybe?" Everyone burst out laughing again. Al-Khidr swallowed the anger and annoyance that was forming inside him.

Al-Khidr could now tell that these men hadn't ever

heard of these countries before. "Never mind. I just wanted to know about the disease. How did it start, and where did it come from?" Al-Khidr changed the topic.

"It was a good joke," Lapis commented. "Al-Eard!" Everyone started laughing yet again.

"You do not look like you're from Lyra. Where are you actually from?" Another middle-aged prisoner with one eye, Baruti, ignored Al-Khidr's question and asked one of his own.

"From the planet near Shamas (the Sun), we call it Al-Eard," Al-Khidr responded. "So, all of you are not from Al-Eard?!" Al-Khidr was confused. They are just making fun of me! he thought.

"He is from Keb!" one prisoner shouted.

At that moment, something inside all nine prisoners changed at the same time. It was fear. Their hearts were struck with fear, and they all got up from their seats and ran to the other side of the room, where the door was located. They left their half-eaten food, although they had constantly been commenting about how hungry they were for the past two hours.

"What is going on?" Al-Khidr shouted behind the running men. No one cared to even look back at Al-Khidr. They banged on the door loudly, and there was a lot of shouting.

"Get us out of here!"

"You should have told us what he was. A disgusting Kebian."

"Save us!"

"Help!"

Al-Khidr was flabbergasted by the sudden shock and terror that had entered the hearts of the prisoners.

"Stop this nonsense!" Al-Khidr shouted at them. He thought it was a joke.

"You shut up. Even your words are possibly poisonous and can cause death!"

"This joke is going too far..."

"Don't listen to his words. Cover your ears. He is trying to get us closer to him. Stay away from him!"

By this point, it was clear to Al-Khidr that something was actually going on. Their frightful expressions suggested they were actually afraid of him. "What happened? Can someone explain?" he asked.

"Don't trick us, you're a monstrosity of a man from the cursed planet!" someone shouted back to the nearing Al-Khidr.

Al-Khidr stopped dead in his tracks when he heard that. He was not sure why they were calling Earth a cursed planet, but what was clear to him was the fact there had to be some sort of truth, because everyone was afraid of him, and not just one man.

"Don't even dare to come close to us!" the prisoners shouted.

The commotion inside the cell alerted the guards, and multiple guards rushed in. They grabbed hold of Al-Khidr and pushed the men, who were trying desperately to escape through the door.

The guards ordered: "Stop this commotion."

"Take us out of here or take this person from cursed

planet out of our cell."

Guards asked men to remain calm and they hand-cuffed Al-Khidr and took him out of the cell. Al-Khidr was flabbergasted by the oddity of the prisoners' behavior. While he was taken out of cell, none bothered to even look at him. Instead, they all were frightened and cramped up on each other in one corner.

***

Al-Khidr was inside a small room. He felt hurt by their rude attitude, but he also understood that they were only afraid of him. "God, help me," he muttered under his breath.

It was almost as if he knew what was about to happen right now, and he needed God's help with that. It had been about ten or fifteen seconds since Al-Khidr uttered his prayer, when suddenly, the large door to the cell was thrown open.

Al-Khidr noticed these new guards were wearing different attire. Their clothing clearly looked a lot thicker and more defensive. They had something in their hands that was sparking. As soon as those two sharp prongs penetrated and stuck to Al-Khidr's body, he was in complete dismay. His eyes rolled to the back of his head, and he was shocked to the point where he was simply a vibrating piece of flesh on the floor. They tased him for about ten seconds.

The unconscious Al-Khidr was then dragged away from the room and into a different cell. The large room where Al-Khidr had been in was then thoroughly sanitized, and they sprayed multiple chemicals over many minutes.

What was wrong with me or my planet? he thought to himself. It was still not clear to Al-Khidr, but it was definitely something dangerous.

# Chapter 11

# The Interrogation

AL-KHIDR was walking in new shoes that had been given to him by the prison guards. They showed some numbers at its base, but other than that, they did something that surprised him by beyond his imagination. One of the prison inmates said that if they tried to make a run for it, the shoes had an anti-run mechanism, locking the movement of the inmates. When they tried to run, they fell face-first on the ground. A

# CHAPTER 11. THE INTERROGATION

few of them had broken their teeth in doing so. Al-Khidr was in no mood to break his teeth, though. He had laughed when someone tried to flee in front of him and fell with a thud. He came out of these thoughts when guards asked him to enter a new cell.

Al-Khidr's eyes opened to a completely new setting. There was no large dining table or even a large room. He was now in a cell—a tiny cell—with no light source. Just a bit of light came from a different room, the only light Al-Khidr had.

He was confused about why everything had happened so quickly. He wasn't even sure why he had been taken away from the other nine prisoners in the first place. It was strange, because Al-Khidr had done nothing to deserve this, and it didn't make sense.

He looked around, as his eyes had now adjusted a bit to the darkness. He saw that he was the only person in this cell, despite there being two bunk beds. He got up from the floor and laid down on the bed.

*What place, city, or country is this? Why does nobody know of Iraq? What is Keb?* There were so many unanswered questions circling through his head, but no way to get answers. He just laid there, doing nothing in particular. There was nothing to do except stare at the bottom of the bunk above. He tried to recreate the whole incident in his head, but he couldn't think of anything he might have done wrong. He might have lost his temper a bit, but beyond that, he did nothing else. He didn't threaten or get physical with anyone.

Al-Khidr had lost his mother when he was only fourteen years old, and helped his Berber father in his business of dyeing cloth with indigo from the flowers of the Nilah plant, which grows in north Africa. There, he became interested in learning about plants and subsequently learned more about alchemy. After his father's death, he inherited a massive fortune, as he was the only heir to his father's business. He sold off the business and moved to Baghdad, where he spent part of his inheritance money in lodging and buying books.

Having spent his life in the desert, Al-Khidr was accustomed to the harsh life, so he knew how he was about to deal with hostile people. But to him, the behavior of the prisoners was still odd, as he had said nothing wrong.

And then it came back to him: cursed planet.

"They were talking about some cursed planet," he reminded himself. Al-Khidr tried to recall if there was anything else they said related to a cursed planet. "But I don't belong to a cursed planet," Al-Khidr said, stroking his unmaintained beard. "It's a beautiful place."

He spent the next two hours thinking and trying to connect the dots, but he couldn't make anything out of the incident. He was deep in thought when a guard brought some food for him. He unlocked the door and stepped inside. Al-Khidr got up from the bed as if to take the plate from the guard, but the guard leaned down and placed it on the floor. He then left, locking the cell behind him.

"That's incredibly rude!" Al-Khidr whispered to himself once he knew the guard wouldn't hear him.

He sat on the floor, staring at the plate of food right in front of him. It had a piece of bread along with some kind of puree. Al-Khidr wasn't starving, but he still dug in. Only, just the first bite spread an expression of dismay across his face. The food had no taste; it was like eating unflavored, soaked wood. "Why do they even eat this?" he wondered. "There is no taste! I wish I had those teal-colored fruits I found when I first arrived. They were good." Al-Khidr still ate the food, because he couldn't take a risk of not eating. Who knew when he would get his next meal, and where he'd get it from? It was best to eat this, no matter the lack of taste.

Once he was done with his meal, he said aloud, "I think this food is just for survival, and not for pleasure in prison."

With his stomach full, a wave of sleep hit him, and he decided to rest. There was nothing else to do, anyway. He let his eyes shut, and soon he was in a deep sleep. In sleep, he found himself at the house of wisdom in Baghdad, discussing his entire journey with his friends. Every sentence that Al-Khidr said sent them into even greater levels of shock. They couldn't believe all they were hearing. Al-Khidr enjoyed it, telling them about how people dressed in the strangest ways. "Everyone dyes their hair some bright color, like pink or blue. I had black hair, and one girl there told me that was her first time seeing someone with black hair! And metals...Don't even get me started on that!" Al-Khidr continued. He told them how there were multiple new metals unknown to the Arab and Berber people, and how they used metals in the most creative ways. He also told them about technology, and gave some examples. He told them how they had moved things on glass. His friends had a hard time comprehending what was being said, but they wanted to hear more.

Al-Khidr went on and on and told them about the camel that had turned into a hovering vehicle. His friends asked him to explain further, as they couldn't understand how something that weighs a ton could float with nothing holding it up.

Before Al-Khidr got the chance to talk more about the camel vehicle, he was suddenly jerked out of his dream. He tried to shut his eyes again, as if wanting to go back to the dream, but before he could, a tap on his shoulder got him disoriented. He propped himself up against the wall, and was surprised to see someone else in the room with him.

Before him was a tall, beautiful lady with light blue eyes and straight, dark blue hair that was tied at the back. Al-Khidr's olfactory senses were telling him that this lady smelled nice. She was dressed in a uniform, seemingly an officer, and was wearing some sort of mask on her face. She also had multiple small metal pieces in her belt. It was her arsenal against any criminal who would dare act up against her.

# CHAPTER 11. THE INTERROGATION

"Doctor, do your scan," the lady commanded someone else.

Al-Khidr tried to see past this woman. Sure enough, there was another woman here as well. The other lady was also wearing some covering over her mouth. The doctor instantly started to do what the first lady had requested, moving forward with a massive chunk of metal that Al-Khidr saw earlier, when he was first brought to this jail. She moved it all around Al-Khidr about three or four times. The metal occasionally beeped, giving some information to the lady. Al-Khidr saw some waves, and then noticed marks appearing on the display panel. "This tablet can inform about bodies?" he murmured to himself in realization. "Scanning completed!" the device said.

The doctor went to the side and stared into the screen of glass and metal. There were few moments of silence.

"All clear, no traces of any disease. Irregular teeth sizes and no brain injury. Body chemistry not identifiable!"

"We need to talk now," the other lady said. The two officers sat and asked Al-Khidr to sit in front of them. It was a narrow room, and that made him even more nervous.

The police officer looked at Al-Khidr right into his eyes with raised eyebrows and asked, "What is your name?" "Al-Khidr Al-Nasir Al-Din Al-Berberi Thuma Al-Baghdadi Ibn al-Tahir," he quickly replied, as if there was a time limit to the answer. "Slow done!

Stop! Give me a short name," the lady exclaimed, her voice raising a bit.

"Al-Khidr!"

"Why did you steal the Amris-tank?"

When she saw that Al-Khidr was confused about her question, she brought out from her pocket the orb-artifact, set it on the table, and then asked again: "Where did you get this?"

Al-Khidr was glad to see the orb. He leaped forward to get hold of the it, but the officer said: "Stop!"

Before Al-Khidr could think of an answer, the doctor exclaimed, "You don't have any sort of ID, nor any planetary record in our files, no previous genetic data, and no birth record! What are you!?"

Picking up where the doctor left off, the officer asked, "Have you landed from the sky?"

Al-Khidr nodded his head in affirmation.

"Okay, now listen to me very carefully and answer my questions truthfully." She paused for effect. "If you do, we shouldn't have much of a problem." Al-Khidr nodded.

"I am officer Nefertiti, and I have been given your case file," she stated. "First question: Are you mad?"

"What?" Al-Khidr tried to think of why they were considering him a lunatic.

"I came to know that you harassed the prisoners in the other cell, and tried to scare them by saying you are from Keb." "I didn't mean to scare them. I told them the truth."

"So, you're telling me that you're from Keb?"

## Chapter 11. The Interrogation

"I am from Al-Eard. It's the third planet from Shamas in the Milky Way galaxy," Al-Khidr said.

"We call it Keb," the officer said. "Do you even know what you're saying? Do you even know how far that is from here? It's light years away!" A frown was forming on her face.

"What do you mean? Don't you know Iraq, Europe, Egypt?" Al-Khidr inquired.

"What are these?" The officer laughed. "You are a strange man!"

Al-Khidr didn't know what to say.

"Fine, just tell me about how you arrived here. We can work from there. Tell me everything; don't skip anything." "This sphere I found inside a pyramid is what brought me here." Al-Khidr pointed towards the orb. "I was looking into it, trying to solve the riddle of this artifact, and it suddenly formed some sphere of light around me. I couldn't escape it. It raised me up to the heavens, and my city was left down below." Al-Khidr paused for breath. "And then it transported me to your country."

Officer Nefertiti was silent. After a moment, she picked up the orb and asked Al-Khidr to follow her. The three of them went through multiple corridors before they finally entered a large room with many machines. These were huge scanning machines, like cubical rocks with different lights coming out of them. Al-Khidr realized that the doctor had vanished during their journey through the corridors.

Nefertiti gave the orb to one of the people in the

room. "Minkah, scan this and give me complete history."

The lady named Minkah took the sphere and nodded. She then placed the orb in a machine. The scan took about two minutes. During that waiting period, she spoke. "I haven't ever seen anything like this before," Minkah stated.

Nefertiti shrugged her shoulders. The scan was completed.

"It is an ancient manufactured device," Minkah said.

"That's strange!" Nefertiti ran her hands over her face.

Then Minkah flipped the orb and looked at it from the base. "The middle hole is not drilled through, and damn, this device is heavy," she said.

Nefertiti nodded her head. "Yes, I felt that too. It's heavy for its size. Looks like part of a machine to me!" Minka brought the orb closer to her eyes.

"There is something written over it in Lyrian. But very small!"

"Is it?" Nefertiti asked Minka to show her where the writings were.

"It's written on the sides of the hole. See there?"
"Yeah..."

Minka took out the lens and looked through it to see what was written around the middle hole of the orb.

"I can read it now...'As...above, so...below!'" Minkah said.

Al-Khidr was watching them and listening with interest.

ₒᏓ ᎓Ꮋᴎᴎₒ Ꭼᎆₒᵻ ᏕᎬᎆᴧₒᎾ

(As above so below)

*"(Amm oflla igat yizdar),"* Al-Khidr uttered in his mother tongue.

"I can see kerker code marks in the hole. It means we should have some record on its manufacturing. There is a code-scanning machine which can give facility or laboratory details," Minkah said as she placed the orb into a different machine.

The clamps in the scanner instantly took hold of the sphere, and then a piece of metal covered it up. Then the machine started to give data in strange symbols. "This is a device from the HSS facility. But no information is coming up. The facility was sealed under royal orders," Minkah said, with an expression of wonder on her face.

Minkah and Nefertiti then exchanged looks. Nefertiti turned towards Al-Khidr and asked, "You know where you landed first?" Al-Khidr tried to recall. "I saw written on the building something about stars and secrets..."

His memory clicked. "It was written there, *Hept Sehetch Sheta.*"

Minkah and Nefertiti looked at each other.

"How did you read it?"

Al-Khidr said, "The device took me to a chamber and then sent something into my brain, which

made me capable of understanding your language."
"So, you're telling me that this small thing helped you travel through space and got you here?" Minkah asked. "Yes," Al-Khidr said.

"I need information for my report on his case file. I guess I need to call another doctor. We need to run some brain scans on him to make sure all things are in order. You know what I mean," Nefertiti said to Minkah.

Al-Khidr, meanwhile, wasn't so sure what this brain scan was.

"Also, contact the Kingdom Intelligence Unit and inform them about this device. It's kind of unusual if we manufactured it and even have kerker code on it, but now have no clues on it. Galactic Exploration Unit could be a good starting point as well, as they took up most of the projects of HSS. Contact them and ask them to send few experts to investigate this device. I want to go to HSS myself to check more. But we need royal office permission to enter HSS." Nefertiti had given Minkah many tasks to do.

Al-Khidr had continued listening to them, but was a little lost on most of the discussions; what still bothered him most was the strange behavior of the other prisoners.

"What about the curse?" Al-Khidr humbly asked.

Nefertiti turned towards him. She sighed, and then said: "According to our history, we went to your planet a long time ago, and unfortunately, your planet gave the males of our mission team Mutmut—a deadly disease—

and so it arrived on Lyra as well. We read in our history books that planet Earth is cursed because a contagion was brought from there, and it resulted in many deaths among our males. In fact, that area where the person from Earth first arrived before getting caught is a forbidden zone." She paused. "That person was caught, but the few minutes he breathed in that area was enough to inflict death upon many hundreds of us."

Al-Khidr couldn't believe what he was hearing.

"You should tell no one where you came from, because that would do one of two things. People will either fear you, or they will want to skin you alive and let you die in the desert." Nefertiti finished the grim story and added, "We are in process of gathering more information on what you have said. If we discover that you have lied to us or that you are a spy, you will remain in prison forever," she said sternly in a harsh tone.

Al-Khidr's head was spinning. He couldn't believe what he had heard. The visions of pyramids of Giza, the black pyramids of this planet, the words of Al-Misri were echoing like hammer in his head, and with each echo he fell more towards the ground until he was unconscious. Someone threw water on his face, and he was back to his senses.

"What...what happened?"

"You were unconscious!"

Al-Khidr was perplexed and in deep thought. With all said and done, Nefertiti ordered guards to take him back to his prison cell.

"Hey, wait a minute. I don't want to go back to the prison cell again. I did nothing, and all I have done thus far is be honest with you guys."

Minkah seemed a bit convinced by this argument. It wasn't like the earthling had committed any crime in the interplanetary system and sought refuge here; it was more a chance kind of thing. Minkah looked at Nefertiti to see if she shared the thought, and she sure did.

Nefertiti looked in deep thought, and seemed to have decided. She looked up. "I am sorry. You will be escorted to the prison cell for now as we think about where to go from here," she said.

Al-Khidr protested, but she cut him off. "Can you return to your planet with this fancy toy? Well, it would be better if you can manage that," she said, raising her eyebrows. "Well, I don't know if it will work again. It's not really something that I invented. I just found it, and here I am," Al-Khidr said, and shrugged. She seemed disappointed by the answer, and Al-Khidr knew what was coming next.

"Well, then you have your answer. Just don't tell anyone that you are from Earth. It will cause a huge panic after the previous mass extinction thanks to patient zero from Earth," she said.

Al-Khidr looked down, as if he had given up. Minkah saw this and felt sad for him. He was an alien to them, after all. She wished there could be another way to handle this situation.

# Chapter 12

# Serendipity

Aʟ-Kʜɪᴅʀ was led back to his prison cell and the prison guard unlocked the gate. It wouldn't budge. He yanked it open as it gave way with a thud.

"Off you go inside," the prison guard said with a light chuckle.

"Yeah, yeah, rub it in. Wait till you visit my planet. I will return the favor. It's the least I can do," Al-Khidr shot back.

# Chapter 12. Serendipity

The prison guard slammed the cell door shut, and it almost hit Al-Khidr on its way back.

"Hey. Watch it, *A' Mis-n-Tkahbacht!*" he shouted in his mother tongue, Amazigh. He was quite angry now.

But the expressionless prison guard only looked at him, made a repulsive face, and left.

After half a day had passed, the second meal of the day came. This time, a new prison guard had come, and he beckoned for Al-Khidr to collect his food. "I heard you're new here," he said as he unlocked the door.

"I guess word goes around fast. I am from a very distant planet," Al-Khidr said, trying to make polite conversation. "I know where you are from, and all that happened to us because of that place. Just keep some distance from me. I heard the last time a man from your planet came, a wave of our people died," he said, changing his tone slightly.

Al-Khidr took five steps back.

The new prison guard placed the meal on the ground and was about to leave when Al-Khidr spoke. "Hey. Wait. What's with the other expressionless guard? He was so incredibly rude, and looked down on me," Al-Khidr said as an afterthought.

"Don't worry about him. He lost his family when patient zero came here. It's been quite a long time since that happened, but some people can't let go," the prison guard said. He seemed deep in thought.

Saying that, he closed the prison cell door and left,

humming a song Al-Khidr had never heard before. Al-Khidr looked at him for a moment and wished he could be back on his planet. The clouds of uncertainty were hovering over his future. He looked at the food lying on the ground. A weird insect was crawling towards it. He stood up and kicked the insect away, and it exploded upon colliding with the wall.

*"Tabkhocht ikhchen! (strange insect!)"* Al-Khidr shouted in his language.

He looked at the plate and saw yellow rice with a red sauce lying on the side. For a moment, his eyes lit up, but then he took a bite of the food. "Lord, not this again. The cooks on this prison have no taste," he groaned with his mouth full.

He was halfway through his food when he gave up and fell asleep.

***

The exhaustion had consumed him. Al-Khidr woke up at midday, hoping this was all just a bad dream. But alas; he was still in his prison cell, with nothing to do. He kept staring at the wall, thinking about his life on Earth. Life had become a nightmare, one freak object turning his life around. He leaned against the wall, thinking about his options. He could be imprisoned here forever—that was, unless God created a way out, somehow.

This world was very different from his own. They were probably a few centuries ahead of his planet, and Earth felt like a distant dream. This world was so, so new to him: the futuristic society, the people and their gizmos, and the overall landscape.

Al-Khidr was lying on the ground as he thought about all this. A thought then came to him like a bolt of electricity, and he sat up. Racking his brains for more, he recalled his time in Baghdad city. During his academic years in the city, a book titled Dying Animals mentioned a mysterious epidemic that had spread throughout the Iraqi animals. They would dehydrate and collapse on the ground after a few hours. This had created a wave of panic among the farmers and livestock owners, who had tried everything under the sun to save their animals. The epidemic continued for a month, until animals became far and few between. This was when a passing old man suggested to an Iraqi farmer that Egypt's plants could cure these animals. He told the farmer to look for a plantation near the city of Qena. The farmer went on his donkey to said location and brought back some herbs. His animals, once on the verge of death, were now given a new lease on life. The news spread like wildfire across the city and nearby villages, and soon enough, the epidemic had cleared the city of Baghdad, and life had resumed to normalcy. Al-Khidr reasoned that, if he could get back to Earth somehow, he could cure these dying aliens—in theory, of course. That same medicine, in some shape or form, could cure their dying breed.

*"O Lord of Universe, where am I and what happened to me? Will I ever leave this place, or am I to be the only human survivor on this alien planet?"* He

groaned again.

More and more questions came to him with fewer and fewer answers. The two police officers had shown him that he had been brought here due to that orb, and now, on second thought, he wished he hadn't ever touched it in the first place. That artifact had unleashed a curse on him, maybe even given him a life sentence in prison. Al-Khidr tried to shove away the negativity and wondered about why God had planned this for him. God must have landed him here for a reason. He decided to find a reason for his coming here, and determined that he would figure out how he could help these dying aliens. Random thoughts and half-baked action plans flashed across his mind, putting him to sleep.

***

Hours whizzed by as Al-Khidr snored loudly in his cell. He woke up the next morning but in better spirits. He had a plan in his mind, and began to fine-tune the details.

He was still in his bed when he heard the unlocking of the door of the cell. It was almost an hour since he has awakened, and Minkah entered with another lady and some staff. This time they had a big box in their hand. Al-Khidr watched them all carefully.

Minkah said to the lady, "Dr. Arit, please start your work."

Dr. Arit smiled at Al-Khidr and said, "Don't be nervous, it will not take very long."

## Chapter 12. Serendipity

She injected some black liquid in his vein, which Al-Khidr found interesting, and he felt like he wanted to pee. But within a minute, the urge was gone. The doctor opened the box, took out a pillow-sized device, connected some wires, placed it on the bed in place of a pillow, and then asked Al-Khidr to put his head on it. Al-Khidr did as advised, and Arit turned on the device. Al-Khidr noticed that a bright light came out of the device, but he felt nothing.

Dr. Arit picked up a tablet-looking device and started looking at it. Within minutes, the procedure was over.

Dr. Arit gladly said, "All perfect. No signs of brain damage. Mr. Al-Khidr is perfectly fine. Now we have confirmed that you are sane!"

"*Tamkhlawt (crazy)!*" Al-Khidr uttered in Amazigh.

"What?" Dr. Arit asked.

"Nothing. Just thinking about my friend back on Earth," Al-Khidr smilingly said.

All smiled, and then they left the room.

***

An hour passed. Al-Khidr felt bored, so he went to the door to see if anyone was coming back.

A passing police officer slid his breakfast through his door and went along his way.

"Good morning to you," Al-Khidr said in amusement. "Talk about human decency and some courtesy, for God's sake."

He took a look at the food, and something weird greeted him. It was a steaming, boiling liquid with bluish bread. He gulped his breakfast; it was so hard to swallow something so tasteless. But at least they took good care of their inmates; you had to hand it to them.

He walked back and forth with determined steps. A plan was forming in his mind that he would now help the aliens instead of running away from them. He realized that it was destined to be like this, that he would arrive on this planet and help them.

Nefertiti wasn't a bad person, really. He was sure that she would lend an ear to him. He could help these aliens out in their predicament and probably arrive back on Earth in one piece.

He called out to the passing police officer, and the expressionless officer came near his cell.

"I need to talk to your superior officer, Nefertiti. I may have some information that might be crucial for your race," he said with urgency.

The police officer ran over to Nefertiti's corner office. Al-Khidr had seen her enter and leave that office on and off during the day. But his enthusiasm started to decline when a few hours had passed, and both the young police officer and Nefertiti were nowhere in sight. Finally, at midday, he saw her walking toward his cell with three male aliens. She looked slightly worried. The sight of her relieved him so much, he wanted to hug her.

"Well, well, well, we meet again. Guess what, the

doctor said I am sane, heeyyyy," Al-Khidr said, smiling ear to ear.

"Yes, I heard. But we still have procedures, you know," Nefertiti said.

The armed guards were following the security protocols. The first armed guard partially unlocked the door by facial recognition. The second armed guard did the same to partially unlock the prison door. Then came Nefertiti, who also presented her face in front of the screen. The lock finally released itself, and in came the three. "It's a three-step security protocol. We have had cases before where one guard released a friend of his out in the open. I suspended that schmuck," she said, and chuckled loudly.

Al-Khidr looked at Nefertiti admiringly. She was so beautiful, and somewhere, after all of this, he hoped to find the real her. She was also wearing a lovely perfume, which was an add-on to the excitement. But her uniform was unlike that of women back on Earth. It looked like men's clothing, more as if she was a warrior. "Oh, well, I'm not really running anywhere. Only if I could return to my planet and let people live in peace here," Al-Khidr said modestly.

"Yeah, I know that. But still, I am only following protocol. Come with us to the police station," she said passively, and turned around.

Al-Khidr entered a huge hall that showed moving images. On the high wall were images announcing the employees of the month. He looked on the other side, and saw that it showed the most wanted criminals in the planetary system. He cautiously looked at the faces to see if his mugshot was also in this lineup. After a while, he heaved a sigh of relief.

"I am not a criminal in your world. This gives me so much happiness. I cannot tell you how happy I am," he said cheerfully. "Yes. We haven't determined your status yet. You are under the 'Intergalactic Aliens B' category right now. This is all I know so far," she replied, still looking ahead.

"Well, that does sound like a reasonable thing to do. Put the aliens in categories, depending on their status," Al-Khidr said, lost in thought. "Well, even if you leave this planet, we can trace you any time," Nefertiti said while looking at Al-Khidr's hand. "You mean because of the thing inside me?" Al-Khidr inquired.

He looked hopelessly at his wrist with the eye symbol and three holes at the vertices of an upward triangle.

"Yes, it's a tracking device. Don't try to tamper with it. It is barred by law," Nefertiti said.

They came to a hall, where Nefertiti stood in front of a screen for facial recognition. The machine approved her entry, and the glass doors swung open for them. She entered her private office and sat on an airborne chair.

Then she started using her hands doing something that Al-Khidr didn't understand. He thought it was some sort of a tablet with lights. She pressed one icon, and the screen presented Al-Khidr's mugshot with his criminal charges.

"Remove all criminal charges for one Al-Khidr with immediate effect," she said loudly, surprising Al-Khidr.

"Yes. Records of one Al-Khidr have been erased. Enjoy your day," said the voice.

Al-Khidr looked around, searching for the voice.

"What happened? Who was that voice talking to you like that?" Al-Khidr said.

"It is Hesb-t—a computer. It can compute and make intelligent decisions, when necessary. I don't think you have such devices in your planet," Nefertiti said, and showed him her tablet-looking device.

"The Emerald Tablet!" Al-Khidr uttered. "Can I play *Shatranj* (chess) on it?" he asked.

Nefertiti didn't answer the question and kept looking at the screen. She then turned it off and asked the other two-armed policemen to leave them alone. They nodded in agreement and left her private office.

Al-Khidr and Nefertiti were now alone in the room. Al-Khidr looked at Nefertiti, thinking of how to break the ice. But Nefertiti did it herself, seeing the hesitation between them.

She turned on the table, which came to life, and then she pressed a button. Nefertiti was recording the conversation for future reference. "Whatever you say will be recorded, and it be part of our Hall of Records, a recorded conversation database between the police and the offenders," Nefertiti told Al-Khidr.

"We can begin now. How did you come to this planet? Start with how all this happened, and finish the moment I took you into custody," she said. Al-Khidr thought for a moment, thinking about where to start. He had to process a lot of things. He then looked at Nefertiti squarely in the eyes and began. "I come from a planet we call Al-Eard. We have not progressed as much as people on this planet, but the human forms here are not any different from the ones on Earth. The technology of this planet is a few centuries ahead of mine. But I can somehow speak your language. That is another story," he said. He had an idea suddenly and spat it out: "Can you find out about my planet in your records?" he asked, surprising even himself.

"We have Interplanetary Data Records, which is a comprehensive database of planets, people, and the habitat. But for people of your planet, Earth...No. The data covers Lyra and its environs. Your Earth is twenty-five light-years away. Meaning, you would have to travel twenty-five years at the speed of light. You realize how far you have come, thanks to one object?" she said, uninterested in the conversation.

Al-Khidr felt heartbroken by this revelation. He was so far away and alone, not to mention speaking to a police officer who was only half-interested in this conversation.

"If it's any consolation, we have a galaxy chart. Your planet is marked here." She placed her finger at one spot on a three-dimensional star chart, which she had made appear after pressing a few buttons on her tablet.

"I have never seen Earth from this far!" Al-Khidr

was amazed by the things her Emerald Tablet could do. "This is so good. We have a lot to catch up compared to your planet," he said.

Nefertiti let the comment pass and resumed her questioning. "Tell me more about your planet and other stuff. What were you doing when it happened, and how did the orb come into your possession?" she asked him.

Al-Khidr nodded in agreement and began expanding on the events back on Earth which brought him here. It would be a while before he was finished retelling the events. From the looks of it, Nefertiti was amazed. Clearly, it was unlike anything that happened in this world. They were both from very different worlds, except that the people in both places were very much alike. At last, Al-Khidr ended his account on the sphere that had accidentally come into his possession and taken him on an interdimensional journey.

"Glass shard. Hmm, that must be Amris...but how did it reach Earth?" Nefertiti was lost for a while.

There was some silence in the room as the two processed their thoughts and the information. Then Al-Khidr spoke again.

"I need to ask a few questions overall, and some about this planet. Should I go ahead?" he asked solemnly. Nefertiti nodded in affirmative.

"What is the name of this planet, and why are the humans here so similar to my own kind? What is the history of this world, and how did you people inhabit this planet in a far-off galaxy?" he asked.

"Those are a lot of questions, not just one," Nefertiti said. "The name of this planet is Lyra. I am not aware of any migration that happened. It does look like that we have a lot in common, as you also noticed during your time in prison. Those prisoners are not much different, either. But, although we look similar from the outside, our scans show that your body composition is different from ours," she said in a monotone.

Al-Khidr listened carefully, then said, "I am curious about the contagion Mutmut that spread on your planet. Who was Patient Zero, and how did he land on this planet? We do not have the means to reach this place unless we used the sphere. What happened exactly?" he said in a serious tone. "It happened quite a long time ago, and records are not available of the event. The officials went there in their aerial vehicles and sealed the area. From what I have heard about the incident—I was a child back then—those people have never been seen in this area again. The Sutekh exclusion zone is still sealed today. You, however, were reported in that area when you broke the transporter vehicle," she said passively.

"You mean to say those people were never seen or heard from again?" he asked. His eyes were wide open. She shook her head. "You see, the southern section of this planet is off-limits. You cannot visit it in ordinary circumstances without the Royal Decree's clearance. I can safely say that the pandemic was contained by putting those people in permanent quarantine. I assume this resolved the pandemic issue, so we never looked for a cure," she went on.

After some thought, she remembered something.

"And no, the cure has not been discovered. We didn't need to go that far. That place is now called the Sutekh, or 'Exclusion Zone.' You can't find the Exclusion Zone on flight charts and consumer transportation maps. The Royal Decree wants people to be safe, so no adventurers are allowed to seek it. It's a no-go area for us all," she finished.

Al-Khidr nodded. He was still thinking about plants along the coast of Nile. This seemed like a moment for Al-Khidr to tell her about his plans, that he wanted to help them and save their race.

"I can save those people with a cure from my planet," he said. "Let me help you. I am an alchemist, after all, and have studied the diseases of my planet all my life. I have a cure in mind that can help those people affected by the disease. But to get the cure, I need to go back to Earth," he said. Nefertiti looked at him for a minute and burst out laughing. He looked back at her, totally confused. It was the first time she had laughed in this otherwise dry one-on-one meeting.

"You come from a society that is still using horses, donkeys, and mules for transportation. Why do you think we cannot find a cure for a disease of this sort? Do you think our medicine is far behind yours?" she said between her laughter.

Al-Khidr felt heartbroken, but realized this probably was not the right time or person to propose this as an option. He just wanted to help, after all. He didn't care much if someone wasn't interested in his services.

He looked up again at Nefertiti. She had stopped laughing, and was now staring at the wall behind him. "Look, I don't mean to offend you," she said. "But we are way ahead of your planet in every sense of the word. If our people were given access to the disease and affected people, I don't doubt we would have found a cure, or maybe many cures. I also know your heart is in the right place. But we can cure a primitive disease. I am sure of that," she said with a finality in her tone. Nefertiti had said what she wanted to say. "You wish to cure it, but you haven't?" Al-Khidr said sarcastically. "There is a difference between wishes and probabilities. You may need something, but not automatically get it. Right?" he went on.

There was silence in the room, and Al-Khidr felt like an outsider for the first time since he had arrived here. The fact that Nefertiti had a low opinion of him sunk his spirits even further.

"The issue is that the records were sealed and locked in the archives. Only by the Royal Decree can we access them. You cannot see the southern part of our planet, since when the pandemic hit, those areas were sealed off," Nefertiti said.

She looked at her wrist and began to stand up. To Al-Khidr, the object on her wrist looked like another screen, one very similar to the one on his shoes or something of that sort. Nefertiti exhaled after looking at her wrist.

# Chapter 12.  Serendipity

"Will that be all?  I need to leave for an urgent meeting," she said.

He had to think of something fast. It was his only chance to make this happen.

"Look, if I can return to Al-Eard, I can find the cure for this pandemic, and maybe those people can live their lives happily like before.  Your government has decided to opt for a no-action approach.  They don't want to deal with them.  Should they be left alone like this?  What kind of society is this?  Do you not care for your own?  Where I come from, we save people as one of our own," he said.  "Last time a pandemic appeared, everyone came together to help each other.  We have a bond that ties us together as one. I am kind of disappointed that your world, with everything it has, is still heartless, cruel, and less human than ours. If you had this disease, would your Royal Decree care for you?" he asked, looking in her eyes.

Nefertiti looked back at him, her eyes searching for an answer. But none came.

Al-Khidr saw an opening and continued further.  "As things stand, I am also sure that God has sent me to this planet for a reason.  He doesn't talk to me, but I can feel it when I have to do something. He has a purpose for everyone and sees everything. If I could, I would have gone to heal God's people myself," he said.  "You are an interesting character. Very interesting.  Tell you what, I have changed my mind about the whole thing. Follow me," she said. It seemed as though she had warmed up to him.

"Thanks. I thought I would be in your prison for the rest of my life or something," he said. "Well, not exactly. The prison population is usually bounty hunters, killers, and scavengers. We send them back to their planet as part of our treaty with the Joint Planetary Commission. Any aliens from the registered planets are sent to their native lands. Your case was pending because you are not a criminal," she said. Nefertiti then thought for a moment.

"Here's what I can do for you. I will escort you to the Royal Palace. The five men will listen to your request and grant it. I should remind you that these men don't take aliens very seriously. It's not the first time an alien has come to them for a request," she said, and laughed a little. Al-Khidr also smiled. Indeed, they were warming up to each other little by little.

He stood, looked at his shoes, and spoke again.

"God has sent me for a reason," he repeated.

"Yes, dear. I heard you the first time. Now come with me," she said condescendingly.

Al-Khidr chuckled. He had taken a liking to her.

The two were about to leave her private office when a young police officer interrupted them at the door. He looked worried and out of breath. "At ease, officer. Is there something you are worried about?" Nefertiti asked.

The officer spoke between breaths. "A wave of reporters has piled up outside our headquarters. They are demanding to see the alien who has arrived from Earth. It's a whole swarm of them. The 'earthling,' as they say, is becoming popular with them.  It will be known to the whole Kingdom of Akhom by the evening—I don't know what to do.  I can't hold them off for much longer," he said breathlessly.

Nefertiti quickly turned on the screen on her desk. The screen flickered to life, showing a massive line of reporters stretching to the last block on the street. They were holding small, black objects, and Al-Khidr couldn't tell what it was, but Nefertiti knew they were mics for the alien prisoner.  The police officers were standing outside the gates, holding off the excited reporters.  Some electric stun guns were hanging in mid-air, in case the reporters had funny ideas.  It was routine police protocol.

"Oh, what in the hell is this now?  How did they know about the goddamn alien?  I told you all to keep information about the inmates inside the police unit. This is the fifth time—"

She was interrupted by the young police officer.

"Pardon me for interrupting.  But it was one of the prisoners who leaked the information to his buddy reporter.  We had to release him after charges against him were dropped after twenty-four hours.  It's just police protocol," he said, and shrugged.  He knew the police protocols hadn't included a clause about leaking criminal information to the public.  It was really out of his hands and Nefertiti's.

"I am your superior officer.  You will never interrupt me ever again.  If you do, I will relocate you to the southern tip," she said sternly.  The young officer nodded and fell silent. She was red in the face and looked away.

Al-Khidr stared at Nefertiti. She was lost in thought now, maybe thinking of something else.

"I see...our circumstances have changed a bit." Eventually, it seemed like she had made up her mind. "Okay. We cannot go through the front door today; it's a whole media circus out there. The news of our alien should not reach other planets. It will mean we have violated alien life rights, and the Joint Planetary Commission will impose trade sanctions and discourage prisoner exchange," she said in a monotone.

Al-Khidr interrupted her. "I have no idea what is happening. What are you talking about? What are reporters and interviews?" Al-Khidr asked. He hadn't heard of these things on his planet. The new data in his mind only gave clues on the nouns or names of objects.

"It's nothing. I don't have time to explain right now. Just follow me, and I will see what I can do," she said. She turned to the worried police officer.

"Remove Al-Khidr's shoes and give him the non-programmed ones," she said.

Police officers removed Al-Khidr shoes and gave him regular boots. Then Nefertiti began to run, and he followed right after her. "Where are we going exactly? Are people looking for me? Did I do something wrong on this planet? I did steal fuel a few days ago. I haven't done anything else, apart from that," Al-Khidr said while running.

# CHAPTER 12. SERENDIPITY

"It'sfine. You are not charged for thefts," she said over her shoulder.

"What about this thing installed in my wrist?" Al-Khidr said.

"It's a long procedure, and now we do not have time for it. We will do that later," Nefertiti said. It would be some time before he understood life on this planet and who was who and what was what. He sighed as he ran with his new, lighter shoes. They ran through different glass corridors, taking many turns. Al-Khidr could see his face in the reflection, and laughed at how he looked. His hair was all messy, but the orange prison uniform he was wearing was still so much better than his own clothes. The corridors lit up as they passed through them, taking him by surprise. He looked above to see white light illuminating the halls as they ran.

"We are going through the back exit. Almost there. I don't want reporters getting there before we escape the police station. Otherwise, you will be surrounded, and I don't want that," she said while running.

They came outside into the open air, and suddenly, Al-Khidr felt frozen to the bone. When the two came outside, a reporter stood alone at the back door. Nefertiti took out something from her holster. Al-Khidr had seen the prison guards wearing it during their patrol hours. She pressed a few buttons, took aim, and pulled the trigger. It released the green light and hit the reporter, throwing him hard against the wall. Fumes surrounded the man. He collapsed to the ground, gasping for breath as he tried to get up.

"Hurry up. Follow me. We don't have time," Nefertiti shouted.

"You killed him?" Al-Khidr said, surprised.

"Shooting a reporter is a federal police offense. I only pushed him aside using a beam. Don't worry, he'll be fine." she said, trying to catch her breath. They climbed into a silver vehicle. Al-Khidr was impressed by the interior. It was white from the inside, and a screen came to life when Nefertiti entered. "Hermes, take us to the nearest safe house, away from the reporters and people. I want to protect the alien for the time being," she said loudly. "Understood. Vehicle taking off in twenty seconds," the computer replied.

Al-Khidr looked around, but there was no one in the vehicle. "Who are you talking to? Who is Hermes?" he asked innocently.

"Hermes is the navigation system designed specifically for the kingdom's police," she informed him.

They were lifted in the air as the vehicle made a loud sound and jetted across the high-rise police station building. The flying vehicle quickly moved towards the city center, tearing through clouds as they gained more height. Al-Khidr couldn't help but admire that he was moving past tall buildings. He saw the high-rise structures stretching higher than the clouds. It was then he noticed that a lot of other vehicles, similar to Nefertitis, were moving at a height above the buildings. "What is this world? I have never seen anything like it," he said to no one in particular.

# CHAPTER 12. SERENDIPITY

"You will get used to it. Give it a few years or so. You can speak our language somehow, and the reporters want to break the story of an illegal alien who arrived mysteriously from Earth," she explained. "I can take you to my home if the safe houses are closed, but let's see. I am not sure yet," she said. As they were talking, a screen appeared in front of their faces. They turned to it, both surprised by the intrusion. "It's not far from here, understand?" she said nicely.

He just nodded his head and crashed into the seat behind him.

"This thing...It's like a flying carpet. However, a flying carpet cannot talk. It can understand you just fine. On my planet, I heard a story about Alladin and the Magic Lamp. This vehicle is like a carpet from that story," he said.

"Uh, what?" she asked, without looking back.

"Oh. You have never heard about him? Well, long ago on Al-Eard, there lived a very careless man named Alladin. He was the son of an impoverished tailor who barely made enough for his wife and naughty son. At fifteen years old, Alladin was on the streets playing with boys of his age when an old sorcerer passed by them. The passion and enthusiasm of Alladin pleased the sorcerer. He laid his hand on his head," Al-Khidr said excitedly.

Nefertiti listened with mild interest; they had some time before arrival.

"The sorcerer asked, 'Was your father's name Mustapha?

He was a tailor, if I recall."

"'Alladin said, 'Yes, he was my father, but he died a long time ago. Only my mother and I remain now. We live at the corner of this street.' "'Boy, will you take me to your mother? I have great things for you. Take these gold coins to your mother. She can buy some clothes, food, and kitchen utensils,'the sorcerer said. 'Tell her I will visit her tomorrow at noon. I am your father's lost brother,' he said dreamily.

"The next day, the sorcerer visited Alladin's house to talk to his mother. She burst out crying when he asked about Alladin and their living conditions. "After his dad's death, Alladin had become an idle fellow. 'His father tried hard, but failed,'his mother said flatly. Alladin sunk his head low, realizing he had disappointed his mother. The sorcerer promised to make things better for Alladin and his aging mom. He took him to a merchant to learn the art of selling. The merchant had a reputation for clothes, ancient artifacts, and precious stones. At one corner of the shop was a magic lamp. The sorcerer's face darkened when he laid his eyes on it." "You have reached the travel limits. Further passage in the police vehicle is not allowed," the computer screen said, interrupting Al-Khidr's story. Both Nefertiti and Al-Khidr were lost in the dusty streets of Agraba when the Hermes announcement came. They nearly jumped in surprise. The two stood up and started to step off the spaceship.

"Oh, God, I forgot to deactivate the travel restrictions on this vehicle,"Nefertiti said. "We need to either remain in this vehicle or go back to the police station. Anyway...Please continue from where we left off,"she said in a miserable tone.

"Oh, I am just getting started," said Al-Khidr. Nefertiti laughed.

"You know, you are funnier than I thought," she said. "My friends say that too," Al-Khidr said. "Oh, I wanted to ask this. If I go back, will I become older?" "We travel from planet to planet, and it does make you older, actually. But our life span is long. Have you seen our queen?" "Yes," Al-Khidr said. "Can you guess her age?" Nefertiti asked.

"Oh, she is very beautiful and young, right? I saw her in Obelisk square in the city center," Al-Khidr said. "No, she is old. We regard her as a mother because she protects us from diseases. Legend says that she was on Earth when this disease first appeared in our males, and Mother lost her husband Usir and son Heru," Nefertiti informed him. "What? On Earth, ancient Egyptians thought that Hathor and Usir were god and goddess," Al-Khidr said. "Hathor is a scientist, and her husband Usir was also a scientist, but unfortunately, he died on your planet due to this disease," Nefertiti continued. Al-Khidr was lost in deep thought.

Suddenly, the Hermes system signaled that something was overriding its protocol. Nefertiti was surprised, and then on screen appeared a man in a royal guard uniform. "Is this vehicle 2098?"

"Yes sir," Nefertiti said. Her tone and stature had changed completely. "Are you Officer Nefertiti Uar?"

"Yes sir, I am," she said.

The representative of Her Royal Highness Queen Hathor spoke in a thick, booming voice. "We are relaying a call from the Royal Guards' office. The earthling is requested to be present at the Royal Palace by 02:00 LPM today in front of Her Royal Highness, Queen Hathor. Please be there fifteen minutes before this time for necessary security clearance. Thank you." The screen then vanished from the air.

"Well, there you go—change of plans. We are no longer going to the safe house at the penthouse. Hermes, reroute your course to the Royal Palace in the central city. We should be there in one hour, if the air traffic is under control," she said lazily.

She looked at Al-Khidr and realized something. "Now, we are going across town to the queen's palace," she explained. He still stared blankly at her. Nefertiti sighed. "I mean to say, just sit down for a while. We will be there in a few minutes," she said kindly.

# Chapter 13

# The Rendezvous

Aʟ-Kʜɪᴅʀ and Nefertiti reached a large square with a black pyramid in the center. It looks like the Great Pyramid in Giza back on Earth, Al-Khidr thought. In front of the pyramid stood a colossal, Sphinx-sized statue with the face of Anubis. "On Earth, we have a similar statue, and we call it *Bahwah*, meaning checkpost. Our *Bahwah* has a passage inside that leads to chambers beneath the Pyramids," Al-Khidr said.

# CHAPTER 13.   THE RENDEZVOUS

"It must have been made by the HSS team which visited your planet," Nefertiti said. "Come, we need to enter the Benben after passing through security clearance!" "Benben?" Al-Khidr said in an inquiring voice.

"This pyramid." She was referring to the Great Black Pyramid as 'the Benben.' Al-Khidr then remembered that he had seen this black pyramid when he entered the Lyra's atmosphere for the first time.

The Sphinx-sized statue was actually a security checkpoint. They had to go through all kinds of searches, and apparently, the Benben had no entrance from the surface. Al-Khidr imagined the Benben as the royal palace of Agraba in Alladin's story, or that of the Caliph's palace in Baghdad. But he had to wait until he was inside to be sure of that. Meanwhile, Al-Khidr was mesmerized by the blue shield at the door of the passage leading to the pyramid. It seemed to be moving slightly, back and forth. Some bolts of lights went through it as the shield moved.

He stepped closer, still amazed by this thing that seemed so foreign to him.

"Don't touch it. Please," Nefertiti shouted from behind him.

But it was too late for that. Al-Khidr's curiosity had gotten the best of him.

He softly touched the shield, and a sudden booming sound came. Al-Khidr was thrown backward and he fell on Nefertiti, who covered her head at the last moment. "Get off of me," she said in aggravation.

Al-Khidr was dazed and muttered a confused bunch

of swear words. Nefertiti helped him slowly get to his feet. He seemed weak and unaware of himself. "Well, why did you touch the stupid thing? There is high voltage electricity running through this shield. Even criminals are afraid of it. You are probably the first person to touch it like this," she growled.

Nefertiti freed Al-Khidr's arms, allowing him to stand on his two feet. Al-Khidr stood for a second, then fell on the ground, face-first.

"It's fine. Just sit down for a while. Hopefully, you will be all right in few minutes," she said softly.

"What was that thing?" he managed to ask. "It was so powerful. My legs are still shaking." "I warned you!" she said plainly.

She knew Al-Khidr was not the first person to talk about hyper-electricity. It was a relatively old invention on her planet, but it once ran the whole planet. A few armed guards greeted them, and they sat on the back seat of the vehicle. They went through an underground passage. As they neared the throne room, the passage grew larger and larger until Al-Khidr had to strain his neck to see its walls. Nefertiti laughed at how Al-Khidr was taking all of it in front of him. Soon, they arrived at the large, brown entrance gates.

"Step inside this capsule," the burly guard ordered Al-Khidr and Nefertiti. Al-Khidr looked at Nefertiti in confusion, and she motioned for him to enter it. The capsule was a square-shaped room. Its size was nearly their height. *It looks like the casing over an Egyptian mummy!* Al-Khidr thought. He stepped inside it and felt the soft floor touch his feet. Nefertiti came from behind.

"Take us to the mother's chamber," the armed guard said loudly. The four of them disappeared from the capsule and arrived inside the queen's chambers. Al-Khidr could not believe what had just happened. He checked his arms, legs, torso, and everything. Well, it was all still there. He felt slightly dizzy and weak from the experience.

He looked at Nefertiti, who was seeing the palace for the first time herself. "How did I come from there to here. We did not fly, walk, or drive. Is it the real me?" he asked, still bamboozled by the whole experience.

She rolled her eyes. Oh, God. "You can visit any place through this portal to the royal offices. It's mostly used by members of the royal palace and forces because they have to attend intergalactic meetings," she continued.

He listened to her intently. "You mean, other people are not allowed to use it on the planet?" he asked, still amazed. "It has been a long debate, but no. Not yet," she said flatly.

As they moved forward, they entered a large hall, at the end of which was a throne. Cat-like feline creatures were standing near the throne, both right and left. Al-Khidr was stunned to see these human-looking cat-creatures, but due to royal decorum, he could not ask what these creatures were. They were dressed like ancient Egyptian idols, with a green skirt around the belly and a pink shawl over the torso. They looked like animals, but surprisingly, they seemed intelligent and had no foul smell. Their eyes looked as if they were watching for an attack.

Beyond them, the queen was sitting on the throne. She was as beautiful and majestic as before, and her flowing hair fell behind her back. She wore a red, ancient-Egyptian-looking dress that covered her from head to toes. She was also wearing a crown with a golden sphere and golden horns on it. The armed guards and Nefertiti knelt in respect.

"My queen," they said in soft tones.

The queen said nothing; her sight was focused on Al-Khidr. Nefertiti, without saying a word, moved her eyebrows so that Al-Khidr would kneel as well. Al-Khidr did not kneel, instead looking straight into the queen's eyes. She seemed to be ruminating. The cat-like creatures standing on her right and left moved a step-forward and growled at the same time, and the whole Benben started reverberating back to them in a haunted way. Al-Khidr then realized that he was breaking a royal decorum, so he knelt while keeping his head and backbone straight.

It was Nefertiti who gathered the courage and requested to say something to the queen. The queen then nodded her head and motioned for Nefertiti to continue. Nefertiti said: "Mother, the Guardian of Wisdom, I come in your presence. I have brought the alien with me. He is from the planet Keb, the cursed planet, as we all know," she continued.

# CHAPTER 13. THE RENDEZVOUS

The word curse shook the queen, and she looked at them, still deep in thought. The queen then said, in a deep, commanding voice, "Yes, child. It was a terrible time for all of us. The origin of the virus is something that troubles me to this day." Nefertiti stood up and spoke again.

"My queen, we have had the alien under our custody for a few days. He was in the quarantine section of the prison. However, I was not ready to take any chances with him roaming around in the streets."

The queen listened to her intently and seemed to be thinking at the same time. "My intelligence has informed me that this alien is not infected," she said. "My queen, our tests have cleared him. The traces of the virus were not found in his body. Secondly, you went to Keb a long time ago, probably when we were using old technology. I do believe that virus would have vanished after a couple of centuries," Nefertiti explained tensely. The mother listened to her reasoning attentively, then turned to face the two.

"It was horrible. So horrible. I still shudder to imagine the horrors of that trip. We went to Keb back in 23000 S.C. I lost my husband, my child, and poor crew on that journey," she said, looking down.

Again, a silence fell over the room. Al-Khidr could hear his heartbeat. He didn't want to interrupt just yet. Clearly, the queen was not happy with his presence on her planet, let alone in her throne room.

"My son was dried up from inside until I could barely recognize him. Poor soul," she said in anguish.

"We panicked and put rest in the quarantine chambers. But it was too late by then, and other crew members were already showing signs of infection. Anyway, I turned on the medical interface to evaluate the nature of this virus. Much to my disappointment, it said 'virus unknown.' The composition of the virus was different, unlike anything I had previously encountered," she continued in a flat voice.

Al-Khidr was waiting for his chance to speak up. Maybe the queen would be open to his proposal. He had to take his chance. "The change in biological composition had started at my face, and I could do nothing with it. We were not exactly expecting an epidemic. Otherwise, I would have installed cryogenic chambers in my spaceship," the queen said. She seemed about to continue, but then stopped herself. "Wait. How did you come here? Keb is far away from here. Your kind has not progressed enough to reach such far confines of space," she said, frowning.

Al-Khidr cleared his throat. "Queen of Lyra, I mean, uh, Mother. I came here by chance. We were looking inside the Pyramid in Egypt on my planet when it happened. I found something, a metallic orb. I put a glass shard into it, and next thing I knew, I was on this planet," he said slowly. Queen Hathor stared at him, clearly knowing where this was going.

"It was a metallic sphere that brought me here. I had found it lying in one of the pyramids. I touched it—" Hathor's eyes brightened. "Ahhhh. The jump-sphere!" she said, looking sad.

# CHAPTER 13.  THE RENDEZVOUS

"I took it from the ark inside the pyramid. Is there a chance the people who put those things in the ark were from your planet?" he asked. Mother looked at him and said, "I left the spheres in the quarantine chambers with two of our very bright star-fleet officers. I don't know what you are talking about," she said dismissively. The queen seemed disturbed by his questions, and she said, "I will decide what to do with you. You may leave now." To Nefertiti, she said, "And I suggest you run another test on him and see if the virus shows its symptoms again. We may have to re-think if it reappears," she said. Nefertiti knelt down, "Okay, Mother. I will do that and send the report by tomorrow."

They returned to the capsule and arrived outside the Royal Throne room.

"Well, that's that," Nefertiti said. "I will escort you to your prison cell as per my orders. I cannot override the queen," she said, and shrugged. Al-Khidr shrugged too, knowing well that it was Hathor's orders.

"What were those creatures?" Al-Khidr asked, referring to the cat-like people by the throne.

"The feline creatures are Shekmets, the Royal Guards, from the moon of Nubrisia. They were trained since their childhood to protect the Mother. They did not belong to the planet Lyra, but were adopted and trained here as per agreement," Nefertiti informed him.

Nefertiti had an idea for the way back. "Hey, how about that Alladin story? We had just started that.

Don't you want to end it?" she said, looking at him.

"Oh, right. I was still furious about my transfer into the prison cell. I know your hands are tied and all," he said.

They looked at each other for a moment. "Well, the story ended. Alladin found the lamp, and I found a sphere. Our lives changed forever!" Al-Khidr said.

# Chapter 14

# The Memories

QUEEN Hathor stood from her throne in a disturbed state. The feline creatures knelt on both sides. For the first time since she had become queen, she felt too old to handle it.

A human had arrived from Keb after aeons. She stepped down from the throne and started walking towards interior chamber. When she reached her chamber, she asked her attendants to leave, and the women with the feline face and figure left the chamber.

# CHAPTER 14.  THE MEMORIES

She stood in front of a mirror, her mind startling. She pulled off her mask and looked at her wrinkled face. She was depressed, and didn't feel like resting in the rejuvenation device today; this device could heal her body from toxic effects of free radicals, restoring a bit of youth to an aging body. But the device could not restore the skin's resilience, and the user got wrinkled skin with time. The life longevity device was only available to the royalties, state ministers, and military generals. In this palace, she was the sole dweller, and she alone used the rejuvenation device.

Hathor had no siblings and cousins. Her mother was from planet Kubrios, one of the few survivors from the dying planet.

Hathor looked at herself and tears welled up in her eyes. Then she covered her face with both hands and cried.

"Usir, Usir! I loved you, but I lost you on Keb."

She remembered well the day she had left Earth. After much loss, she was in her cabin, and Asiua arrived and told her that one of the males had experienced the same symptoms they had found on the Earth.

"Hurry up, Princess, into the sealed chamber. The rest of the males will be sealed on the other side of the ship," Ehsis ordered. "What's going on?" Princess Hathor asked.

"Amenhotep contracted the disease, and we have isolated him in the secluded chamber," Ehsis said.

"What a cursed disease it is!" she said. "We must

save Amenhotep. How are Siesi, Hori, Ubania and Tutkaman?" Hathor asked. "We cannot lose them like Anpu and Thoth," she continued.

"They are fine, princess," Ehsis said.

"I want the protection of all, including everyone and baby Heru," Hathor said in a scared voice.

"Amenhotep suggested that he can go into hibernation, and probably by the time we reach Lyra, he will be fine," said Ehsis.

"Let's hope so. Oh God, help us all," Hathor said in nervousness.

The disease was a curse on planet Earth. It dried up the body from inside, all bodily fluids started oozing out, and the body started to look like a dried tree trunk, turning the skin tone dark.

***

Hathor woke again from her disturbed sleep. Long ago, she had shouted at her crew in a spaceship as it moved through the vastness of space: "Open the door, you blasted idiots. My child is in there. Try to understand. We cannot leave him like this. Open the door," Princess Hathor shouted. But Ehsis and other women held her back. Princess Hathor was a strong woman, and Ehsis was not enough to keep her back, so she called for reinforcements, who came running.

The eyes of her child were closed. He was locked in this chamber within a chamber to contain the virus. Princess Hathor looked at her firstborn son. The chamber continued to move in circular and diagonal motions.

Ehsis had shut the chamber after one accidental test had revealed a trace of the virus in Heru. The child continued to roll around for a few days. The scientists of Lyra had come up with the idea of rolling chambers. According to them, as long as the chamber rolled circular and diagonally, the patient remained very much alive and breathing. A beeper would go off if the breathing patterns were problematic, lighting up the chamber. When Ehsis had put the child inside, things were fine. The remaining crew members gave a blood sample to test for the virus again. They were clean so far.

It was Ehsis' idea; she had not told Princess Hathor about it for fear of hindrance. The test results showed the virus metamorphosing, originating from the stomach. The virus sent alarm bells ringing, and Ehsis had locked the child inside the chamber. She knew she also had to change the access code, because Hathor would go berserk. As it happened, she did go berserk.

Princess Hathor came stomping her feet after few hours of her son's isolation.

"I want to see my son, Ehsis," she barked in front of everyone.

Ehsis took a step back.

"That will not be possible, Princess Hathor," she said calmly.

"May I ask why? Give me the access codes. The child has not eaten in days," she said, pushing past her.

"I am afraid that will not be possible either," Ehsis said calmly.

This was strange. Hathor had never seen Ehsis so rigid about anything.

"Ehsis, is my child alive?" she asked.

Ehsis looked down; she had her answer.

"I did not have the heart to tell you. We had enough trauma as it is," she said, disheartened. She removed the frosted glass over the chamber for everyone to see. The chamber had ceased moving.

"I declared Heru dead yesterday. He had passed away in his sleep, without seeing the world," she announced to everyone.

Princess Hathor stood looking at the chamber with sobbing eyes. The tears were falling from her cheeks. Could anything be worse than this? She had lost everything on this mission. Her child, husband, some lovely lifelong friends, and who knows what else!

"Can I at least take a look at Heru?" she asked Ehsis, already guessing the answer.

"There is no way I am letting you inside the chamber. I have lost enough crew members already. I am not in the mood for another casualty on this dreadful mission," Ehsis shouted.

But her words resonated with Hathor's agony. They looked at the dead child; a victim of circumstances that befell them. The two then stared at the darkness ahead of them. They were leaving the outskirts of a galaxy. An asteroid belt was visibly clear by now.

# Chapter 14. The Memories

Ehsis broke the strained silence. There were other things to do.

"Princess Hathor. We have to release the child into space. Keeping him inside is too much risk. When we re-enter Lyra, there is a threat of a virus outbreak. We cannot take that chance. The chambers will open, which could unleash the virus," Ehsis warned her.

Hathor realized that she could not fight her destiny. She said, "Release Heru into space. The risk is too great to take—it could cause a huge uproar. People will demand answers. We have questions ourselves," she said, staring into space. A large, bluish star was visible in the distance. Its blue sunlight had lit up the spaceship as they moved past it. For a moment, Ehsis and Princess Hathor were blue. That did lighten up the mood.

Hathor looked at the ceiling.

"Moses. Dispatch the chamber into space. We no longer need it for any purpose. We are better off without it," Ehsis announced.

An alien male appeared in front of them, and the dead body of her child Heru was placed in a pod and released into space as they traveled.

"Ehsis, state for the record the reason for dispatching the chamber," he said in a soft voice.

Princess Hathor and Ehsis gave each other a look.

"The child's name is Heru. He is a victim of an unknown virus that owes its origins to Keb. The infection spread rapidly in his body. A point came when his breathing ceased. We do not wish to endanger our planet with the virus," she finished with a heavy heart.

"Thank you, Ehsis. The conversation is in the archives for retrieval," Moses said.

With that, the chamber broke the connection with a loud thump. They could see the chamber floating away into space. The loss of one chamber had significantly increased the speed now.

*** 

Hathor turned over, but she still could not sleep. She remembered when the spaceship landed on Lyra, the princess and her crew were put in quarantine, and the males were taken out of hibernation.

"I had no choice. The fear of the curse of Keb could have spread across the whole kingdom, and stories of the misadventures were told generation after generation," she said to herself. "Oh God, please help me! I can no longer stand the fact that I hid so much from my own people. I should gather my courage and tell the truth," Hathor murmured.

She also recalled that strange mummies had appeared in the town where Amenhotep, the survivor of Keb's mission, had stayed. The horrific disease had appeared on their planet, so the southern part was sealed as no-man's-land called Sutekh. It was now highly guarded, and it was forbidden for anyone to trespass in that area. King Ptah had known his daughter going through an emotional trauma after losing her husband and child, suffering betrayal and mission failure. He became fearful that people would not regard her with respect anymore if people knew she brought the disease to Lyra. So, King Ptah sealed off all access to the HSS facility, stopped exploratory missions, and sealed access to the galactic data, including the health records which were collected during the trips over the years. He wanted to safeguard his family's reputation as patronage of the kingdom. Perhaps that was the correct decision to avoid controversies which could harm the reputation of the future queen.

The king eventually died, and he had no other offspring to take the throne of the planet. So, Hathor was made the queen of Lyra. Hathor took Seth's son under her tutelage and gave Seth's wife a false story that Seth had died helping Usir. In textbooks of the kingdom, planet Earth was described as a cursed planet, full of diseases and fatalities.

***

It was well after midnight when Ehsis received a phone call. She checked the caller ID and sat up straight in bed.

It was Hathor's staff. Why would she call her at this hour of the night? Was someone attacking?

She picked up the call, and shrugged off her shoulder-length white hair.

"We are calling from the Royal Guard's office. Your presence is required in half an hour in Queen Hathor's chambers. Something urgent has come up, and needs to be discussed with you. The queen apologizes for requiring your presence at this time of the night. How-

194

ever, she says it cannot wait till tomorrow," the woman said. Ehsis nodded her head lazily. The screen vanished in the air as it usually did.

"Goddammit. I know it has something to do with that alien from Keb. It could have waited till morning. You are just scared," she said, annoyed. As the Secretary of State, Ehsis had to be at Hathor's beck and call for emergencies. So far, it had been calm in the galaxy clusters, and most of the bounty hunters were serving time in their prisons.

Ehsis was as old as Hathor. She cared little about her looks, and had a slightly wrinkled face with brown eyes. She trusted Hathor with her life, having known her for a long, long time.

Like Hathor, Ehsis was also the survivor of that unfortunate mission on planet Earth. She still remembered how she and Hathor had tried their best to save Usir and Heru. But in the end, they decided to abandon some of the crew members on the foreign planet, fearing an outbreak on their own planet. Soon after the disastrous mission, Ehsis had resigned from the space exploration program, Hept Sehetch Sheta (Higher Space Surveillance, or HSS). After the traumatic mission, she and Hathor became very friendly, and Hathor offered her the Secretary of State position. Ehsis had secured several strategic alliances with the larger planets and created a framework for criminal prosecution in her role. Creating the interplanetary criminal database was her initiative, making the identification and deportation of criminals much easier.

195

## Chapter 14.   The Memories

Ehsis had known Hathor before she was awarded the title of Princess of Kingdom of Akhom. Ehsis had sought refuge on Lyra when her planet's reactor malfunctioned, which resulted in an explosion that shook her galaxy. She took an escape pod from the laboratory, and the cataclysmic explosion happened as she left the planet, thinking of everything she had lost. The escape pod crashed on Lyra after its nuclear fuel ran out, thanks to the intergalactic distances she had covered. Hathor found the escape pod in ruins and took the lonely survivor to the health facility.

There, Ehsis was nursed back to health under Hathor's supervision. Soon enough, Ehsis joined the Higher Space Surveillance (HSS), launched by King Ptah, which would explore distant and livable planets in galaxy clusters.

King Ptah congratulated Ehsis for her brilliant initiative, and thus Lyra began exploring distant livable planets and collecting data. It wasn't long before Hathor found the space project appealing, and she came on board as well. Successful voyages and mapping of the galactic clusters pleased King Ptah, and he bestowed Ehsis an honorary title of the princess' protector. The title came with a big responsibility. However, Ehsis was up to the task. Her prior military training helped them evade primitives and bounty hunters who would often chase them for their spaceship.

King Ptah passed away after living a long and fulfilling life. He had ruled Lyra for a long time, establishing communion with the galaxy clusters, trade unions, and prison exchange program for safe deportation of the felons. Hathor then became Queen Hathor, but she preferred to call herself Mother. She looked after her people like her own children, facilitating them as much as she could. She remained a part of the space mission, frequenting new lands on and off Lyra. She also took the lead in some of the missions and trained the crew members. Ehsis privately agreed that Hathor was a great leader in her own right, a watchful protector of the kingdom, and a great ambassador on the galactic front.

The death of Usir had left Hathor aggrieved and in pieces. The painful memories of her dead child gave her many sleepless nights, and now, with this sudden call from the palace, she had to go.

***

As Ehsis was preparing to go to the Great Benben, she recalled Hathor on planet Keb, calling the team to gather around her. She had an announcement to make—a briefing, of sorts.

They all stood looking at her. Hathor cleared her throat.

"My fellow crew members. We have successfully arrived at Keb. Congratulations to you all. The planet's climate and atmosphere make it habitable for our population to establish our first outbound colony. Keb is a very young planet. Certainly, much younger than ours. Its star is less powerful and radiant than our

197

star, Vega. Vega is fifty-four times brighter than their central star. It means we need to create big batteries to store the power which we need. "Life on this planet has merely begun. We do not expect to see signs of sentient beings like us. So, I can safely say that we are under no hostile attack," she said, breaking into a smile. Hathor looked at the ground for a while before speaking again.

"Oh, yeah. Another thing. This young planet is going through a period of major thermal changes. My heat maps show abnormal heat levels on one side of the planet. The volcanic activity is huge on that section of this planet, so do not fly over that area. Am I clear on this?" she asked.

Heads nodded in all directions, including that of Usir. Hathor was the Team leader, after all—always a step ahead. She continued further: "Okay. Aside from that, the conditions here are very different and unlike Lyra. So, I advise you to run anything and everything by me before taking a step. I am available on the communications network. It's there for you to reach out. We are all on the network. Be responsive when someone asks for help. Communication is key. Also, tracking chips are embedded in your spacesuit. Hopefully, using these, we can reach you in time. Am I clear on this?" she said again. Everyone nodded in agreement. They were with her so far.

"We are not to harm any lifeforms. Let them be. This planet has extreme temperature waves sometimes. Use the temperature thermostat in your spacesuit to manage the heat and cold. We found this to be an ideal landing site because the climate was perfect, with a huge water reserve flowing nearby. It's the only place with fresh drinking water, as far as I am concerned. You should check it out. It is beautiful. The Milky Way is also visible from here—the nascent galaxy housing this small planetary system," she continued flatly.

She clapped her hands, signaling she was coming to the end of her speech. "If you come across fiery gusts of heat, just duck down for a moment. Our signals shows that the animals here usually take refuge in the water, but your spacesuit will protect you. Oh, yes—do not touch the plants, since we don't know their biological composition. More tests are needed for that. Class dismissed," she said. The group scattered and everyone went on their way.

Hathor was so satisfied with herself; everything was going according to plan. She went back to the spaceship to check up on something. Tomorrow was going to be a big day for everyone and the project.

Usir was an engineer on Lyra, and nobody was a stranger to his contributions to their planet. He was nicknamed Ra by his fellow engineers, and the man was loved and adored by one and all. Young mothers looked up to him, and children wished to be something like him one day. He drew the envy of other women in Lyra—something Hathor often teased him about. He was a tall and handsome man, with black eyes and curly black hair. However, Usir was not to be distracted by the finest beauties on the land. His first and last love was Hathor.

Usir had previously designed a system that could direct a short-duration, high-voltage discharge of electricity from lightning bolts to the batteries. He also knew the necessary technology to create the Aakhut (pyramids), which, with water from the river and the right chemicals extracted from the nearby valleys, could form huge batteries. The water that boiled due to passage of the high-voltage electricity could then be drained back to the river, if needed, using underground tunnels. In case of no blitzes or lightning, the energy from the sun could also be stored as a battery.

A team of engineers was ready to help Ra in the pyramid-batteries construction project. Seth, the son of Geb, was one of the engineers helping Ra with the pyramids and their construction. They were using Lyrian technology to cut different types of stones and to shape them. Some of the types of stones needed were not nearby, but only found at a distance of 26,300 Supris (866.6 km). Supris was the Lyrian unit of distance they were using.

At first, things were going smoothly on every front.

"All right, guys. I want no mistakes here. We are here on a mission. If you have a problem or something is difficult for you, let me know. I am always here. We are making the Aakhut not only for energy, but also to connect our jump-sphere to the docking station installed on top of it," Ra said kindly to his crew. "Understood, sir," his crew said, and they left for work.

Seth had previously worked on the pyramid project with Ra, so he understood the process quite well. On Ra's instructions, their first monument would be huge. It was a mythical creature with a head that looked like a Lyrian Anpu and had the body of an earthly lion. When they had finished it, they stared at the masterpiece, in awe of it.

Hathor could not be happier.

"Well done, Ra. The monument will stand as a testament to our individual entity and excellence in space. Great job," she said, and left. The construction was moving at a brisk pace, the monument giving the team more motivation to speed up the project. But then one day, Ra wasn't feeling well. He called it a day and resigned to his chambers in the spaceship. Seth, meanwhile, was doing quite well. While putting the components of the electromagnetics together, he reversed the polarity. He was not precisely sure how to go about it, and Ra was sleeping when he needed his help. "Screw it. Let's do it," he said.

He sat back and watched the device come to life. It moved in the opposite direction it was supposed to and slowly spiraled out of control. "What the—it was not supposed to do this," he said with a confused look. He then had an idea.

"Let me bring Ra here. Maybe he will know what to do with this. What he told me does not seem to be working," he said, and shrugged. He casually began to stroll out of the pyramid when a sound stopped him.

He turned back. The scene horrified him. A hot ball of fire had erupted from the cable shaft, indicating that there had been an explosion in the central chamber. Amenhotep, Seth and many others ran towards pyramids.

They immediately entered the pyramid and found that the blast had cracked the roof of the central chamber. The water in the moat surrounding the Aakhut was draining fast.

"Oh, my God. What has happened?" Amenhotep said, putting his hands on his head.

"You ruined it all!" Amenhotep shouted at Seth.

Seth's face turned scarlet red. This could not be good news. Suddenly, Ra came running behind him. He was crestfallen at the sight. Seth looked at Ra, thinking of his facial expressions. Something was going through his mind. "This cannot be happening. We are doomed. We are doomed," he said. The fear in his voice was evident.

"The roof of the pyramid's main chamber is cracked. This means the electricity grid will be down and out in a few minutes. Oh, no," he said, putting his hand over his mouth.

Just as Ra had said, the electricity in the complex started to go out one by one. Within minutes, the whole colony was engulfed in darkness. Ra was livid. He turned to look at Seth, who stared back meekly. The one source of fuel they had left was that of the ship; the Amris. But if they used that, they would not be able to return home. It was a rare liquid on Lyra, not found on this planet. This shiny, glass-like substance was the source behind their impossible interstellar speeds. Thanks to it, space travel was now ridiculously easy.

As Ra was thinking all of this, he sunk his head.

"Our mission has failed before we have even begun. What will we do without power on this planet?" he said to no one in particular. "Are we stranded here forever, Mr. Ra?" Seth whispered.

Ra ignored his question. "Great. Look what you have done here," shouted Usir angrily.

Seth looked at his feet, wishing the young planet would just swallow him at that moment. "We cannot establish a colony now. Do you understand that? Do you understand that, Seth?" he thundered.

The others took notice and started coming towards them. Hathor was the first one to reach the spot where Ra and Seth stood.

"What happened here? Usir, you are supposed to brief me about any matter rather than taking them into your own hands. I was very clear on that," Hathor said defiantly. They both looked at each other. Usir was still fuming.

"At ease. Feel free to speak," Hathor roared.

Usir was not very keen on explaining the disaster and instead stood silent.

"Now would be a very nice time to explain the matter. Everyone is here," Hathor insisted softly.

# CHAPTER 14. THE MEMORIES

"Yeah, yeah. Rub it in," Ra said. He explained to the crew members the mess they were in right now. Their chances of establishing a colony had vanished into thin air. However, the space mission could still safely return to Lyra if all else failed. Hathor listened intently.

"Calm down. Let me think. We came to this planet for fuel and energy sources data, didn't we? I suggest looking for fuel or energy sources on this young planet. Hopefully, we can get back on track. Otherwise, it's Lyra for us all. Be soft on Seth. That is an order," she said, raising her voice. She decided to leave them, glaring at Seth as she went.

"As the power is down, we need to record something important. The most important thing is to carve on a rock the positions of constellations and stars around this planet. This way we will track the movement of the planets and star Vega, and this will eventually help us in finding the way back home," Hathor said. Hathor then looked at one of her teammates and said, "Toth, you engrave on the rock near the monument the constellations passing through the intersection of equatorial plane of this planet, and the elliptic plane of the nearest star. Use the star's positioning software, and this should be ready within few hours. On the rock-engraving, keep this monument at the center," Hathor ordered further while pointing towards the monument made by Anpu. Toth nodded in affirmation and left the scene.

The rest of the day passed without an incident.

Because the communication network was disabled, and the ongoing research was put on hold, People were left with nothing much to do. They sat with each other, sharing the fun times at Lyra. Hathor joined them, laughing and teasing Usir and others. Their flaring tempers had cooled off as evening drew.

The next morning, they split into groups.

Hathor presided over the morning meeting. The crew members huddled around her. "Listen up, people. We will scour the nearby area for any possible fuel source. As things stand, we may get lucky. Ra can work his magic with the conversion. We just need a raw source. That's it," she said cheerfully.

The group scattered after her meeting. One took the monument made by Anpu, and another went along the riverbed while Hathor went into the desert. While walking along the river, Ehsis sat for a while. The majestic river flowed in front of her, its blue water mesmerizing her. At once, an idea came to her like a bolt of lightning! What if they could use the water as an energy source in a different way? Why had not they thought of this before? She stood up and ran towards the station.

Digging a tunnel under the monument of Anpu was an uphill task. Ra's equipment pointed at a possible fuel source buried underground. It was scorching hot that day. "Dig, friends, dig," shouted Ra at the others. "This is gonna be a long day," said one of the crew members. "Yeah. I know. We would not be here if Seth had asked me about the polarity. It was so simple, and yet so hard for him," Ra said with a smirk. Seth ignored the remark and continued digging. It was not all his fault, but he didn't want to disturb the renowned engineer. People were confusing his compassion with negligence. "You said it, Ra. We had our orders. Clear orders," one crew member said. "Well, I did not know it was so easy to get the polarity of the charging system wrong. I mean, that is amateur hour. Not sure Geb taught him all that well," Ra said, the acid dripping in his voice.

A wave of anger went through Seth. He threw his mechanical shovel at Ra, who just managed to duck. "I care for you. I did not come because you were sick and resting in your chamber. I was not negligent. It was the goodness of my heart," he roared, shaking with fury.

"Shut up! Look where your compassion got us," Ra said, smirking.

Seth was staring at Ra, still infuriated. How could someone be so rigid and full of himself? He could not believe that his compassion was mistaken for his negligence. The air had become uncomfortable. The people digging in the tunnel had now formed a circle around Ra and Seth. "We must not fight like children. Let's take this issue to Princess Hathor. She is a fair and impartial lady. Hopefully, our queen will judge this better," one of them said from the circle. The others nodded in agreement.

This sent Seth into a heightened rage. He tried to break free of the circle, but Ra was not much far away, either. "Oh, yeah? Who do you think she will favor? Her husband, or someone she barely knows?" he said at the top of his voice. "You don't know the lengths people go to save their loved ones," he shouted.

"Was not the princess fair to you yesterday? She saved you from Ra when he was scolding you in front of everyone," one of the others shot back. Seth considered the answer for a while. He then took out the mechanical shovel and started to dig again. This is not over, he thought. The matter should be taken up to Hathor. She would help him out.

The evening was falling fast on the new planet. After coming to this planet, Seth had realized that the Vega cycles on Lyra were so, so long. Their day-star was very young and luminous. This new planet was pretty close to its sun, which made its day relatively shorter, but hotter. Back on Lyra, their day lasted for forty hours, which meant that the nights also lasted for the same time frame. Their lifestyle revolved around these long days and nights. Something had to be done about Ra. Something serious or maybe sinister, Seth thought.

"That is a wrap, everyone. Go to bed. We have a long day ahead of us. Everyone needs their rest," Ra announced as dusk was falling over the new planet. "Thank you all for coming and sharing the workload. Only heaven knows if we will find what we are looking for," Ra said. Some people laughed at that and started to walk back to their chambers. Seth also picked up his mechanical shovel and followed them close behind.

# CHAPTER 14. THE MEMORIES

Something was cooking up in his mind. Maybe he was onto something.

*** 

It was pretty late at night when there was a knock on the door of the lab, taking Ra by surprise. Surely, Hathor had slept by now. Why else would anyone knock at his odd hour? "Who is it?" Ra shouted.

"It is me, Seth. I brought you something," he said nicely.

The electricity of the grid was down and out for the facility, and only given to the lab. People were sleeping in their chambers with the doors open. But for Ra, he just preferred the time he had to himself. It was good for his own introspection and thinking things through.

The name of Seth soiled his mood and spirits. The last thing he wanted to do was see the kid and talk to him.

"Just a moment. I am in the middle of something," he said in a soft tone.

He shut down the screen in the air, deactivating it for a while until Seth went away. The latter was not privy to sensitive information. He opened the door, and Seth was standing there, smiling.

"What do you want, kid?" he asked him sternly.

Ra was in no mood for fun and games. As things stood, they probably would not find another energy source, which would compel them to return to Lyra. This was the first setback for the HSS in all these years.

Their missions had been very systematic and planned thus far, but now Seth had left a smudge on the legacy of the space mission itself. King Ptah would be unhappy about it and demand an answer for the failure. Upon full disclosure, Hathor and Ehsis would be called into question. They had not taken 'the ring'— an emergency power source often kept in the storage unit. Hathor, Ehsis, and Ra had all forgotten about this source, realizing it halfway through the mission. But by then, it was too late. This could result in sanctions on the space mission. "We had an ugly spat this afternoon. The temperature on this planet is too much for me to take. Maybe I spoke too much. I thought I should make something for you. Here," he said, smiling.

Ra looked at him with a stupid look on his face. Then his face brightened. Seth had brought his favorite snack—the one he was often seen eating back on Lyra, with vegetables inside a crispy pastry. Who knew Seth and he had such similar tastes in food?

"Oh, you brought this with you from Lyra. You got me off guard. This is fabulous, I must say. Good thinking on your part," he said, patting his shoulder. Seth broke into a huge smile. Finally, they were back on good terms. And all it took was a snack that Ra liked. How easy was that? Ra went back to his bed and starting munching loudly, irritating Seth. Lord, he liked them a bit too much.

"They taste a bit different than what I had back on Lyra," Ra complained.

## CHAPTER 14. THE MEMORIES

"How is the taste any different from that on Lyra? Maybe the storage has changed the flavor, or the atmosphere has reacted. I don't know," he said. All at once, Ra felt as if he had missed a breath. Something strange was happening to his body. He looked at Seth, who was checking something on the screen in the air. Ra tried to speak his name, but failed miserably. Nausea and abdominal cramps followed after his loss of voice. He put his hands over his stomach, trying to shout in agony. He dropped on the ground, holding his stomach. Seth turned to look at Ra and broke into a smile. "Well, well, well, what do we have here? It looks like you ate something bad. Very bad. Was it something in the snacks?" he said, laughing. Ra was trying to stand up, but it proved very difficult with his body failing.

"I was walking into the desert—it was windy out there. You should take a walk sometime—and I came across some plants. I plucked them and gave them to passing animals. Well, it was a sight to behold. I was seeing things that horrified me. It was painful to see those animals drop dead to the ground," he said, chuckling. He stared at the floor, thinking for a while.

"Though, I will be honest. I was just keeping it to show it to my friends over in Lyra. But that will come later," he said. Ra had now managed to stand on his two feet. This worried Seth slightly.

"Look. You don't have a lot of time. Maybe if you have something on your mind, better do it fast. The poison will kill you in the next few minutes," he said, and started for the door.

"Any last wishes?" he asked, turning back once more. "No? then fine," he said. He slammed the door shut behind him. Ra was left alone, standing in the room. In his agony, he had to think of his next course of action. Like Seth had said, he had been poisoned. With that thought, he dropped to the ground. Painful convulsions started to happen to him. The poor man was wildly shaking and writhing on the floor, and it continued for another minute. He managed to stand up and look for Hathor in her chambers. Slowly and gradually, he moved towards the door and fell again. It was increasingly hard for him in his current state.

Walking towards the chambers, he suddenly had another thought. What if this was a virus of some sort? Maybe it was a deadly virus. Seth could have infected himself with it without knowing about it. Ra had to get out of the chambers—and fast. He could not risk endangering the lives of Hathor and other crew members. Ra walked, limping along the corridor, trying to exit the space crew member chambers and get out into the open. The last thing he could do was save the lives of the crew members, who would live to tell the tale of murder and blind rage. The Pyramids of Giza were a no-go area for him. He had to get as far away as possible. As he reached outside, Ra saw the magnificent monument of Anpu ahead of him. That was it. This would be the safest place for him to die. He started to inch slowly towards the monument of Anpu. The magnificent statue stood in all its glory, inviting Ra towards it.

***

Hathor was lying on her bed, wondering what was taking Ra so long in the lab today.

The troubles of the previous day had merely begun, thanks to Seth and his inexperience. But Usir was wrong to scold the young guy. It was his first mission, after all. Their new plan was to look for fuel sources and tap into earth's magnetic field somehow to carry on their mission. She decided to talk to Usir about this and get things straightened out. But when she tiptoed to his room, she found it empty. Some snacks were lying on the ground. This gave her a clue that Seth had been in his room only recently.

She looked at her wrist and tapped Ra. A screen sprang from her wrist. It was a map of sorts showing people—a snapshot of everyone on her space mission. A look of horror crossed her face. Ra was deep inside the monument of Anpu—somewhere in the mining shafts. "What is he doing in there at this time of the night?" she said, fuming.

She ran at full speed towards the monument of Anpu, following her screen's virtual directions in the air. Maybe Ra's adventurous spirit was taking over his mind. But he had gone inside the mining shafts; they had been digging there in the morning and left the site at the brink of the evening. Reaching the end of the mining shaft, she saw the water pool and Ra's body in it. His eyes had left his eye sockets, and his body looked like a trunk. But he was not dead yet. She took him out of pool; the poor man was shaking and writhing on the ground.

"Ra, what happened to you?" Hathor said, kneeling. She took Ra in her arms, but he had no sense of who was there. It seemed he had only a few moments left before the last breath would leave him. Tears welled in her eyes; this was not happening. Ra was about to die in her arms. "Seth," he said.

Hathor looked at him and understood what he meant.

Uttering these words, Ra was paralyzed. He was not moving at all. His face remained expressionless. Hathor slapped Ra's face for any sign of life, but none came. She checked his breathing—it was slow, and he struggled.

Hathor tried to lift him over her shoulders. However, he was twice her weight, and she crumbled under his weight. In a fury, she tapped her wrist to activate the communication network. It was time to call for help. "Ehsis, where the hell are you? I need you right now inside the monument of Anpu mining shafts," she screamed. It would be a tense one minute before Ehsis responded in a sleepy voice.

"Yes, Hathor. To what do I owe the pleasure?" she asked in a sleepy voice.

"Ra is almost dead in my arms. It would help if you got over here right now. I need an extra hand to pick him up and take him to the Pyramids," she screamed. Ehsis panicked. This could not be happening. Had Ra been attacked by animals, or had he accidentally fallen into the tunnel? There was no time to think.She rushed through the chambers and took one more member with her. They could help bring him back, she reasoned. They found Hathor in tears. Ra's body was not moving much. Ehsis came and put a hand on Hathor's shoulder. "Come on, my Princess. There is no time to waste. We can take him to the first-aid unit. Give me a hand," Ehsis said tersely. Ra was a bulky man. It took them twice the time to bring him back into the chambers. His breath was very slow and labored. Once they got him in his chamber, Ehsis and another crew member examined him for the strange symptoms he was showing.

"I will be right back," Hathor said, and ran off.

Hathor went into Ra's chamber once again to see if she could find anything. She found a note written in a rush. She opened it to find some terrifying details that took Hathor by surprise. But the last line caught her attention.

Seth has poisoned me, he had written.

Hathor's fears were confirmed. She returned to the room where Ra was lying. She looked at the others, and they looked away. Ehsis preferred to stare at the ground. "What is it?" Hathor thundered.

"His breathing has slowed. His pulse is also too low," she said.

"What does the report say?" she pressed further.

"It does not show anything in his system. That is what I kind of find strange. No signs of death," Ehsis replied plainly.

Hathor was lost in thought. This changed everything, and something had to be done right now.

"What is it, Hathor?" Ehsis asked worriedly.

"I have some more bad news. It was Seth who did this. But I am not worried about that right now," she said, still lost in thought. "Why?" Ehsis pressed. "Usir has warned of an impending virus that could infect every crew member. He says Seth could be responsible for that. The instructions in his note are to leave the planet as soon as possible," she said.

# Chapter 15

# The Changeling

HATHOR took out the note and showed it to everyone. Ehsis was the first one to read it, and her facial expressions changed as she read the note. The terrified look on her face said it all.

"We need to move out of this planet, and fast. As it stands, our preparations to counter an epidemic are next to none, thanks to the explosion. It's time to move," she said.

"What curse is this? I cannot leave my love on this planet, and I also will never be mother of his child!"

she cried. But after a few moments, her tears were gone. An idea had come to her mind, and Hathor's face brightened as it did.

"I need to impregnate myself. But to do that, we need to test the semen for virus. Check the sample and let me know. I will be right back," she ordered, and ran off again.

Hathor needed some air. Stepping outside, she cried her heart out. A little enmity could go so far. It was unimaginable.

"There is good news. Ra's semen is untampered. We can impregnate you with his semen before he dies. But if you become pregnant, we should expect a child in the next few weeks, as all Lyrians bear children fast,"Ehsis said.

Hathor said, "I am ready to impregnate myself with my husband's semen."

Two doctors and one nurse approached her, and they did the necessary procedure to fulfill the princess' desire. Hathor then had an insertion near her navel, and the nurse used a device to put in the sutures. The device did its job immaculately. Another alien nurse approached and sprayed a healing spray on the wound. Within minutes, the wound healed, and she removed the sutures. Doctors ran the scans and found no anomalies. The whole operation had been completed successfully within twenty minutes.

Hathor returned to her compartment. She was ready to give birth to her child very soon; maybe within a few weeks. Now, for her, the safety of the child was the foremost thing. She had to choose the baby's name with Usir, and she was engulfed in worries about him.

"Oh God, save us from this calamity!"

Suddenly, a nurse arrived and said, "Hurry Princess, Mr. Usir's heartbeat is not stable."

Hathor ran to triage room. Ehsis was already there at the door. The room was sealed, and inside, doctors in full body gear and protective suits were trying their best to make Usir's heart beat again. Ehsis turned and stopped Hathor from coming close to the window installed in the door of the triage area. Hathor could only see Usir's fingers, which looked like dried twigs.

Hathor's head was on Ehsis' shoulder, and she could see through the window that the doctors had turned as well, and they were hopeless. There was no heartbeat. Ehsis was crying. "We lost him. He is gone." Hathor was not crying. Her tears were already dried up. She released herself from Ehsis' hands and shouted with full voice, "I, Princess Hathor, vow that I will kill Seth!"

\*\*\*

Seth held a bident-looking weapon in his hand as he limped fast along the Nile, moving away from the colony as fast as he could. He was breathing heavily, and his sight was blurred. "Curse this planet. The plants have affected me!" he muttered under his breath.

# Chapter 15. The Changeling

Behind him, he heard loud shouts coming from the colony.

*Oh, I must hide before they find me. Ra must have died by now*, Seth thought. He heard the voices of Ehsis, Hathor, Anpu, and Toth, who were using tracking devices and tracking Seth's footsteps. The infrared cameras showed that Seth was already half a mile away from the colony.

Seth fell to the ground, and when he managed to stand up, he found Anpu growling at him. He was the jackal-looking monster from planet Kebirum and had a body like a Lyrian. Anpu was growling at Seth from a distance. Seth threw his bident in an attack, but the bident went into the sandy pit near the pyramids. The bird-looking Toth also arrived at the scene and said to Anpu, "He is cursed! The indicator says that his temperature is rising."

"He must had contracted the virus!"

Seth laughed and said, "You will all die on this cursed planet! You will never get back to Lyra."

"You are deceived. Murderer!" Anpu said.

The whole space crew that had previously been deep in slumber now arrived on the scene. Seth did not feel like himself. His arms and feet slowly moved as he tried to fight the two military-trained males, but he was too weak for both of them, let alone one. Hathor and Ehsis also arrived. Hathor wore her crown, and all were horrified to see her in this form. She wore her judgement attire and was raging with fury. Hathor looked at Seth angrily and said, "Only one question,

Seth. Why?"

Seth looked her in the eye and gave a wicked smile. "I put Ra in his rightful place. I don't think he should be a crew member, nor a team leader," he said in a satisfied tone.

"And who gave you the right to be judge, jury, and executioner?" Ehsis said, fuming.

"I did. I showed him the error of his ways. He might have lived to see the next day, had he been nicer to me inside the monument," he said, now growing tired. Seth fell to his knees, his two hands caressing the desert sand. A look of sadness passed over his face.

"I think something has infected me. Maybe it was the plant I brought from the desert fields," he said, feeling weak.

Ehsis eyed Hathor, who returned the look. The decision had been made. "Your son and wife will have to live without you," she said.

Seth looked up at them, and his face turned scarlet.

"Oh, no. Please have mercy. I don't want to die like this. It was temporary insanity—a rush of blood. I feel sorry for your husband. He did not have to go this way," pleaded Seth. But the end was nigh, it seemed.

Hathor spoke, breaking the uncomfortable silence in the air. "Your crime is capital murder, Seth. Call it a mercy killing or whatever you want. But I do not think people will take your gruesome murder of my husband very lightly back on Lyra. It will land your son in hot water for the rest of his life. I do not want that for him, even though you could not see that in your fit of fury,"she explained calmly.

"Long live father Geb," shouted Seth into the night.

The wind took the passion from his voice. At the same time, Hathor activated her weapon. Electric surges started appearing on the horns of her crown, and an intense laser beam burned Seth. All watched it with utter horror.

"For survival of our civilization, it was necessary," Hathor said to herself while looking at the dead Seth.

Ehsis said nothing. She was so not interested in talking about such a fiend like Seth; a monster among people. They nodded to each other and started making their way back to the colony, leaving Seth's half-burned dead body near the three pyramids.

***

Hathor wished Ra had stayed in his room if he suspected a deadly virus had infected him. The male crew members had been tested one after the other, and except for Toth and Anpu, they had all contracted the virus. It must have happened when Ra passed through the corridor. The females were somehow immune to the virus. Ehsis reasoned that the virus must attach itself to DNA that was not found among the females. This attachment made men a host for the virus, infecting them slowly. Anpu and Toth were luckily immune to this new virus, so they decided to make the best of it. They put on their protective suits and lived in a separate chamber. The two studied the virus, its strange origins, and tried to figure out how to cure it, if possible. Hathor feared a mutation of the virus. Having studied viruses and microorganisms, she predicted a new wave of virus that would infect the female space crew. Ra's semen had been transferred into Hathor using their existing technology while Ra was still alive. She had decided to name the coming child Heru. As Hathor saw things, Heru would arrive in a tense world.

After Ra died, they buried him on Earth, between the pyramids and the monument at one of the excavation tunnels. The water was poured into the tunnel after burial to prevent the spores from spreading in the air. The baby Heru was still in her belly, apparently unaffected by virus. "Ehsis, we need to leave this planet right away. I fear the virus will grow into something more. Let's protect the handful we have left," Hathor cautioned Ehsis. Ehsis agreed, and they began preparations for the launch. They would have to use their fuel reserve to return safely on Lyra. This was, of course, if something else did not come their way.

"Ehsis. We have a problem," Hathor said worriedly. Ehsis looked at her.

"We don't have enough fuel in the reserve tanks. We might run dry somewhere before the Clara galaxy. Our best bet is to contact the galaxy for fuel," she said. "And we cannot stay here, either. The virus could mutate here. Even we may not survive," Ehsis said, thinking of their options. "We also cannot take Apnu and Toth with us, as it would jeopardize everyone's life. What do you suggest?" Ehsis asked. "We can give them jump-spheres. That is the only device which may bring them back, if they survive this disease. The sphere, once charged with dark matter, will not need further charging for the next four million rotations of planet Keb, due to its unique magnetic field. Maybe it will just need a little push from Amris," Hathor said.

"But princess, this will lengthen our travel time," Ehsis said. "I estimate that we can go back, but we will need to hibernate a part of crew," Ehsis informed further.

They exchanged a look, and each knew what the other was thinking. "Okay. I will inform Anpu and Toth," Hathor said. "You do your thing," she said to Ehsis.

*** 

The spaceship roared to life. Anpu and Toth watched as it prepared for the launch. As it flew above them, the shockwaves threw the two men back towards the monument. They saw the spaceship until the last faint light showed it moving out of the Milky Way galaxy. They were thankful that the female crew had abandoned this cursed planet. However, Toth hoped that Heru would survive the journey. There was no telling if the child had contracted the virus, putting his mother at risk.

Soon enough, Toth and Anpu had also contracted the virus. Before they died, they decided to pay homage to their cursed journey. It was Toth's idea, though. He reasoned people from Lyra who came here later would recognize their work for King Ptah. The destiny sphere and the paltry fuel left by Hathor would come to their use; not that they could use it for space missions. These two things were put in an olden stone ark in the center of the Aakhut pyramid. After doing this, the two sealed the pyramid. Someday, someone might open the pyramid and unlock the secrets of Lyra. They then inscribed the story of their unfortunate space mission on Keb on a brick wall.

The male crew members who died were buried under the Great Monument of Anpu by the still-alive alien males. It took some time to transfer the men's bodies and bury them inside. The spaceship had taken the tools, which would have made things easier. Anpu and Toth were left on the planet Keb. It was expected that they would arrive back if their bodies healed; however, that had not happened. The space crew would remain unaware of their fate to this day.

***

The Amris fuel in the reserve tank had been exhausted, leaving Hathor with a new challenge. On top of that, they were in a distant galaxy that was at daggers drawn with Lyra. King Ptah had made his hatred for the planet known throughout the galaxy. Unfortunately, their communication systems were down, and they could not contact their neighboring cluster for help. Help would have come immediately if only the communication network was working. A bluish light came from the planet, putting Hathor's spaceship in full view. The spaceship had been at a standstill for a day before the planet, Honkira, noticed it. Soon after, a military convoy surrounded Hathor. It took Hathor and her spaceship into the planet, pushing it forward with a force field around it. Hathor was taken to the king's palace.

"Princess, we were not expecting your arrival here," King Phi said in bitter tone. "We had no plans to visit your planet and its environs, but destiny forced us to come to you for help," Hathor said. Ehsis was right at her side.

"I could invade Lyra and teach Ptah a lesson, but you made my life simple. Instead, I can imprison you," King Phi said while moving hand over his black beard. "I am sure that king will not do any dishonoring of the royalties of other planets. Besides, we are mostly women on board, just on a scientific mission, and have no hostile intentions," Hathor said. "I request only fuel, as our Amris is gone!" she said further. "Ah, Amris—the most efficient fuel present in the entire known galaxy," King Phi commented "Preciously guarded, but used in useless things." He laughed and looked at his courtiers, who joined him in laughing.

"King Phi, I know that many want Amris, but it was never denied to be sold to others. We, the Lyrains, just don't want other planets to attack us just to take over our fuel mines," Hathor said.

"Well, let me think about your condition and consult with my ministers," the king said.

King Phi ordered the military convoy to take her

back and leave her into space's deep voids. Hathor shook her head, thinking of a dark future ahead. Ehsis, Hathor, and her crew sat silently. They had no hope of returning to Lyra. Their only possible help had made it clear that they were on their own. It was nighttime when another space crew approached them, sending a blue light. Hathor was awake at the time, still mourning the death of Ra, so she heard when the head of the military convoy signaled for them to open the latch. He was coming inside alone. Hathor opened the latch for the military commander to enter.

"It seems your luck has run out. First that epidemic on the planet, and now you have a fuel problem," he said. Hathor nodded, looking at the flight trajectory. They still needed a lot more fuel to get home. "I have decided to destroy your ship. It will be a message to your tyrannical father," the commander said. Hathor looked up, and her head sank. This was the end for the crew. At least everyone was asleep, so it would be quick and painless. "I was kidding," the commander said. "We are refueling your ship. The look on your face was something," he said, still laughing. Hathor stared at the commander and then hugged him.

"Oh, it is no bother. I will be executed for disobeying the orders of the king. It is what it is," he said. Hathor and the military commander looked at each other.

"Thank you very much. We are indebted to King Phi. Please inform him that I will consult my father to give Amris to you for free for a full year!" she promised. The spaceship started with a jump, roaring past the hostile planet. Hathor did not wish to stay, since King Phi could send another convoy to destroy her ship. As he had predicted, military commander was executed as per the orders of King Phi.

***

After a week of intergalactic travel in Lyrian years, the space mission arrived successfully on the planet. The crew was received with great fanfare and cheers. People came and congratulated Hathor and Ehsis on returning from the mission.

King Ptah was standing at the far corner of the space station, beaming with pride. His daughter was doing so many great things; he could not be more proud of her. Someday, she would make a wonderful queen for the people of Lyra. Queen Hathor would be her name. He grinned at the thought. This gave the king an idea. He gathered the people of Lyra; it was time for an important announcement. He noticed something, but it slipped his mind among a bunch of other things.

The sky lit up, showing the face of King Ptah smiling at the people. He cleared his throat to say something important. It was his usual routine to do that so that people would have some time to quiet down. People everywhere on Lyra looked up when King Ptah addressed his fellow people. "Citizens of Kingdom of

Akhom, it is with great pleasure to announce the successful return of my daughter Hathor to Lyra. Every time they head off on a space expedition, I am the only one worried about them. I breathe a sigh of relief when they return without a hair harmed on their bodies," he said, and chuckled. The crowd started to applaud while some chanted the king's name with an unparalleled passion. King Ptah held up his hand to maintain silence.

"Many thanks, my fellow Lyrians. Your love and support keep me coming back for more speeches. Now, let us talk to everyone's favorite Hathor," he said at the top of his voice.

The crowd cheered, applauding loudly. Hathor made her way to her father, blushing.

"I am so glad you are back on Lyra. This space mission had me very scared, dear," he said to Hathor.

"Yes, dear Father. I was also scared during this journey. It was the farthest we had gone to date. Strange surprises awaited us," she said, looking down. King Ptah just remembered what he was going to ask. "Say...where are some of your crew members? I don't see Ra here. Seth is also missing. What happened to that poor child? I always thought he was a kind of a loose cannon," he said, and laughed. Hathor looked at the people. She didn't know what to say; it was hard for her to announce the bad news.

She sunk her head. An uncomfortable silence prevailed for a few minutes. "Hathor. Speak your mind. Maybe we can help in some way," King Ptah said.

# CHAPTER 15. THE CHANGELING

"Father...Ra passed away on the planet. It was an epidemic that we could not detect. The alien virus had strange origins; it spread at a very fast speed among the other space crew members. Anpu and Toth also caught it. We had to leave them back on Keb, because I could not risk more infections. The virus spread at an accelerated rate. I wish we had time to arrive on Lyra and disinfect my crew," she said.

*I cannot tell my father that his grandson died too*, she thought. Oh God, should I tell him? Hathor had no idea what to do. A deafening silence had prevailed among the audience. After all, people on the space crew had died. Seth's mom and wife were listening among the people, and they broke into tears as the news of Seth's death was uttered. Geb, the father of Seth, was standing with the crew members as the tragic news was told to the audience. King Ptah thanked his daughter for the bitter truth and took over the podium.

"In the memory of the deceased crew members, the flag will be lowered. We will mark this day as an unfortunate incident in the history of Lyra. I am announcing a public holiday in light of these events," he said authoritatively. "My wishes are with the deceased ones and their families." The screen turned off, which usually meant that the king had finished his announcements.

Hatathor, the son of Seth, was growing up into a skilled warrior during these years. However, he was as unaware of Seth's mystery as his son. Geb raised

230

him like his own son, telling him all about his deceased dad's fate on the cursed planet Keb.

Some of these things Hatathor did not agree with. Maybe the official narrative of Seth's death was too convenient.

# Chapter 16

# The Aftermath

PRINCESS Hathor sat in her chambers. She had never felt so miserable in all her life on Lyra. "Oh, Ehsis. Where are you when I need you?" she said pleadingly.

She tapped her wrist to open the virtual interface. Maybe Ehsis was there. But no answer came, much to her annoyance.

King Ptah entered Hathor's private chambers with a solemn look on his face. She knew her father better than others; the man had come to give her some much-needed moral support. He sat beside her, lost in thought. A stern silence prevailed between them.

"I am so sorry for his death, darling. I wish there were another way to undo all this. I wish that going back in time was possible, as we could have saved Ra," he said in a low tone.

Princess Hathor shook her head and patted his arm. Her father was still terrible at this, especially in circumstances like these. She let him do it his way. "Father...time will heal all wounds, I suppose," she said. "It was a dreadful mission. Things went from bad to worse. We had to leave in a hurry. Our time was short, and people were getting infected left, right, and center," she said, recalling the harrowing incident.

"I know you better than most people—Ehsis aside. Why couldn't you contact me for support? I would have sent a convoy when the virus had infiltrated. You could have just left a message for me," King Ptah pressed.

Princess Hathor looked at the floor and shook her head.

"The communication network was down. We could not communicate beyond the planet. And Seth had accidentally blown up the Pyramid of Giza. This deprived us of the energy source we needed to execute the mission. That set us back, and as things stood, only internal communication was possible. We made the most of that. Even then..." Princess Hathor went mum.

King Ptah noticed the sudden pause. He knew his

only daughter was hiding something. Maybe there was more to the story than she wanted to let on. "Even then, what? Is there more to the story you had told just now?" he asked in surprise. "Father, I don't have the stomach to talk about this right now. Can we drop it? I do have a lot of things on my mind..." Then she uttered the name "Heru," and started crying.

"What is Heru? Who is Heru, my dear daughter?" the king asked.

There were more and more questions and fewer answers.

Princess Hathor looked at the ground. She was not ready for a series of startling revelations; her heart did not wish to relive the unfortunate series of events. It was harrowing for her—a mark on the space mission and herself. "Just leave me alone, Father," she said, turning away from him.

King Ptah softly patted her head. He was about to leave the room when she spoke again.

"I am sorry, Father. I have changed my mind. Come here. I will feel much better to get this off my chest," she said, looking into the distance. King Ptah smiled at her. His daughter was a mess.

The two sat silently as Princess Hathor figured out where to start with the series of unfortunate events. "Seth, the son of Geb, killed Ra," were the first words she uttered.

King Ptah's jaw dropped. "You cannot be serious. We had a murder during the space mission? In all these years of our missions to far-off planets, it's the first time. Why did Seth kill Ra?" he asked in surprise.

Princess Hathor opened up regarding the events that had transpired on Earth. She spoke a lot about the rage that had boiled inside Seth when Ra said things he did not like; the poison he had given to Ra in the guise of friendship. The disturbing events brought tears to her eyes—it was too much for her. One man alone had spread havoc on the space mission.

"Does Geb know all this? Who will tell him about the actions of his silly son?" he asked himself.

"No, I did not have the heart to tell a father that I had killed his son. He is on very good terms with me—I was honored by his loyalty when I told him everything. He did not raise one eyebrow. There could have been a rebellion on the space mission. Only Ehsis and I were in the know," she said in a monotone. "So, where did Seth go?" he asked, even more, surprised.

"Seth was a threat to the mission, so I executed him," she said.

It was late for bedtime. King Ptah stood up and started to leave when his daughter spoke again.

"Father...one more thing. We need to have a grand funeral for Seth. The truth should never come out in public—people will lose faith in our kingdom. Our dynasty is at risk if it comes out in the open," she said.

King Ptah nodded in agreement and left the room.

The next day, King Ptah announced a grand ceremony to commemorate Seth. Attendance was mandatory at this public event. It had been centuries since

Lyra had such an occasion. This time King Ptah spoke from his private chambers; it was a common sight for the people. The extravagant interior was a sight to behold. For a moment, the audience stood in awe—it was always as beautiful as the last time.

Once again, he cleared his throat before speaking. A wave of silence fell over the audience, and the king smiled a little. "We are all gathered here today to mourn the death of commander Usir, son of Shatu, and his teammate, junior engineer Seth, son of Geb. They both died on the mission to planet Keb. As I have been briefed by the mission team, I learned that commander Usir was investigating the rocks on a mountain. Seth was trying to help Usir, who slipped from the mountain and was hanging on the cliff. Seth tried to help him, but he slipped, too, and fell into the pit. We lost both of our very bright and talented engineers. Geb and Minerva can hold their heads high, because their son laid down his life for Lyra," King Ptah explained. King Ptah paused a moment to let it sink in.

"We will remember both in our memories as long as the kingdom of Akhom remains—and long live Akhom!" he said in a measured tone. The silence was palpable. A slow wave of applause filled the arena, and the audience began to chant Usir and Seth's names unanimously. The King found the window to slip in his favorite part of the speech.

"As I see things, it would be fitting to honor the memory of the both Usir and Seth with bronze statues at the city's center," he announced. The crowd cheered wildly. The king had made the right decision, everyone thought.

Seth's name thus went down in Lyra's history as the person who gave his life for the greater good. The official narrative ran for a week, making him a national figure. Geb and his wife, Minerva, could not have been prouder of their son. They went away after the king's speech, thoroughly content with what he said. As they walked towards their home, Geb had a thought. "You know what is greater than a hero?" Geb asked his wife. "No, I don't know. A hero known for his ideals?" she said, but shrugged.

Geb smiled at her. "No. A dead hero," he said with smug satisfaction.

*** 

Ehsis was walking outside of her residence near a river on the planet Lyra, enjoying the open air. She came to a point where the river was flowing near her ankles. Lost in thought, she decided to sit down for a while. The first month after their landing had stirred another havoc, she recalled. It was the first time she had seen the manifestation of the virus up close and personal.

A man named Amenhotep became patient zero on Lyra. He was part of the unfortunate space mission that would return to the planet with half its crew. Upon the advice of Amenhotep, the space crew was keen on the idea of a separate colony. The plan was in part a wise one, since it would save the population of Lyra from infection. Ehsis was sleeping when she got a distress signal from Amenhotep. The hastily recorded message went into Lyra's cloud database.

Ehsis reached the location where she had last received Amenhotep's call. There were dried woods, twigs, and marshy land near the sea. Mangrove-like outgrowths were also there.

The sound of the body rubbing against the dusty ground was accompanied by a disturbing sound that resembled something fluid. It was a combination of squelching and leaking, the sound of something being forced out of a body. It was a sound that made the heart pound.

She saw Amenhotep's body on the ground but she could only see his hair; the cloak had covered his face, which was fluttering in the winds. "How are you, Amenhotep? Are you okay?" she said and ran towards him, but he didn't respond.

She reached his body and immediately removed the cloak from Amenhotep's face.

"Aaaaah," Ehsis shouted in distress, and she moved back in utter shock. She turned her face and saw the pile of dead Lyrians around her. Gathering courage, she then looked back at Amenhotep. In front of her was the undead skeleton of Amenhotep. His eyes were wide open, and his lips parched. His skin looked like the bark of a tree, and his fingers like twigs. The smell of death and rotten flesh was pervasive; the odor, caused by the pungent mix of blood and meat, was too much to bear. "Stay away!" a broken voice erupted from Amenhotep. He moved his finger to warn Ehsis to not to touch him. Darkness pervaded over the town.

Ehsis set foot in this now-desolate place. She stepped on something, and her jaw dropped in horror. At her feet was one of the space crew members. The dead body was dry, except for the head—it had exploded, leaving the body down from the neck. Ehsis had only recognized him from his attire. Luckily, she wore a bio-protective suit to protect her from viruses and other contaminants active in the area.

After walking through the entirety of the town, one thing was clear: there were no survivors left. They had had to seal this small town to prevent the spread of the epidemic. Ehsis returned to her spaceship; her first destination would be Hathor's private chambers. She was the princess, after all. King Ptah was away on a foreign mission, so she had to confide in her.

Princess Hathor gave one look at Ehsis, and she could tell it was bad news. She looked at her expectantly. "This better be good, Ehsis. I am in no mood to hear about death and doom. Please, just this one time," she said flatly. But Ehsis was distraught. "Princess Hathor, this cannot wait. The epidemic hit the small town where Amenhotep was quarantined; we need to contain this immediately. I just need your permission to get started. There is no time to lose. We may not have people after a month," Ehsis said cautiously. She tapped her wrist to show the pictures Ehsis had in her database. The screen opened to reveal a panorama view of the town. The remains of Amenhotep were easily recognizable, while several other bodies lay here and there.

Princess Hathor looked at the harrowing pictures. Tons and tons of dried, dead bodies were on the ground. Their heads had seemingly exploded, and some people hung from their windows while others had crashed. This was disturbing.

She turned her face; it was too much for her. Ehsis could see the faint heart of the warrior squirming like a little girl upon seeing people like this. "Take them away. I cannot bear this for the life of me," she said.

Princess Hathor buried her face in her hands. It was terrible. She could not bear the deaths of so many innocent lives on her conscience. Seth had changed the lives of everyone—people were dead on the other planet; people were dead on this planet. Families were led to waste, thanks to one rascal. An idea came to her mind, and Hathor turned around to call Ehsis.

"Ehsis, come here. We need to do something," she shouted.

Ehsis had reached the door when she heard her.

"Listen to me very carefully, Ehsis. The news of these deaths should not reach anyone other than us. I don't think Ptah will take a liking to his news. The colony will be off the maps—I will make some excuse when Father asks," Princess Hathor said menacingly.

Ehsis nodded. She had known all of this well before. Though the map idea was something pretty unique, she had to admit. This meant that she would need to remove the mission to Keb from public records and the cloud database. Any person asked about Amenhotep and others would meet a dead end. Amenhotep had helped the narrative somewhat, as when he arrived back on Lyra, he had made it clear that he would leave the space missions to live a quieter life. On the orders of Ehsis, the town of Amenhotep was declared as Sutekh, an Exclusion Zone. Public access was denied to anybody and everybody, and the forces of Lyra would guard it under the guise of protecting the wildlife in the region.

# Chapter 17

# The Space

AL-KHIDR was sad and gloomy as he anticipated being brought back to the same uncouth prison cell. Queen Hathor had been annoyed at his presence, and they were sent away from her royal chambers without a word or promise of anything. This artifact had really stood as a test for him. He gazed out to see the city for a bit; it was the same congested prison cell again. Queen Hathor was unkind, sending him back to the correctional facility. His patience was being tested. In light of the hate and disgust he carried for his prison cell, he wished that he had never touched the sphere at all.

"Ahhhhhh. The sight of that small and hideous prison horrifies me. Can I stay on the road? It's still better than in that cell," he said in disgust.

Nefertiti looked at him in shock and mild amusement. She wished she could take him to her home, but alas, it had just one room. "Can we reverse time so I can go back to Al-Eard? Anything but that prison will do," he exclaimed annoyingly.

The worried look on Al-Khidr's face brought compassion to Nefertiti's heart. He was far away from his home, stranded from his family and friends. The jail sentence wasn't doing him any favors.

She patted his arm. "Cheer up, I am sure Queen Hathor is doing the right thing in her mind. We do have a planet to save, after all. One more thing—when she is confused, her usual route is to take opinions of high council members. I know her. She will do that today," Nefertiti told him. This did not bring any comfort to Al-Khidr. He was still going to prison.

"The queen cannot hide you from the people forever. There is a clear and looming danger in doing that. I think she will send you back to Al-Eard. She does not want people to know what you are," she explained further.

Al-Khidr listened to her, hoping that something about not going to the prison would come up.

"It's a temporary repose," she explained, still patting his arm.

244

Al-Khidr did not answer. He was still thinking about his options. The thought of prison gave him a headache.

"I need some fresh air. Do the windows open in this—this thing?" he asked timidly.

This made Nefertiti laugh. "Of course they do," she said. She pressed a button, and the windows of their vehicle opened. The fresh air was oozing in, easing Al-Khidr. The fresh air really cheered him up, and the thoughts of the gloomy cell were forgotten for a while.

In the meantime, Nefertiti placed a call to her subordinate to make arrangements for safeguarding Al-Khidr. She did not want the press and journalists marauding the premise. The confirmation that the journalists and press wouldn't be there relieved her tense nerves; they were told to seek the queen's permission. This was a lie, as the queen would never sign the release form allowing them to interview Al-Khidr. They put two and two together, and, disappointed, the journalists had left the premise.

The two relaxed for a while. Things were slightly better now, and this gave Nefertiti an idea. "Let's do something interesting," she exclaimed excitedly. The vehicle changed direction, going right rather than straight.

"Where are we going? Not back to the queen—I don't want to see her again," he said in irritation.

"You said you wanted some fresh air. Well, that is what I am doing. We are going to the river. It will refresh your nerves," she explained.

# Chapter 17. The Space

Lyra had a river called Iteru. They moved past the high-rise buildings and floating towers for a while until they reached the city limits. The natural landscape started from here, and the traffic thinned out as well. The river was visible from a distance, and Al-Khidr could see the line of the river flowing downhill. He recognized it from his last encounter; it was the same place where the energy sphere was hovering and moving as he entered Lyra.

Nefertiti stationed the vehicle a short distance from the river, and they walked towards it, enjoying the scenery all around. The river's water was clear, and Al-Khidr could see fishes inside. Quickly, Al-Khidr took off his clothes and jumped inside.

"No, wait!" Nefertiti shouted. But Al-Khidr did not hear her. He went into the water with a splash, throwing water on Nefertiti.

"My clothes," she screamed, taking a step back. She could see him swimming with the fishes. "Oh, no. What are you doing?" she stated in horror. "I will be charged with failure to keep the prisoner safe," Nefertiti muttered under her breath. Nefertiti's heart raced; she could nothing to stop him. "Hey. Come out of there. I will be suspended from the police force. Dammit," she screamed.

Al-Khidr looked at Nefertiti and saw that she looked annoyed, so he came out.

"It's beautiful. There is sand and fishes inside," he said.

This made Nefertiti laugh; it was a strange subject

to talk about.

She shook her head at the sight. Al-Khidr's hair was wet, and his body was shining with water. Nefertiti noted that he had sculpted body. With wet hair that reached his shoulders, he looked much alluring than the Lyrians. She then blushed and started looking at the river. Meanwhile, Al-Khidr drank some water from the river. The fresh water lifted his spirits. He then put his clothes back on.

"It is so sweet, even better than River Nile," he said. He turned to look at Nefertiti, who was smiling.

"The water has a scent to it, and it is pretty addictive. Like, I simply cannot get enough of it. It reminds me of the hawkers selling Itar in my planet," he explained to her.

"What is an Itar?" Nefertiti asked him.

"Itar is a perfume, extracted from flowers which grow in my planet," Al-Khidr said. Nefertiti looked at him blankly.

"Well, you can get scents from the bazaar. It gives a good scent when you pass by someone. It's a sign of good hygiene," he added hopefully. "Okay. I get what you mean," she remarked, looking at the sky above.

He joined her in looking at the sky; the view from Lyra was way more beautiful and dramatic than he had seen on Al-Eard. "How come the sky above Lyra is so mesmerizing?" he asked. "Look at it—you can see a multitude of stars, moon, and more planets. When I studied in Baghdad, I learned that we have six more heavenly objects, apart from Earth. The star Vega was used as our northern pole star, through which we got directions in sea," he said while looking at sky.

"Your planetary system is different from ours. You live in a planet which is located in the end of stars of Anart, which will be visible soon in the sky." she explained to him.

Al-Khidr was amazed by her knowledge. "Oh, interesting!" He responded, chuckling a little.

"You do have planets as well. You may not know this, but none of the other planets in your system is habitable," she stated, relaxing a bit. A puff of cold air hit her face.

Al-Khidr was about to ask something when she cut him off, pointing at a distant star in the sky. "Can you see those clusters of stars over there? It's the closest to Lyra, and also has the brightest star after Vega in this system," she exclaimed excitedly.

Al-Khidr looked at the stars. There were many stars clustered together, like a Milky Way.

Al-Khidr said, "Is it Al-Majarrah (the Milky Way)?"

Then he stood up as an excited child and said: "Yes, it is Al-Majarrah!"

"We call them stars of Anart. It give looks like the milk of stars dripping in the river Iteru," Nefertiti said.

They sat silently by the river, enjoying the fresh breeze and starry night. Nefertiti broke the silence again.

"At night, the river Iteru seems to connect with the stars. It goes on and on; it's a really beautiful sight. Come to think of it, I have spent many lonely evenings here all by myself. I will never get tired of it," she stated with smug satisfaction. "Tell me what you know about it?" "I have seen this a lot myself, back on my planet," he shared. "Families gather at night to stare at the sky above River Nile. There is a point where we stand and stare for hours. You tend to get lost in that sight," he exclaimed longingly.

"That sounds nice, I must add," she remarked, sounding impressed.

After a moment, Al-Khidr had another question.

"The sight of stars makes me wonder. How do we see the stars? Do they connect us in some way? How did people come around here?" he asked, wondering loudly. His questions were met with silence. He looked at Nefertiti and saw that she was doing something, but he was unsure what it was. She appeared to be drawing something on the dry white sand using a piece of wood. He took some powdery-white sand in his hand, and found that it slipped out of his hand pretty quickly. It was just like the sand in Egypt back on Earth. Come to think of it, the combination of turquoise blue water and white sand looked so beautiful. Al-Khidr suddenly noticed a rock behind him, which gave him an idea. He stood up and turned around.

"Where are you going?" She asked.

"Just to watch the scenery. Relax; I am not going anywhere dangerous," he assured her.

"Don't go far. I have not seen most of the area

myself," she exclaimed worriedly.

Climbing the rock for a few minutes, he looked at the view ahead of him. It was truly awe-inspiring.

"Nefertiti, you should come and take a look. It is heavenly from here," he said, lost in the sight's beauty.

"Been there, done that, partner. Enjoy the view. When you are done, come down here. I have to show you something," she replied.

He stepped off the rock and came near Nefertiti. She was sitting beside a huge drawing of sorts.

"Oh, wow, what am I looking at?" he asked.

"The answer to your question. Behold the power of the wooden needle. It is a snapshot of the world around us," she replied, opening her arms. "These are all the planets, stars, debris. Each one is folded in seven layers over one another. It is how the world outside your planet Keb works. This is only a gist of it. I cannot explain everything here," she added with a bright smile.

Al-Khidr looked at the sketch. It seemed like a bunch of marbles were lying on a wavy line drawn on sand. But there was more to it. It looked like a planetary system. "This is amazing, Nefertiti," he stated in awe of the sketch.


"This is a map of the stars and planets. We call your planet Keb, located here. This planet is pretty below us in space. But what you call Al-Majarrah is somehow connecting us. We went through the Milky

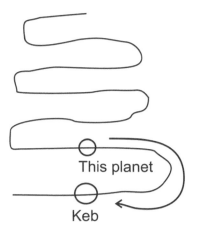

*Space is like a fabric folded in layers*

Way when the space mission landed us on your planet. This is because your planet is inside a cluster within the Milky Way. I learned planetary science back in school; that is how we see the space outside Lyra. I do not know how you came here so fast with the sphere. I did not study that in school. But maybe Mother knows—she is a space scientist, and she knows many things and many secrets not taught to us at all," she explained in detail. Then a look of sorrow emerged on her face. She looked at the ground for a while.

"Most of her space crew has died now. Some by Mutmut, some due to age and some by accidents. Only she and a senior member of the space mission still survive. That member's name is Ehsis—the Great Ehsis," she said, looking up.

"What does Ehsis do in Lyra?" Al-Khidr asked.

Nefertiti looked at him and answered, "She is the

most important person after the queen. She is the secretary of this kingdom—handles the administrative issues. I am sure Mother will consult her before deciding your fate. She is one person aside from Mother who knows as much as her," she answered. Al-Khidr had an idea upon hearing this. Ehsis was the woman with the right connections and resources. She could help Al-Khidr with his project. "I need to meet this woman. Can you take me to her? I may have something to tell her," he said.

"What do you mean?" she laughingly said. "If she wants to meet someone, it's her prerogative. It's the same as the queen you met today. Though, I can say that she will know about you by now," she replied, and shrugged.

Al-Khidr got annoyed for a moment. "Is there anything you can do? It seems like you are a servant of the state. Is that so?" he said in mild annoyance. Nefertiti was just a police officer, after all. But she looked hurt by the remark, Al-Khidr noticed as she looked at the white sand, upset by it. "That is what I am—nothing less, and nothing more. I serve the kingdom of Lyra to the best of my ability. The queen and Ehsis are beyond my reach. They can contact me only on a need-to-know basis," she exclaimed dismissively.

Al-Khidr did not want to upset her. After all, she was already violating her duty by taking him out for some fresh air. Al-Khidr changed the topic and posed a question to divert Nefertiti's attention. He felt an attachment to her. "How are you parents and siblings?"

Al-Khidr asked.

She kept quiet and looked at stars and said: "My parents also died from the disease Mutmut." "By God, I am sorry to hear this," Al-Khidr said.

"Life is weakest thing to sustain this universe. There is no such thing as a superhero, super-human, or super-alien. All are bound to die. This we learned, but in a hard way. With our technology, we thought that we would conquer all ventures. The sky was not a limit, but a doorway to different stars and planets. We knew this very well, but sustainability is the thing we missed. It easy to leave your planet, but surviving on any other planet won't be easy," Nefertiti said. "Who took care of you?" Al-Khidr asked. "Do you have relatives?" he inquired further.

"I grow up in Misraim after my parent died, and the government took the orphans into its protection," Nefertiti informed him. "My parents are from Domvar. Now it is a city in ruins," she said. "We have many such places in Lyra." "Do you think Earth is a curse?" Al-Khidr asked.

"I have no hard feelings for the people of Earth, and nor do I consider the planet a curse. It is just a notion that unfortunately spread in our society, and even educated people started using these things in their conversations," Nefertiti said.

"Tell me about the economy of Lyra. What does it run on? Back at Al-Eard, we mainly do farming and raise animals. Later on, we sell those in the bazaar to customers," he said shyly.

Nefertiti stifled a laugh over that. She did not want to criticize this way of life or make fun of it. Al-Khidr went on. "What does Lyra produce, and who purchases them?" he asked.

"Now that you mention it...this area is a fuel mine, actually—we call this fuel 'Amris.' It is a glass-like substance that we mine from the planet. I recall you tried to steal this glass. Am I right?" she exclaimed laughingly. Her laughter grew louder and louder, diffusing some tension in the air. Al-Khidr felt slightly embarrassed by the remark. It was true; he had been apprehended on charges of stealing fuel for his return back to Al-Eard. He had felt enchanted by the fuel—the substance was something that he didn't see on his planet.

"Yes. I remember. It happened a few days ago. The plan was to put some of it into the sphere and head back to Al-Eard. It was a small price to pay for a peaceful life back on my planet. And it's not like Lyra was running out of fuel," he said, clearing the air. She was still laughing.

"It's fine. I was messing with you. Amris is a rare commodity in the Universe. This is why it is always in high demand—the rest of the planets buy it from us. That alone makes us the wealthiest planet in the system. We are the sole sellers of the fuel. Lyra holds the key to everyone's survival," she stated proudly. However, her excitement slightly dwindled.

"But then again, there is so much we can mine.

At some point in the future, we will run out of this fuel. When that unfortunate day comes, we will be just another planet in the system. We will lose our bargaining chip," she said, looking a bit discouraged.

Al-Khidr nodded in agreement. "This fuel is very different in shape and form compared to what I use back on Al-Eard. We burn wood, coal, and animal fat to provide heat and cook food. These are important for us. Survival is not possible without them," he said. "I was surprised that the Amris immediately fired up the ancient artifact. It was strange and unlike anything on my planet," he said, remembering his surprise.

"It is what it is," she said.

"What else do people on Al-Eard do for a living?" she asked earnestly.

He thought for a moment. There was not much to tell; nothing interesting, that is. "We do sell birds and medicines. Some men raise the birds, and others extract medicines from plants," he said.

The word 'medicine' made him think of something else.

"Tell me something—do you have hospitals on Lyra?" he asked.

"Hospitals? What is a hospital?" she asked, surprised.

"Well, they are treatment centers to cure the young and old. People get medicines from there and use them to get well," he explained. Suddenly, Nefertiti's beeper sounded and she said: "Okay, prisoner, get up—time to go. We must get moving, and I need to get home. There is a lot of work pending for the weekend, and I would like to have some time for myself." She stood up, staring at the turquoise blue river ahead.

"It's a sight for sore eyes. that is for sure," Al-Khidr said, still lost in the beauty of the scenic landscape.

Nefertiti turned around to walk back to her vehicle, but as she did, she slipped on a stone and fell hard on the ground. "Ouch—my ankle; my ankle," she cried in pain.

Al-Khidr saw Nefertiti fall and came running towards her. He examined her ankle for a while. The moment he laid his hands on it, a burst of pain went through Nefertiti's insides. She let out a huge scream again.

"Don't touch it. Just don't. I am in pain here," she said, moving here and there.

Al-Khidr stood up straight. He could remember something about ankle sprains, and he had learned to fix them over the years. He brainstormed and searched his memory for the right information. Slowly, he could recall a procedure.

"Okay, Nefertiti. I want you to relax and distract your mind towards something else. Can you do that for me?" he asked her in a serious tone. "Don't come near me. It will heal itself," she protested in return.

"It can. But I have a better solution here. All you have to do is stay quiet and let me do my thing," he remarked and went for her feet. He took her ankle and looked for the right spot; it had to be done correctly the first time around. He twisted her ankle a bit, and Nefertiti let out a bloodcurdling scream, which was drowned by a sudden gush of wind. No one heard it except Al-Khidr.

"Allah, Allah. My ears are bleeding. Where did that voice come from?" Al-Khidr exclaimed while laughing loudly. The pain went away as quickly as it came. Nefertiti stopped screaming and felt her ankle for a while. It did not ache anymore. She stood up and walked around; a smile crossed her face. "You really are something," she said, now smiling broadly.

Al-Khidr bent low to say thanks. "It is all I do. No need to mention it," he explained, returning the smile.

Nefertiti gazed inconspicuously at Al-Khidr; he seemed like an alright guy. He may be from another planet, but he had a heart of gold. He kind of reminded her of Queen Hathor. She was still looking at him in admiration when Al-Khidr suddenly looked at her. "Hey, is everything all right? I thought you were getting late for something," he remarked.

Nefertiti recovered from her trance and nodded in agreement. "Well, I thought you should enjoy a few more moments of this scenic view," she lied sheepishly. She stole another glance at Al-Khidr and then smiled.

Al-Khidr had noticed the look on Nefertiti's face. This was something odd, coming from her. He had a feeling that something was up. Suddenly, some birds caught Al-Khidr's attention. These birds were very

# CHAPTER 17.  THE SPACE

different from the ones on Al-Eard; they had the stripes of a leopard, singing in their language. It was a truly mesmerizing sight for Al-Khidr, who was lost in the beauty of the moment. The birds left the river, heading over to the mountains, still singing the song. He turned to look at Nefertiti, who was smiling. She nodded at the sight.

"Come on now. We are getting late," she stated, and began to walk back.

# Chapter 18

# The Truth

MUDDLED in thoughts of their past, Ehsis entered the Benben Pyramid and met Queen Hathor. As usual, Ehsis had reached the Great Throne Room through the same old underground corridor. Ehsis continued to walk, thinking about the recent events which transpired on Lyra. Queen Hathor, being Queen Hathor, would certainly need her advice.

The Benben Pyramid was a windowless construction, as security was of utmost importance. King Ptah had decided to keep it that way during the time of its construction, which had happened during the madness of another time. Lyra was the center of attacks from space pirates and bounty hunters. The discovery of rare fuel on the planet had brought thieves, soldiers, and terrorists from all over the galaxy, looking to get a piece of the pie. Kingdom of Akhom was forced to go head to head with these outsiders. Sometimes ransom threats were made in exchange for the fuel. These situations were difficult to tackle, mostly because they were in a weak bargaining position when a civilian was taken hostage. The night is darkest before dawn.

Ehsis snapped back to reality; the corridor was taking too long to end. She cursed under her breath—damn this stupid corridor. She met some guards along the way, who stared forward.

At long last, she reached the access corridor which led her inside the Great Hall. It had been built by Queen Hathor's father, who was into majestic and exquisite interior decorations. Irrespective of Ehsis hanging around this place for a long time, the black granite walls and floor never ceased to amaze her. The glint of the granite tiles hit her eyes as usual; She could see the chambers at the far end of the Great Hall, and there was Queen Hathor on her golden seat, with her feline creatures before the throne. The feline creatures gave Ehsis a scowling look and frowned. Queen Hathor smiled at the sight.

"Do not worry, Ehsis. My cats have never warmed up to you for some reason. I don't know why," she said warmly.

Ehsis nodded. She then knelt to the queen and did

the routine ritual. "Lofty is your presence, queen!" said Ehsis with her head down.

The Royal Guards were inside the room as well, and were armed. Some stood at the entrance gate, while others stood behind Queen Hathor.

Queen Hathor dismissed the whole thing.

"Oh, come, Ehsis. You know I love you so much. How many times I have told you not to do it?" she remarked, half amused. "Your Majesty, I still serve you, and just like the people of Lyra, I am your loyal subject. Paying respects is part of the law as written by your late father," Ehsis explained.

Queen Hathor thought for a moment. "Come to think of it, I need to remove that blasted law. Maybe ease people of their miseries. I am tired of this line as much as the people of Lyra doing it each day," she reasoned.

Ehsis did not answer her judgment. This was also a part of Lyra's law.

Queen Hathor clapped for everyone to listen to her.

"I want to discuss something with Ehsis, my old friend. Leave us be," she stated with a tone of finality. The second she spoke, everything started moving. The feline creatures stepped down from the throne; the still guards also started moving, and all began piling out of the room. They bowed to Queen Hathor one last time before leaving the room.

There was now silence in the room. Ehsis and Queen Hathor looked at each other.

It was the queen who spoke first. She had not met

Ehsis in a while; it seemed like she had gained some weight. "At ease, Ehsis. Come here to the throne. We need to talk about some important issues here. Let's not stand on ceremony today. You are the only friend that I have had all these years," she said plainly.

A moment of silence passed.

"I trust your judgment on matters like these. That is the reason you are here today," she beamed at her.

Ehsis passed a weak smile. She then stood up to look at her queen. Hathor was making her way towards Ehsis. Apparently, she wanted to talk in a more friendly climate. She came near Ehsis and held her hands, examining them. This was weird, as Queen Hathor had not done anything like this previously. She still held her hands, thinking about something.

"I know you recall the unfortunate incident 23,000 cycles ago on that cursed planet Keb near Shemesh," she remarked, imploring with her eyes for an answer. Ehsis could sense that she was taking a detour. The harrowing memories of that mission still tormented her to this day. The incident had happened around 23,000 cycles ago on that ill-fated planet. The space mission had come with so many hopes and dreams. Unfortunately, it then became a race against time to escape. Ehsis nodded her head.

"Of course, dear Mother. I still remember that mission and its darkest moments. We made it out alive, and I am so glad for that. That DNA saved us. But the lives lost took a huge toll on my conscience," she stated, recalling the incident. Then, after a bit,

Ehsis spoke again.

"We can never forget that Heru and Usir died during those missions. It was the only space mission that left us distraught for millennia," she said. The mere mention of Heru and Usir sent the queen on an emotional rollercoaster. Tears fell from Hathor's eyes, and Ehsis saw the emotional side of her queen once again. She had not changed after such a long time—no one could corrupt her ever-adorable and soft heart. Ehsis felt a bit pleased with that thought; this implied that the planet was still in great hands.

Ehsis had to change the subject. She had come into the throne room for a reason. However, the queen was still hung up on her past—their past. "My queen, you called me here for a reason. I want to know what is troubling you at this time of the night. We can resolve this thing." Ehsis motioned, hoping that Hathor would remember the purpose of this meeting.

"Ehsis, good thing you reminded me. I forgot about the alien," Hathor exclaimed, drying her tears. She cleared her throat. "There is an alien from Keb among us. He landed only a few days ago, in the HSS docking facility. He seems harmless and friendly, by the looks of it," Queen Hathor said. By her voice, she did not seem worried. However, Ehsis had known this was coming, and her protective instincts came back in full flow. She decided to formulate a plan for the earthing. It was for the greater good.

"Your majesty, we should take action immediately. We cannot have another Keb-like incident. Our whole population could go extinct," Ehsis said a bit loudly. Queen Hathor raised a hand to interrupt her speech. She was not finished.

"Hear me out first. The alien from Keb came here using a jump-sphere. Remember the jump-sphere? We left two of them on Keb. Well, he has brought one of the jump-spheres back. I am not sure what to do about his arrival on our planet. You are one of the oldest surviving members of the space mission. I am open to your suggestion on this matter," she explained in a plain voice.

Ehsis was equal to the task. "My queen, there is nothing to think about. We have a very clear plan ahead of us. The protection of the Kingdom of Akhom should be our utmost responsibility. Nothing more, nothing less. The alien is a threat to our well-being. Does he carry the disease? If he does, the threat may have begun already," she said.

Ehsis could see a brief smile on Hathor's face. "Initially, this is what I thought as well. However, the doctors have scanned the human with our systems. His tests came back clear—crystal clear. There are no traces of the diseases in him, not even on the cellular level," Queen Hathor replied. Ehsis seemed satisfied with her answer, and was pleased overall. In her mind, there was no danger from the little alien. But Ehsis had a political concern. Perhaps Queen Hathor had not thought about it just yet.

"My queen, grant me permission to speak freely," she asked.

The queen nodded her head. Even though they had known one another for a long time, Ehsis did not break protocol. Hathor appreciated this quality in her. "It is the first time in the history of the Kingdom of Akhom that an alien from Keb has arrived. The situation is a bit more complex. As far as I know, the prisoners in his former jail cell know that he is from Keb. The news has also spread, and media stations have been standing outside the prison. Police Officer Nefertiti did well," Ehsis said, explaining the details of the past few days.

Queen Hathor listened to this, but she was still unfazed. Ehsis stood waiting for an answer. She could feel that Hathor would plead her case the way she knew best. "Well, I have been told a lot about the alien. His genetic makeup is quite different from ours. Even though he has the same physicality, skin, and exterior, he is different at the DNA level," Mother said.

Then she spoke again. "Oh, and another thing— his life energy is very low. It is nothing like what we have. I bet if he had the virus, he would have met his end a long time ago. This shows that he does not have the virus in him," Queen Hathor said softly.

"My queen, we can protect the people of Akhom and avoid propaganda. Command me, and I will personally escort this little Kebian to the Sutekh Exclusion Zone. I am worried about your future as a queen. Please, let me do this," Ehsis stated quietly.

Queen Hathor then said something in a soft tone that Ehsis could not hear.

# CHAPTER 18. THE TRUTH

"My queen, can you speak a bit louder? I cannot hear you," she explained as politely as she could. "Tell me about your plan. What is it about? I will think about it if it sounds good," she said, a bit louder this time.

"My queen, I want to take this human, Al-Khidr, to the Sutekh Exclusion Zone and imprison him for good. We will give him food—I will make arrangements for that. The usual routine will follow. No person will be allowed inside or outside. Al-Khidr will be a prisoner. He will not see the rest of the Misraim city. We will keep him alive for as long as we want. One alien intruder cannot disturb the peace of the Kingdom." Ehsis had made a convincing argument; she saw the queen nodding her head in agreement. After contemplating for a moment, she turned around and looked at the high walls of the throne room. They looked magnificent.

"I am not a monster, Ehsis," Queen Hathor finally announced in disgust.

Ehsis could tell that the queen had changed her mind. She initially liked the idea, but unfortunately, it went against her ethics. "He did not do wrong to any of the people on Lyra. He seems to have a good understanding of our people. Something tells me that he can be a good citizen during his stay on Lyra," she explained in a low tone. Ehsis nodded; the queen had a point here.

The queen thought for a moment, then said, "I respect all life forms. The last being that I did kill was a very long time ago. I cannot take another life. It is just not in me. Every life form should live. Therefore, let Al-Khidr live with the people of Lyra. Something tells me he will be good with us," she remarked with a tone of finality. "I will call the alien again. You and I will talk to him and see what he can do for us," Hathor said further.

Ehsis nodded. "Yes, Queen. I agree with this idea more than my own," she stated, and she left the throne room.

Queen Hathor lay in her bed that night, thinking about Al-Khidr and Nefertiti. The two seemed very comfortable around one another, even though the human was still not happy with his imprisonment sentence. She felt bad for doing that, but the people of Lyra still did not know about Al-Khidr. An idea came to her mind. She had to know more about the human who used the jump-sphere to arrive here. There was something about him. She was now more determined to see Al-Khidr again after managing some of her political duties.

\*\*\*

Nefertiti begrudgingly dropped off Al-Khidr at the prison. She then radioed her subordinates to pick up Al-Khidr without anyone's notice. She apologetically looked at him. "You know, when all this is over, I will offer you a place to live in my home. It is the least that we can do to make amends for your treatment on this planet," she stated, talking in a low tone. Her tenderness and humanity touched Al-Khidr.  Maybe she was not like the rest of them—she stood out from the crowd.  One heavily-built prison guard came out, bowed to Nefertiti, and took Al-Khidr inside.  "Have fun.  Don't lose hope yet.  The queen may call you again," Nefertiti said from behind.  Al-Khidr looked back and nodded.  Or maybe not, she said to herself. On her way back home, Nefertiti thought about Al-Khidr.  He seemed like a decent enough lad—he carried no weapons and had no murders or extortion to his name.  His intentions were peaceful thus far.  But he was caught between Lyra's strained history with his planet.

***

The morning after Nefertiti and Al-Khidr met the queen, Nefertiti was cleaning her desk when she received a message.  She clicked to see the identity of the sender, and saw it was from the Royal Guards' office.  She sat up straight as the holographic image opened in front of her.  Queen Hathor suddenly stood before her, smiling.  Nefertiti bowed her head to the queen.  It was very unusual for her to come here, of all places.  "At ease, Nefertiti.  No need to bow in front of me.  I want to say something.  That human from Keb is a bit interesting to me.  Why don't you bring him to me this evening?  I will also call Ehsis, and together we can think of something to do with him," she remarked, beaming at her.  Nefertiti's wishes had come true.  For a moment, the excitement on her face was clearly visible. Then she quickly hid it, fearing the queen would change her mind. However, Queen Hathor had noticed this. The excitement on her face was palpable—it all happened under a few seconds. "I see you are happy with my decision to call him again; no need to be afraid of hiding your emotions. I will not change my decision on this matter. But I do believe justice should prevail," she stated, expecting an answer from her. "Thank you, Mother. I was afraid of what might happen. Al-Khidr is not happy inside the prison. He wants to see you again, but I told him that it's not possible unless the queen demands it herself," she explained. "Well, I am demanding it myself. Let us see what the kid has got for us," she said to Nefertiti. "Very well, Your Majesty. I will escort him to your royal chambers. He said something about a cure—I'm not sure what it is about, though. I think you should hear it from him," Nefertiti said. The queen seemed to consider this for a moment. She made up her mind and looked up. "Okay. Then it is done. I will arrange a meeting with Ehsis and the two of you. Let us hear his proposition. I'll see you in my chambers later in the evening," she said. With that, the queen's holographic image disappeared.

\*\*\*

Al-Khidr was fast asleep in his cell when the screen on the wall flickered.

"Hey. Al-Khidr. Wake up. Wake up," Nefertiti shouted excitedly.

# CHAPTER 18.  THE TRUTH

Al-Khidr looked at the screen with his sleepy eyes. He was surprised to see a screen on the wall, and even more to see that Nefertiti was screaming on the screen. "I have a message from Queen Hathor," she explained cryptically.

Al-Khidr had a mini heart attack. He turned around to see the screen. "Why didn't you tell me this before?" he remarked angrily.

She was unfazed by his outburst. "I have been yelling your name for the past fifteen minutes. Now, shut your mouth and listen to me. Queen Hathor wants to see you for something. I am not sure what, but it is time to tell her about that cure. Ehsis will also be there at the table," she exclaimed excitedly.

Al-Khidr could not contain his excitement. Maybe things were looking up for him; perhaps he could return to his planet and tell his friends all about this strange planet.

"You just say the word. I will be ready when you are. When is the meeting?" he asked, still feeling surprised.

"It is this evening. You had better be ready when I come. The queen does not like latecomers. Are you a latecomer?" she asked laughingly.

"This evening? Is she in a hurry or something?" he questioned her incredulously. "Not really. I told you she talked with Ehsis, the Secretary of State. They may have decided something about your future. That is what I think. Maybe they could be willing to listen to your idea," she said.

"That's good. I am ready for the evening, then," he said.

"Good. I will pick you up from the police cell," she exclaimed tauntingly, and turned off the screen.

"Yeah, yeah, rub it in," he remarked, and went back to sleep.

# Chapter 19

# The Promise

Evening happened very fast. Al-Khidr had prepared a speech for the queen, a sort of proposition for both her and Ehsis. Mistakes were out of the question today. One misstep could result in Al-Khidr spending the rest of his life in the prison cell, or some colony Nefertiti had told him about previously.

He memorized the speech in his head over and over again. Going over the trivial details was pretty important to him, as far as he was concerned. Ehsis and Queen Hathor had the decision-making power. Depending on how he played his cards tonight, Queen

Hathor could imprison or send him back to Al-Eard. When evening came, Nefertiti was smiling from ear to ear. Something exciting was on her mind, and Al-Khidr decided to ask precisely what it was. "Hey. What happened? You seem a bit too excited about the meeting today. Anything I should know?" he asked in a worried tone.

"No. no. It is nothing. I am just glad that Mother did not cancel the meeting scheduled for today. As far as I am concerned, you have more to lose if she cancels this affair. At that point, I can do nothing except follow state-sanctioned orders." She chuckled, making the matter somewhat lighthearted.

Al-Khidr considered this for a moment; she had a point. Queen Hathor was the undisputed ruler of this planet. Anything that irked her would change her mind. *That is true. It is the only chance I have to leave Lyra peacefully, after all,* he said to himself.

"Yeah, yeah. Come on now. We cannot keep the queen waiting here. If something important comes up, like the intergalactic meeting or border patrol monitoring, she could be gone for days and days," she stated timidly.

She opened the prison cell and let him out. After drinking water from the automated vending machine, he followed her outside the station.

The air was quite cool that day, and Al-Khidr stretched himself for a bit to take in the cool air. Nefertiti pushed him into her vehicle. "Come on now. We don't have all day for this. I will let you stretch after we come back," she exclaimed earnestly.

Al-Khidr did as he was told. The vehicle moved at a brisk pace through the air, allowing Al-Khidr to enjoy the beauty of the landscape that was years ahead of his time. At long last, Nefertiti and Al-Khidr reached the Benben Pyramid. It was situated outside the city and barely visible from a distance.

"This royal house was kept far away for a reason," Nefertiti explained. "The history of the planet has involved wars, pirates, and bounty hunters. The king moved the house from the heart of the city to the mountains, as it would give them enough time to prepare counterattacks and so on." Even though Al-Khidr was hardly listening to any of this, he was repeating his speech again and again in his head.

In a few moments, they reached the entrance of the Benben Pyramid. Nefertiti knew her way around the pyramid, as the queen called her on and off due to security meetings and prisoner exchange. They stepped off the vehicle and started making their way inside the pyramid. It was the same route Ehsis used a week earlier, when Mother called to ask her opinion about the human from planet Keb.

A gush of cold air greeted them on their way to the throne room. They entered the room, but the queen was not there. One of the armed guards inside the room stopped them and said, "You will see a door behind the throne. Open it, and it will lead you to the queen," he stated to both of them. Nefertiti and Al-Khidr looked at each other. She shrugged to let him know that this was also new for her. The palace guard motioned the younger guard to escort them through the place.

"Come on, follow me. The queen is not that far away," he stated in a reassuring voice.

Al-Khidr and Nefertiti walked behind the armed guard. They walked and walked, reaching the center of the pyramid via a ramp that was going downhill. The fully dressed Sekhmets led them to the queen's chambers.

Al-Khidr was still recapping his speech when he entered her chamber. Queen Hathor was indeed there, along with another lady. Nefertiti recognized her, and Al-Khidr guessed her name.

Ehsis and Queen Hathor didn't notice them entering the room, as they were in the middle of a deep conversation when they silently entered her chambers. "My queen," said Nefertiti, kneeling. She motioned for Al-Khidr to do the same, and he bent his head in respect for the queen. "Let's not waste time on ceremony here. Come here. We should do a few important things," she said to them.

Nefertiti was glad that Al-Khidr was quick to follow in her footsteps. If he went with her, Queen Hathor would be on his side. Al-Khidr looked at the middle-aged lady standing beside the queen, and Hathor noticed the look on his face. "This is our Secretary of State and a dear friend of mine. Ehsis is her name. She handles the political affairs of the state when I am preoccupied with something else," she exclaimed while smiling widely. Ehsis nodded towards Al-Khidr. He looked pretty innocent and remarkably young.

They approached the seats arranged around the table. Two of these seats were occupied by the entourage. Al-Khidr followed Nefertiti as she sat on a chair, and then he did the same. The queen and Ehsis looked quite serious, and silence prevailed at the table for a few moments.

Al-Khidr looked at Ehsis, the new person in the chambers. She was scary, and carried herself with an air of importance, unlike the queen. She was wearing green kalasiris made from a material similar to linen. His proposition needed to go through her as well.

Ehsis had noticed his scared face, and she smiled at him. This relaxed some tense nerves. Al-Khidr had forgotten his proposition in the heat of the moment. "I know who you are, don't be worried," Ehsis reassured him. "Come, have a seat here. We have something important to discuss," Ehsis continued, repeating what her queen had said earlier. "Yes. I need to clarify something as well. I will speak with the permission of Ehsis and Queen Hathor, of course," Al-Khidr explained.

Queen Hathor nodded, but she spoke first. "Did that disease, which we are calling here Mutmut, ever spread on your planet?"

"No. I have never witnessed such a disease in humans before. I only read in a book that such a disease was once spread among animals, and then they were cured when some plants from Egypt were fed to them,"

277

he replied casually.

"The disease killed off my entire space mission, except the women. Perhaps you are immune to it or something. The jump-spheres were in the hands of two of the male space crew, who probably died because of the disease," Queen Hathor explained.

Nefertiti used this moment to clear the air. "We have checked him several times. He does not have the virus in his bloodstream. The cellular structure of his body is very different from ours; I think this is why his people did not catch the virus. They did not have a host to attach to," Nefertiti said, explaining the reason behind his immunity.

Ehsis listened with great interest to Nefertiti's story about this alien.

"I have a feeling that this virus can be cured only with something that belongs to Keb; nothing else. The cellular life forms, same as yours, are quite different for us," she remarked to no one in particular. "There has been a menacing spread of the disease. It came from your planet, and the cure still eludes us to this day. In order to protect the people of Lyra, we had to take a hard step. A separate colony was made for the victims of the disease.

"We have superior technology and medicine that is the best in this galaxy. However, we have not yet been able to find a cure. Our scientists have tried for many years to find the cure. Unfortunately, the virus is immune to our medicine. After losing at all fronts, we contacted other planets in the neighboring galaxies and planetary systems. It was to no avail; they were as baffled as us. If we can find the cure somehow, those people can be cured," she explained extensively to Al-Khidr. "All that said, I have decided to send you back to your planet, as people here view you as a man from the cursed planet. We cannot guarantee your safety at all times. Therefore, you should leave Lyra," Queen Hathor said straightforwardly.

Al-Khidr was in deep thought. He looked at the heavens and thanked God for being here. Perhaps this was his calling after all. He was supposed to help the people of Lyra and save them from an epidemic. He kneeled down this time, taking Ehsis and Queen Hathor by surprise. This was new. The human was learning the customs and traditions of Lyra pretty quickly. "My queen, I wish to speak freely here," he stated.

She nodded quickly. This child was interesting. "I believe that my God has sent me here. There is a purpose for my journey, I believe. Surely, why else would God not choose someone else for this mission? I believe God has given me the mission. There were thousands of people exploring those pyramids. However, I was the only one of the lot to get the magical sphere. I appreciate God for this chance," he exclaimed in monotone with some excitement.

Queen Hathor and Ehsis looked at each other and felt satisfied. Something told them that the human was onto something important. They waited and listened. "The Caliph gave me the sphere of all those people. Maybe he did not know what would happen, or whether something would happen or not. However, God surely knew what was about to happen. I am indebted to have such kind people around me. Nefertiti and you have both have been nice to me so far. This brings me to my next idea. It is something I figured out since I was in prison," he said, and went silent for a moment.

The three women waited for him to speak. Nefertiti already knew what it was. She would step in if required.

"I am an alchemist. My job is to find cures for new and unknown diseases. I have been looking for the disease which was responsible for my mom's death. But I think this is more significant than anything else. My mom passed away a long time ago. I am survived only by my dad. Anyhow, I believe Al-Eard has cures for all kinds of diseases. I have a faint idea that this disease is caused by something back on Al-Eard. I could be wrong, but I could try and ask others. I am sure that the cure is still back on Al-Eard. I want an opportunity to return to my planet and search for the cure. I will then return with the cure. When I find the cure, I will head back to Lyra and cure the diseased population," he stated with a lot of conviction.

Ehsis and Queen Hathor were surprised at his confidence. This kid was kind.

"Please grant me the approval to search for cure on Al-Eard. I will return to Lyra with the sphere," he proposed. It was Ehsis who spoke first, surprising everyone.

"How do we trust you? What if you bring more people from Al-Eard? Maybe you will carry a new disease to our planet, if not the old. The risks are too high for us if you return with the cure—if you even find it, that is. And how do we know that you are not lying? Do you know that we can take your primitive life force? It will be over in ten seconds," she said, almost sounded menacing by now.

Queen Hathor looked at Ehsis in surprise. There was no need for this. The human was trying to help, after all. Al-Khidr considered this for a moment. It was a plausible and fair question. "Yes. I agree," he said. "This could be an elaborate plan to escape the planet. I do miss my friends and relatives here. However, I believe that I can genuinely do something for this planet—your planet. Consider this my gift to the people," he exclaimed with a beaming smile.

Ehsis and Queen Hathor thought about this for a bit. Al-Khidr still felt that he needed something more to convince the two women. Nefertiti was staring with a blank face; she was not clear what to say yet.

"Also, our planet is far behind yours. Perhaps we can cooperate on a technological exchange somehow. However, that is a plan for some other time. I first want to help the diseased population in this colony," he exclaimed earnestly.

Ehsis was surprised by that suggestion. Queen Hathor just smiled at the idea; the man wanted a lot more than a cure. Then he, too broke into a smile.

# CHAPTER 19. THE PROMISE

"Besides, your planet is extraordinary. I have seen and used the technology of this planet. It is unlike anything I have seen before. Our planet will take centuries to come close to anything like this. I would also like to help the people of Al-Eard, if I can," he remarked while smiling. "Look at the quality of water, the technology, and the clean and hygienic water. It is possible that I may stay longer on Al-Eard. Back on my planet, I could catch a disease and just die. However, people of Lyra live for thousands of years. If I talk about Al-Eard, people live for sixty to seventy years there. I want to live longer and help mankind. I believe God sent me here for this and many other reasons. May Allah help me in my mission," he remarked, looking above.

Queen Hathor was touched by the compassion of Al-Khidr. He reminded her of herself. She knew then that she could not kill such a person. The last murder she committed on his planet was during the madness of another time. "How do you know that you will find a cure for the disease that was there ages ago? Is the disease still there?" Ehsis asked, surprising herself. Al-Khidr was not expecting the question himself. "I do not know that yet. However, I will try not to catch a disease. Actually, Nefertiti can put me in quarantine if something does happen," he exclaimed while thinking to himself. Queen Hathor smiled. She knew that he would be vaccinated before heading to his planet. Nefertiti also smiled at the thought. "I humbly promise that I will find the cure on my planet and return to

Lyra. Allah Almighty will help me in my search. My words are etched in stone. May harm come to me if I do not abide by my promise," he exclaimed seriously.

"That won't be necessary, and we certainly do not hope that. You may visit your planet," Queen Hathor stated in a loud voice. Finally, it happened: she had granted him permission to leave for his planet. Al-Khidr could not contain his happiness. His face brightened, even as he was still kneeling before the queen.

"Thank you. Thank you so much, my queen. I will not let you down. I will search the ends of Al-Eard to find the cure," he remarked, getting a bit carried away. This made the queen smile. "That will not be necessary. You can still return to my planet. I give you my permission," she responded wholeheartedly.

Al-Khidr looked at Nefertiti, who was hiding a smile. She did not want to screw it up. However, Ehsis and Queen Hathor had noticed her expression as well. Hathor then realized she and Al-Khidr had talked about this plan quite a bit. It was THEIR plan all along.

At last, Ehsis decided to break up the conversation. It was getting a bit too chummy.

"We left your planet around 84,428 years ago, in Al-Eard years. I do not think that the alien colony would still be there, or any remnant left of it. We will brief you on the necessary details before you leave for the planet," Ehsis exclaimed sternly. Ehsis pointed to the tracking device holes still in Al-Khidr's wrist. "With our tracking device, you won't go out of range of our system. We can track and hunt anyone," Ehsis said further.

Queen Hathor looked at her as if she was disgruntled, and intervened: "I believe we can give him the basic details about the space mission and people that were involved in it. Why not? After all, he is spearheading a mission for us. It is only fair that we tell him the story of the mission and the dangers we faced. The human has been very truthful with us. We should return the favor, Ehsis," she stated clearly.

Ehsis could not disagree with Queen Hathor, at least not in front of these two. It would send a very wrong message about the ruler of the planet if she was talked down to by her Secretary of State.

"Why, of course, Queen Hathor. Anything you like. Foremost is your command, and then comes everything else," she exclaimed while bowing down. "Thanks for the buttering up, but there's no need for that. We have known each other for a long, long time," she reminded her. Ehsis kept her head down in respect for the queen. As a result, Hathor opened up regarding her encounters on Al-Khidr's planet. Even though it was a long time ago, tears still formed in her eyes as she went along, narrating the events that transpired.

Al-Khidr thought about the queen. He stole a look at Nefertiti, who was listening as intently as him. Clearly, this was the first time she was listening to the personal account of the events that had unfolded on the primitive planet.

He looked at Ehsis for any expression that would

say something different. However, she was just listening with an impassive look on her face. It was nothing out of the ordinary for her; it felt like she had gone over the events a few times over the course of millennia.

"Al-Khidr, I need to tell you something at first. The information I am about to give you must be kept in complete secrecy for reasons I cannot reveal. It is something only I and Ehsis know and rest of the planet are unaware of to this day. Mission-sensitive details are not in the public records, after all. Some people want this information, especially people in the military wing. Curiosity runs wildly among the people. Our space missions are very well-known, except the one on Al-Eard. Senior generals still smell some foul play, though I have made my stance on the matter of secrecy final to them," she explained.

Al-Khidr nodded in agreement. "Queen Hathor, nothing will go beyond these private chambers. I am a man of my word. Also, I think my only point of contact is dear Nefertiti, who has been so kind to me. I have not talked to anyone else except these three women in the chambers," Al-Khidr exclaimed confidentially.

Queen Hathor seemed satisfied with that explanation. She began to narrate the story, looking briefly at Ehsis while the Secretary of State nodded.

She began her story, from the time the mission took off from the planet Lyra to the sudden spread of the disease among the male crew members. She told of how the female crew members had panicked and decided to abort the mission and return to Lyra.

# CHAPTER 19. THE PROMISE

"Oh, one more thing. We had intended to do a complete study of the plant life on Al-Eard, but before we could do that, the virus hit us. We were in damage control mode then. Maybe if we had more knowledge about the plants, we could have contained the virus," she exclaimed while talking in a low tone. Al-Khidr listened intently, trying not to miss anything.

The final bit of the story involved the problem on Al-Eard. Lyra's technology was ahead of their time, which allowed them to develop a changing map of Al-Eard and its altering solar system. But thanks to Seth, they had lost their power source on the new planet. Now they had to rethink everything they wanted to do. The return of the diseased population was important.

"To make things easy, the statue of Anpu was established as the reference point. We created a star chart on a rock nearby with the reference of it. We coded the star positions when the stars of water (the constellation of Cancer) appeared on Keb's plane and the closest star plane's intersection. Maybe the star chart is still there, or maybe it was moved to some other location on your planet. You may check," Ehsis informed him. "It would have helped the dying astronauts retrace their steps back to their planet, if it had been possible. The colony on the planet was abandoned, as Queen Hathor, I, and others left for Lyra," Ehsis said further.

Al-Khidr learned what few people of Lyra knew, and he was proud of it. He remembered that in one of ancient Egyptian temples in Egypt, there was a star chart that nobody knew the purpose of. That temple was now in a place called Dendara, Egypt. Everything now made sense to him. The Sphinx, the pyramids, the zodiac chart; they were all connected.

He was lost in his thoughts when Queen Hathor clapped, gaining everyone's attention.

"So, it looks like everyone got what they deserved. You may leave the chambers now," she stated with a tone of finality.

They both bowed and departed from the chambers. As they entered the air-conditioned corridor, Nefertiti spoke first. "Well, that went better than expected." She could not contain her happiness.

"I agree. Queen Hathor is a gem of a person," Al-Khidr remarked, thinking for a bit.

"Oh. She likes you, actually. The way you talk and created a connection with her to tell the story...a few months, and she will like you as much as she likes Ehsis," she explained with an air of confidence.

Al-Khidr agreed with her. She then changed the subject.

"Well, we will receive the go-ahead for the mission later this week. You want to do something? Take it from me—You are not in prison anymore. We can sit, relax, and enjoy the evening air somewhere else. Oh, oh—I have an idea. There is this revolving restaurant up on the 200th floor. Want to try that?" Nefertiti exclaimed enthusiastically.

Al-Khidr did not understand the concept of floors yet, but he went along with it anyway.

"Sure thing. Anything that is worth your while is good for me. Does it serve great food?" he asked curiously, feeling his stomach. "Oh, it is one of the best, if not the best in the main city," she exclaimed brightly.

Al-Khidr smiled and nodded his head. Sounds good, he thought.

Nefertiti was now like a whole different person. She had dropped her serious look and demeanor, taking on a more friendly and sweet persona. *Oh, God, he thought. She is so beautiful. Just look at her.*

She twirled her hair to one side, leaving Al-Khidr in a trance. Something caught his attention. His olfactory senses were sharpened, as the perfume worn by Nefertiti was captivating.

"Hey, Al-Khidr, look." She turned to look at him, and he was caught looking at her.

"Are you alright? Why are looking at me like that?" she asked him.

"It's nothing. We don't have your hair color back on Al-Eard," he managed to lie.

She laughed and turned her attention to the object. *He likes me,* she thought.

# Chapter 20

# The Sceptics

IT was morning in the kingdom of Akhom, and Queen Hathor had called the military high command today for a special announcement. The agenda of the meeting was not mentioned, as the mission involved great secrecy. The people of Lyra could not be told about this information, as otherwise, it would raise an outcry.

The military personnel sat in their seats, waiting for the queen to arrive. As they pondered over the agenda for the meeting, Queen Hathor entered the chamber wearing a teal-colored kalasiris, not looking at the military personnel seated there.

The guards, in blue uniform, announced in a stern voice, "All behold; Queen Mother Hathor, the protector of Kingdom of Akhom, is entering." Queen Hathor gracefully sat on her royal chair, which was twice as wide and laden with ornaments. It was a sight to behold for the military personnel; some of the young ones were coming inside for the first time.

The men stood from their seats in respect for their queen. These generals were a different breed than the average population. They were pretty strong, their muscles quite visible underneath their tough uniforms. Queen Hathor looked at the men, and a smile crossed her lips.

The men saluted her, still standing up. She beckoned them to take their seats. Some of these men looked much younger, since they were newly inducted into the forces. The men hailed from the related government offices and military ranks, as the concerned matter was about the health and security of the kingdom. Most of the men were middle-aged generals, except Major General Hatathor, who had recently been appointed as head of weaponry design.

Akhom had gained a reputation regarding the recruitment of these tough men who kept the planet safe. The Kingdom of Akhom bred and raised warriors from an early age, and the training sessions and hardened routine of these men were a secret. It was no wonder that these soldiers took down bounty hunters and thieves with their bare hands. Sometimes, these soldiers were sent to neighboring planets to maintain peace and ward off small terrorist groups. The men were the pride of Lyra. Queen Hathor raised her hand to collect her thoughts. She thought for a moment before speaking up.

"It is an honor to meet you in flesh and blood. I am proud of the brave and reliable men who protect our kingdom day and night. Everyone trusts your expertise, and it gives me great pleasure to see you all here. As it stands, I seldom have to interfere in matters of the armed forces. Our able scientists, generals, and major generals can look after these matters themselves and make wise decisions. I am fine with how they run things," she finished her opening monologue. The men in front nodded their heads, recognizing the praise. She paused for a moment and then resumed. "But that is not why we are here today. I am here because of a different mission; one that does not really affect Lyra in any way. Yet, you will see the mission through," she explained vaguely.

The queen pressed a button, and a wall enclosed her and the military personnel sitting inside. It hid the chamber guards, who looked at each other in surprise. However, they nodded their heads. It left only the queen and the military personnel. Perhaps the queen wanted to talk about something top secret—maybe something of national security.

"This problem will not leave the room, ever. People will not like us keeping things hidden from them, but still, I feel some things aren't really important for people to know. It is a matter which should be handled quietly," she exclaimed impassively.

The general recognized these walls—they were used in times of war. The walls were specially hardened with metals, alloys, carbon fiber, and special Lyrian-designed materials to protect them from aerial fire and ground forces. These shields were also present in military compounds, ammunition barracks, and other military bases. In times of war, Lyra had the policy to protect its reserves and military personnel. Should an onslaught continually hit these shielded targets, the Lyrian military units would be prepping inside to unleash a counterattack.

It also meant that battalions and their soldiers could not leave the room until they were cleared. It protected Lyra from spies who could release sensitive mission details and compromise the mission, and the walls also protected the occupants from radio signals.

However, the general, having seen several wars on this and other planets, saw no reason for this action. Although he understood that the queen did not want this information leaking outside, a spy could be sitting inside right now. The queen smiled.

"Perhaps it was not necessary. But if a word of this goes out, I will know who to target. I don't like this any more than you do," she exclaimed with a smile. The senior generals returned her smile. If they could get on with the issue at hand, it would be better.

"Something important has come up. Bear with me

for a moment. I have been aware of this intel for a long time, along with the Secretary of State and some police members. The military was not in the loop regarding this matter. We thought that it would resolve by itself, but since it's a matter of national security, I wanted to inform you as well."

The men in the room looked at Ehsis, who had been standing there for a long time. However, the men had not noticed her somehow. She walked near the queen and stood beside her. It was a show of force—a message that this was coming right from the top.

Ehsis nodded her head to acknowledge the presence of these esteemed men, but she kept silent. The queen briefly looked at her, then continued to speak. "Some of you may not know about the planet Keb. It is also called *Aitenn* and Earth. Our mission under Higher Space Surveillance program failed on that planet considering reasons which aren't worth the discussion. After that failure, we disbanded the HSS Program. The sheer loss of Lyrian males' lives was just too much to take on my conscience. After losing HSS staff, we started new space program, the Galactic Exploration Unit (GEU), which was more for the defense-related jobs, mainly for the space weapons system design, as we were facing continued threats from the planets Sovidos and Honkira. However, it was always my dream to restart the HSS facility for the greater benefit of our race," she explained thoroughly.

The generals knew that the GEU approved space

missions after evaluating the equipment and inspection procedures. It was a routine with GEU, who would arrive each year to recheck the equipment. But after the last failure of the HSS, the GEU ceased visits to Keb, allocating their resources on other space exploratory missions. "Some of you are new to the military, but Ehsis and I have seen the challenges faced by our kingdom. Some of you were not even born then," Hathor said. One general wanted some clarification, so he raised his hand. "Where is the space mission going this time? Why is our help needed in the matter?" he exclaimed straightforwardly.

Hathor kept silent and looked at all generals, who were anxiously waiting to hear the reason for this top-secret meeting. "I would like to send a human back to Keb. We feel that he can help us in getting the cure for Mutmut," she replied in a serious tone. There was silence in the room as the men looked at each other. There was a human on their own planet, and they had no idea! "Why were we not informed about this? This is a matter of national security, isn't it?" boomed Senior General Dodvan, Head of Immigration and Border Entries. He was annoyed that he had not been informed of the arrival of the human.

Dodvan was a general in his middle age, but he was not nearly as old as Queen Hathor. Why did Queen Hathor and Ehsis make this decision by themselves? They were there to backstab the standing army and military generals. There was tension among the military generals, who frequently inquired one other about the alien on their planet. This was a legitimate security threat.

Queen Hathor did not answer this question. However, she felt that, as the queen, some questions could be left at her discretion.

"I believe some decisions should be left to me," she said. "And yes, we do have an alien on the planet. A harmless one, at that," she finished.

"But that is impossible. We installed illegal immigrant shields at all entry points for nothing. We haven't found any trace of an alien entering or leaving the planet. Are you sure there is an alien?" he asked again.

Queen Hathor nodded seriously to make sure the question was not repeated again.

"Of course, we are sure we have an alien here. First, he arrived here not on a ship, but inside an energy field. Secondly, he arrived here accidentally," she explained further.

"How long has the human already been here? Has he been inspected? He could be a spy or might carry a disease," asked General Osevia, Commander of Land Forces. Osevia was livid with both Ehsis and Queen Hathor. *They made a habit of keeping the Lyrian Army in the dark. To them, they were just soldiers. In their minds, the men would enlist in the army, get combat training, and maintain peace on other planets. What nonsense!*

Major General Hatathor was sitting, watching this situation unfold. Hatathor was tall—eight feet—with

CHAPTER 20. THE SCEPTICS

sturdy arms and a face with elevated jawbones, which gave him a manly appearance. His deep, guttural voice echoed in closed chambers. His skin was reddish-brown, with a strong jawline and menacing look. Hatathor's hair was tied into a round rope and he wore a blue uniform at all times. It was a military uniform.

General Hatathor was the son of deceased Seth, who was the one Hathor and Ehsis shot dead on Al-Eard. He had turned into a rather handsome young man, but one with a brutal temper. Tales of his misdemeanors were quite common in Lyra. Ehsis and Queen Hathor were no strangers to this behavior, with the history they had. Some laws were changed, while others were created to stop Hatathor from misusing the planet and its laid-back rules for the people. Of course, all of this was different for the outsiders of Lyra.

Hatathor's mom had found her son's antics slightly unnerving. She thought maybe something more rigorous and work-intensive would have her son in control. As luck would have it, some openings appeared in Lyra's newspapers, and Hatathor enrolled in the foot soldiers of the Lyra Galactic Force. The man had become a warrior with the Lyra Galactic Force, rising through the ranks as the best of the best, and now working as head of new weapons design. He was handed a commanding position in the army in his later years. Queen Hathor and Ehsis followed his progress closely over the years.

Ehsis hated his guts; his face reminded her of Seth, and the horrors of their previous mission. According to her opinion, it was important to watch over him, as the two knew he was a loose cannon of sorts. Yet, for some reason, Hatathor returned a dislike of Ehsis. The queen understood the intelligence and capability of both Ehis and Hatathor. However, they were both ticking time bombs. She feared the day when the two started fighting one on one.

"Mother, what if the alien is a spy from Honkira? We cannot rule out the possibility of spies landing on the planet, for obvious reasons," Hatathor stated straightforwardly.

Ehsis eyed him with suspicion and couldn't stop herself from intervening "And you think you know more than we do? We checked his flight paths. The alien is clean as a whistle. He came directly from his planet to ours. He made only two stops: Keb, and Lyra. I am quite a lot older than you; I have seen many things. I even designed your training," Ehsis talked down to Hatathor.

Hatathor was about to say something, but General Oseria, Commander of Land Forces, spoke up, asking his question delicately. "There is nothing wrong in sending an alien-human back to his planet. But may I ask why we should send him back to Keb? He should live in incarceration, as he entered without permission," he offered as a solution.

But Major General Hatathor was not done yet. The lingering question was still on his mind. "How the hell did he enter Lyra without our notice? How did he get inside? Is there a problem with our systems?

We need to fix that first," he exclaimed cautiously.

Queen Hathor looked at Ehsis; it was her cue again.

"As it stood, he entered the galaxy and then our planet through Maft-Shespt," Ehsis explained calmly this time, giving the name of the device. "Maft-Shespt?" The generals looked at each other. Major General Hatathor looked up in surprise. "Maft-Shespt meaning, a jump-sphere? What is that?" he demanded more information.

Everyone shook their heads.

Ehsis came to his help again.

"The Maft-Shespt, translated as a jump-sphere, is an old technology of ours. We used them several times during reign of King Ptah. Long before Hatathor or any of you were here, this was our technology to reach planets, light-years away planets. It creates an energy field on the spaceship and warps the space. "But you may ask, how does this work? Well, it is too complex to explain to you, as it requires many aspects. I will tell you simply that it is a device that creates a cosmic-tunnel space. Back on Keb, we left two of these jump-spheres. We were in a hurry and wanted to leave as fast as possible. Our men were dying, and two of our most talented male officers contracted the lethal Mutmut disease. We could not keep them on board, so we left them with the spheres. It looks like they didn't survive, but they sealed them inside the pyramid."

Ehsis stopped with tearful eyes. She did not want to give too many details to military. She looked at Hathor and continued. "Obviously, we could not keep track of everything. The arrival of this human was a trip down memory lane," Ehsis explained nicely. Ehsis said further, "We did not think that the people of Keb would ever be able to use the device. It is not a simple technology. Our team of scientists had designed it. Unfortunately, most of these scientists were gone, as they contracted the disease," Ehsis informed them sadly.

A stunned silence filled the room at the mention of earthlings' abilities to use the jump-spheres. Racism and looking down on other races were against Queen Hathor's policy. Queen Hathor realized this, and she motioned Ehsis to keep quiet and let her take over.

"Forgive this mistake by Ehsis. I hope she speaks highly of other planets who have yet to go through technological development. We should not look down upon other species. It is unbecoming of a superior race like ours. But now that we have covered this part, there is something else. The disease Mutmut originated from Keb. The human-alien is planning to return to his planet. Unfortunately, we cannot find the cure, even though our technology is far superior. This is because of a slight drawback: our science is established on our own cellular structures. People on Earth have molecular and genetic structure different from us. We probably need another kind of biology department to understand them, and, we can cure the epidemic through them," she explained in detail. General Kityr, Head of the Kingdom Heath and Safety department, spoke up. He was heading the science division on Lyra and was the scientist of virology. "I have something to say. Can I?" he asked the two women.

Queen Hathor looked at him. "Yes. I am aware that you and your team have been working at it for years. Keep up the good work," she said. General Kityr felt embarrassed, but still spoke up. "Hear me out. Our planet mostly has a desert landscape. The plants in this region are few and scarce. But God gifted us Amris. No one else in known planets has it. What we lack is the plantation. We analyzed our homegrown plants and those which were bought from other planets. They do not contain the right compounds which can control the pathogens associated with Mutmut. I strongly believe that we should explore other planets for the cure," he finished his pitch to the queen.

Queen Hathor held her face in her hands. Another pin drop silence ensued into the room. Everyone knew that she did not like this line of questioning. Ehsis started, "But what if..." Queen Hathor interrupted her. "I am not interested in speculations. I am tired of these ideas. You can visit the planet, by all means. Just tell me when you will have the cure," she remarked dismissively.

She continued, "For centuries, the cure has eluded us. I think we must have a different approach this time. The epidemic came from a planet far, far away. I believe that the cure is also on that planet. The biochemical elements are present there. It is the right thing to do. Go to planet Keb and get the cure." "Oh," the generals said collectively.

Queen Hathor and Ehsis shared a tense look. The surprise was palpable on their faces. Ehsis tried to explain the developing situation. "It sounds dangerous, but we also cannot just seal off city after city, region after region. Sealing off is not a long-term solution. So, the right solution is to send the human back there. We cannot go there, but he can survive, and hopefully, he can find the cure. After all, he has offered to go on this mission on our behalf. We are glad that he is doing this for us," Ehsis exclaimed happily. The military generals looked disturbed, and murmurs started among them. They did not agree with the decision taken by the high command. Some of them passed scornful looks at the two.

It was Major General Hatathor who spoke up this time. "This proposal is very dangerous. There is no telling if the human alien will bring another epidemic to our planet which we cannot possibly cure. What if the plants he brings have a new kind of deadly pathogen? It is a risk too great. We should not make decisions in silos," he said agitatedly.

Ehsis stepped forward, clenching her fists. "Can we talk about this privately?" she said, irritatingly.

Queen Hathor raised her hand and stopped both. Another military general spoke up. "He is right. I was thinking about the same possibility," the old man exclaimed.

Major General Hatathor took this moment to speak up again. "Keb is a cursed planet. The unknown and untested pathogens could cause havoc on our planet.

# CHAPTER 20.   THE SCEPTICS

We cannot take a risk like this," he exclaimed further. The other generals nodded collectively this time.

"Already, Ankhamon, son of Heka, and his brethren are gaining popularity underground!" said General Eli, Head of Internal Affairs and Security.

"Ah, Ankhamon son of Heka. He is nothing. I can crush him and his supporters any moment like insects. It is my mercy that I allowed them to go out of civilization and live in the mountains," the queen said.

The whole hall went into silence. The queen was getting annoyed, and to the generals, she was not a person to argue with rationally sometimes. "Al-Khidr can go and bring plants. We analyze them, and if it is not feasible, we will destroy the pathogens instantly," Ehsis broke the silence and looked at queen. The queen nodded, indicating that she could continue.

"Who is al-Khidr?" one general asked.

"The human from the planet Keb," Ehsis said, and continued: "We know that our DNA is the best. Our males can lift heavy weights, climb mountains easily. The human we analyzed is weak, meaning that if they survived on Keb, then they must have developed the immunity over time, and we can learn from it. Also the Ar-t Heru kingdom tracking unit is installed in the human's hand." "I am not convinced, Madam Secretary!" Major General Hatathor said. "I want to talk to the human." Ehsis looked at the queen.

***

"Hey, wake up, it already too late." Nefertiti was standing over the head of Al-Khidr, who had been sleeping since yesterday. Al-Khidr woke up and was surprised to see Nefertiti in regular Lyrian dress for women. She looked stunningly beautiful. He sat on the bed and asked, "Where are we going? To some party?"

"No. I am taking you to this new place I found. You will like it, trust me on this," Nefertiti exclaimed excitedly. "I bought new clothes for you." She showed him the new clothes.

Al-Khidr took the clothes and started feeling the fabric material. Apparently, the fabric was soft. The clothes were a pair of brown trousers and white shirt. He was also fed up with the prison clothes he was wearing. He sniffed the clothes, and found they smelled good.

"Thank you," he said. "I don't wear such soft clothing...but since you bought it for me, I'll put it on," he said further. "Hahaha, that's because we can make such soft fabric," she laughingly said, and went out of the room and closed the door behind her. When Al-Khidr came out of the room, Nefertiti stared at him. He didn't look like a human, but like a Lyrian.

"You look so handsome!" Nefertiti remarked. "When do we remove this?" He showed her the three holes in his hand—the tracking unit. "Soon. I suppose tomorrow we can do it. But not today. I don't want to go to office today," Nefertiti said.

# Chapter 20. The Sceptics

\*\*\*

He almost felt dizzy. The restaurant was at such a height that he could not see the people on the ground. The clouds moved around him as he looked below. The air traffic today was very hectic. He could see shuttles, cars, and police patrol vehicles moving at breakneck speeds. This society was way ahead of his own in several ways. Often, a beam of light would blind him as a shuttle emerged from thin air and joined the heavy traffic. He was amazed at the lifestyle of Lyra and its people. It would take half a day for Nefertiti to return and find the prisoner sleeping. She broke the awkward silence.

"There was a council meeting today. Queen Hathor and Ehsis presided over the council meeting and laid out some important points for the military command," she explained while driving.

Al-Khidr nodded. He could sense that the meeting was about him, most probably.

"We don't know that happened in meeting—but I am sure there were disagreements," she remarked confidently.

The vehicle entered into a lush, green belt, which was floating in the air as strange birds flew around them. Suddenly, an animal jumped on the vehicle and Al-Khidr screamed in horror. The animal looked at them and disappeared back into the trees.

"What was that thing? I didn't know animals can jump that high," Al-Khidr exclaimed shockingly. Nefertiti smiled.

"I came here deliberately to scare the hell out of you. This is what we call a Naar. Naar can jump very high, almost twice as high as this one. This one was just a curious baby. The larger ones can jump extremely high. They live in the trees down there," she explained.

They came into a clearing, and Al-Khidr could see that they were above Misraim city. This was a sight to see.

"This is a great restaurant in outer space. People come here for the view, just like us. Look over there; that is Vega, our star. And, down below, you can see Misraim. Well, the place over there is where we live," she exclaimed like a tourist guide. Al-Khidr was surprised by the place and its elevation. Suddenly, a big, circular door opened in front of them. Nefertiti went inside and parked her vehicle in it. A voice announced, "Vehicle number eighty-four." Eighty-four vehicles today, she thought. "Dammit, there are a lot of people here today. I hope we can find a table," she exclaimed worriedly. Al-Khidr had no idea what tables were, although he thought he would find out soon.

Nefertiti took out a chair and told Al-Khidr to sit down. "In our kingdom, women take out the chair and allow their men to sit," she exclaimed playfully. They finally sat down. The whole restaurant had glass walls, and they could see the Misraim city on their left and Tehuti mountains on their right. "Yes, let's get back to the council meeting. They discussed some important points today," she stated sternly. "My gut feeling is that some of the military Generals may not be happy that this information was kept hidden from them. The alien-human could have infected the population and caused havoc of unimaginable proportions. I think if you also view this situation as an outsider, you might agree on it. If, by any chance, you carried a disease, we could have problems," she stated, thinking about the scary idea.

Al-Khidr was listening intently. He did not show it, but he was a bit worried inside. His promise to help this kingdom was a difficult one. This meant that he could have some problems for a while. Ehsis and Queen Hathor were on his side, as far as he was concerned.

"Besides the military, the brethren might also take note of your presence in the Akhom," Nefertiti said.

"Brethren?" Al-Khidr repeated, surprised. "The Brethren of Awakened Consciousness. Their ringleader is Ankhamon, son of Heka," Nefertiti said.

Al-Khidr raised his eyebrow. "Who is this Ankhamon, and what did he do?" Nefertiti understood his confusion and smiled. "Nothing to worry about—I agree with Queen Hathor. Can you see the mountains from here? This guy Ankhamon and his tribe, they live in the Tehuti mountains. Ankhamon is a journalist turned politician. He used to write in the newspapers. When disease broke out and the government failed to bring in the cure, a lot of people in the city died. The queen sealed the affected quarters and declared it Sutekh, or Exclusion Zone. The people from Sutekh were only given food which was dropped from air. Slowly, they all died. But this created chaos in our society. The survivors disagreed, and Ankhamon wrote articles against the whole procedure. Sizeable populations started supporting Ankhamon, and he formed a political party. They called themselves Brethren of Awakened Consciousness. Some people like them, and some don't. If the government decided to, it wouldn't take more than an hour to bring them down in those mountains," Nefertiti finished speaking.

Al-Khidr started connecting the dots. "We had the same problem in our planet. Abu Muslim Khorasani had supported Caliph Al-Saffah initially, but then he rebelled and the government killed him." But Al-Khidr was confused about Ankhamon; something didn't add up. "What did they do, exactly?" he blurted out. "Ankhamon has a cultist kind of mentality, so much so that government got worried and for the stability of kingdom. He and his supporters were asked to either accept government policies or leave the capital. The government had a fear of rebellion, and our intelligence informed us that they might overthrow the government. It was one of their brighter ideas. The queen decided to expel them from the capital and send them into the mountains in the north. These people live in Tehuti mountains. In my view, they do not pose an imminent threat to us," she exclaimed, laughing mildly.

Al-Khidr lost interest in this whole conversation.

Instead, he nodded and stared at Vega. Nefertiti realized that she didn't order the food yet. "Well, I am starving right now. Let me decide the food so that we can talk and eat," she exclaimed intently. She tapped on a button on table, and a menu appeared in front of them. Nefertiti picked a few things and showed them to Al-Khidr.

"Look at this," she stated excitedly. Al-Khidr touched it, although his hand passed through the image. She opened a sizzling, black drink in front of him. He was feeling thirsty and snatched it. Yet again, his hand went through the image.

Nefertiti was giggling hard, with her hand on her mouth. She was toying with Al-Khidr, who realized this a lot later. "Well, thanks for doing that. I am hungry here. All this talk has made me sleepy. When will the food come?" he asked anxiously. She was still giggling.

"What do you mean when? It is coming right now. Look behind you," she said enthusiastically.

A female employee was coming towards them with their food. She was flying, he noticed. He looked at her feet to see she was hovering in the air as he moved. She set the food on the table, smiled at them, and left. The aroma of the food was tantalizing. Nefertiti forgot about her briefing for a while as she dug in immediately. Al-Khidr looked at the food. It was not something he had seen before.

"Back on my planet, it takes over an hour to cook the food. It depends on the wood we have. Sometimes the wood is wet after rain or flooding, so it creates a problem. We usually kill animals and skin them. So, it can take a few hours before we eat," he said, explaining his life back on Al-Eard. Nefertiti looked at him blankly. "What?" she said.

"Nothing," he stated brashly.

As they eat heartily, Nefertiti said, "Soon, you will be flying back through the stars!"

"That was frightening, that I can tell you!" Al-Khidr started remembering his last journey. "Will you remember me, once I go back?" Al-Khidr asked Nefertiti. "Yes, maybe," she said with tearful eyes.

***

Ehsis and Queen Hathor were looking at each other, thinking the same thing. The issue troubled them yet again. Perhaps they had to reduce the role of the army from this point forward.

Ehsis spoke up, breaking up the chain of their thoughts.

"Hatathor, you will not take any action without my approval. If you do, you will violate section 421(b). That is a criminal offense under our constitution. You are a senior member of the standing army. Please do not make me arrest you. The prisoner is with police, who is safeguarding him as we decide on the matter," she exclaimed in an insensitive manner.

She turned to the room. "This goes for everyone sitting here. No military personnel should directly talk to human called Al-Khidr without me saying so. The

309

queen has already spoken and made her decision. We gathered you here to inform you what had been decided," she reminded all the generals.

The room went silent yet again. The generals did not murmur this time, but looked at Ehsis and then Hatathor. Were they missing something? Queen Hathor stepped in to break this confrontation. "I understand that our generals have served us well over the years. But protocols are protocols, and I strongly suggest that we abide by them. So, we will take things into our control from here," she said definitively.

The queen looked at all and said, "I do not want to listen more arguments. I am here to announce to you what I have planned. Act on my orders. General Lukmas, as head of Space Operations and head of the Galatic Exploration Unit, it is your job to activate the HSS facility. I will visit soon. Make sure that the facility is properly disinfected. Thank you all for coming. We will get in touch with you soon with the mission preparations and other important details," the queen said sternly. General Lukmas was a bodily weak man, but was always high in spirit. He had seen his share of battles and had even been injured a few times. When Ehsis, as Secretary of State, recruited him to be the head of Space Operations, he immediately accepted the new job. He couldn't think of anything more exciting than working on the defense of Lyra.

The military generals stood up and started to leave the chambers. Several murmurs ensued as they left the chambers. Once they were outside, one senior general came up to Hatathor and whispered, "What is the deal with Ehsis and you? It seems like there is some bitter rivalry underneath. Tell me the history between you two. What happened? Why does she address you like this? She talked down to you twice today. For someone of your rank, I hardly think you should be a target," he said. Major General Hatathor was annoyed by the question. "I have no idea what Ehsis wants from me. I did not say anything to her. I only asked if I could talk to the human and understand what plan he had in mind. Even though it was a simple matter of permission, Ehsis made a mess of it. She is a bit emotional and lets it out on me," he explained as they sat in their hyper-drive shuttle.

The senior military general was skeptical. "I don't believe you. There is more than meets the eye. Is there some history between you that I should be aware of? Perhaps we can discuss the matter with our queen," he offered. Hatathor laughed loudly. "You think she didn't notice that? She sees the tension each time and chooses to remain silent. Now, what kind of queen is that? I demand an answer," Hatathor replied.

"Well, that is downright favoritism right there. We can talk this thing over with her if you like. Do let me know if I can come with you," he exclaimed seriously. Hatathor laughed again. "I am not going to talk about this issue. She cares and understands that this is a problem. She should call a meeting and get this thing behind us," he roared.

The senior general did not respond to that. It was

probably best that the matter was left alone. So, he started the turbo drive feature, and they disappeared from the queen's chambers.

That was that, thought Hatathor as they flew towards the army barracks.  Al-Khidr was out of his reach.  However, he could talk to police about him, and hopefully, some information would come through. The police station was under constant monitoring with cameras.

"Whatever these two women do...Huh...Military has a solution for every problem.  We will save Lyra!" Hatathor said to himself.

# Chapter 21

# The Just Cause

MAJOR General Hatathor was back in his military headquarters. He was sitting in his chair, confused. His table had several files on the design of new weapon systems. He had to check and approve many designs, but today he could not focus much. You cannot eliminate a virus with a bullet or a laser, let alone a missile. He felt he could not save his country if the epidemic struck again. Even Dr. General Kityr, a very accomplished virologist, was unsuccessful. Under these facts, asking a human to bring a cure from Keb could have devastating and unsurmountable consequences for Lyra.

He couldn't believe what had transpired in the meeting. With such a high position as that of a Queen and Secretary of the State, they would even suggest that the military high command accept sending a human back to Earth to bring the supposed cure for the disease Mutmut.

"Is it some fairytale which the queen and Ehsis have told us, and we all believed in like gullible children?" he asked angrily. "How come they are both so irrational? Were they always like this?" He was still raging at the thought. He was agitated that the queen was not listening to him, persistently supporting Ehsis. "We listened to them because we thought that there would be a talk of intelligence in the whole dialogue, but we found that superfluousness has overwhelmed their mundane minds. This is a matter of national security," he said to himself. "Look at their proposal. Send humans back to Planet Earth? I hate that planet. It took my father away. He died there in an accident while helping the queen's husband," Hatathor said in his deep voice.

He was sure that something had not been told to the military, which only the queen and Ehsis knew. "I need to gather information on the space mission undertaken by HSS. Who could help me?" he asked himself.

A thought then came to his mind. Hatathor called

General Oseria.

"Good afternoon, General Oseria," he thundered.

"Good afternoon, Major General Hatathor," General Oseria said sweetly.

"You were there in the meeting today; you know how complicated the situation is getting. You worked before as head of the intelligence unit. I need a piece of information from you. I do not want to ask General Eli at the moment," he said dryly.

There was some silence.

"General Hatathor, I hope I can help you with this," Oseria said.

"I need access to HSS-related data. I need to know. Where is it?" Hatathor asked.

"General, the database has been sealed off since the time of King Ptah. After that, there were many heads of the intelligence unit. Each one of them moved the data from one repository location to another. I tried to do some data mining, but you will be shocked to hear that the data has been completely sabotaged. If you insert the recorder into the Hesb-t computing systems, nothing useful comes out. There was no proper record of destinations, no trajectory data, no exploration data. Nothing—it looks like it has tampered intentionally. I have the feeling that the original data might have been removed to some other secure location that I am not aware of," Oseria stated.

"Oseria, you mean you don't even know where the data is?" Hatathor asked in dismay.

General Oseria nodded.

"Who might have removed the data?" Hatathor continued.

"Them!" Oseria whispered.

"You mean the queen, or Ehsis?" Hatathor tried to narrow down the culprit.

"Ehsis, who else!" Oseria said impatiently.

Hatathor thanked Oseria for receiving his call.

He was back into his muddled thoughts. Now, he was sure that there was something that was hidden from the military.

"All this time, the two idiots were playing around as if we are children," Hatathor grumbled. "I willl not let this go on any longer. I will dig out the truth!" Hatathor said with conviction. Suddenly, a name came to his mind. "Ankhamon!"

He knew that Ankhamon was a journalist long before starting the Brethren. He was also a fierce opponent of the queen and the Secretary of State. A mischievous smile appeared on Hatathor's face. He knew what has to do.

***

Vega was already set, and the moons Villio and Umria were brightening the firmament over the city of Misraim. The interplay of different lights on the sky of Lyra was fascinating, as always. It was already night when the military helicopter of Hatathor hovered over the needle-shaped building in the Tehuti mountains. The helicopter lights were not on, and it was in no-transmission mode with the Lyra forces. Hatathor was on a personal visit, which was equal to treachery according to Ehsis. But Hatathor was now fed up with constant surveillance by two state-nannies—Hathor and Ehsis.

This place was known as the Tekhenu. It was a strong base of the brethren of Awaken Consciousness. A white flag stained with blood was flying on top of it. Every year, the flag was changed when all brethren stained their hands in their blood and marked the flag. The ritual started to show others that brethren were united in blood and would die together if attacked.

They were famous as Brethren, but they had a sizable female population. Although the people of the group wore shabby clothes and had faces with strange tattoos, they were armed with weapons. Warnings were issued from the Tekhenu. "You are warned. If you land without permission, your helicopter will be destroyed, and you will become a slave of Master Ankhamon, son of Heka," came a voice from below.

General Hatathor contacted the tower.

"Major General Hatathor here. I come in peace. I want to talk to Ankhamon," he spoke with authority.

A woman with a broken tooth and tattoo on her face turned and looked at her master.

"Master, shall we allow the military helicopter to land here?" she asked hesitantly.

The man thought for a moment. "Who is on board?" the master asked.

"General Hatathor!" she said skeptically.

The master smiled mischievously and nodded his

head in affirmation.

General Hatathor came out of his helicopter in a blue dress with a red cape, a mandatory part of the military uniform of the Kingdom of Akhom. He looked at the Tekhenu from the ground till the top. He was asked to hand over any weapons, which he did, and he stepped towards the door, which looked like the mouth of some space creature.

Hatathor was taken by an elevator at the top of the building. As he came out of an elevator, he entered a large, dimly lit hall. Incense was burning behind the elevated metallic structure, giving the entire atmosphere a murky appearance. The Brethren's master was sitting in it like a ghostly apparition. He was a bearded person, with black eyes, pierced ears, and a tattoo in the middle of his forehead with a picture of a semi-closed eye in a vertical position. He was wearing some beastly hide and helmet with a laser weapon installed on it.

"Welcome, general. Finally, someone from the south came to see us!" he said in a sarcastic tone. Hatathor said nothing, but looked around on both his right and left side. There were around twenty men there, all watching Hatathor's every move. "I am General Hatathor. I come here in peace," Hatathor said while walking.

"Hahaha, peace is a deceptive word from the mouth of a general," Ankhamon laughed. "These men on your right and left are my assassins. They are trained to fight generals like you. You are here. What a day indeed!" he shouted.

"Sambi!

Sambiii!

Sambiiiii!"

Ankhamon was calling his man. Each time he called the name, the tone increased.

"Yes, my lord?" Sambi appeared out of nowhere.

"Note this day. We will celebrate it every year," Ankhamon ordered.

Sambi moved a gadget on his wrist, and the gadget transformed into a multi-layered device. Then Sambi entered some numerals in every level of the device. Strange beeps were generated, and the device became a wristwatch, like before.

Ankhamon gave a signal through his eyes to one of his men sitting close to him. The man stood and left a chair for Hatathor. "Sit down, general," he motioned to him.

Hatathor did not sit, but said: "I need your help!"

Ankhamon laughed like a snorting pig and said, "The most trained general of the kingdom of Akhom is here asking for my help?" He seemed surprised, and then laughed. With him laughed all who were present.

"What do you want, general? Just say it," he asked curiously.

Hatathor said cautiously, "I want to talk with you in private."

"What makes you think, general, that we will help you? We are the brethren, bound in a single conscious-ness. We are pure, and we are the ones who left the filthy politics of the kingdom. We are enjoying life here in the mountains. We grow our food, make our own medicines, and even weapons," Ankhamon reminded Hatathor. "It is top secret," he said impatiently.

"Very well, Hatathor. All leave. Only me and the general," Ankhamon ordered. All left the room.

Ankhamon left his seat and came down. He started walking around Hatathor while he stared at his antics. "I know you were a journalist. I have also heard you were also a good hacker. I want your help to get data related to the HSS," Hatathor said. Ankhamon laughed again. "A servant of a kingdom like you could get all the data from...girls—Hathor and Ehsis," he said snidely. Hatathor realized he would have to first clear the air. "They sabotaged the data. It's no longer available. That is why I need your help," Hatathor said weakly. "I lost my father in the last mission bound to Earth. I heard many stories from my mom and others, but now I want to know more—the truth," Hatathor pleaded. Ankhamon's mannerisms changed. He softened. "Who was your father?"

"Seth. He died on Keb, supposedly helping the mighty Usir," Hatathor replied weakly.

"Ah, I see. Well, boy, the truth could be bitter," he said darkly. "Hathor is a cunning woman. She and her father, they divided our nation, weakened our kingdom internally by concocting lies and distorting history. She was the one who intentionally brought the disease from Keb to our planet. What else do you expect from that cursed woman?" he explained.

Hatathor turned and looked at Ankhamon. "What are you saying? She was the one who brought the disease intentionally on our planet?" he asked blankly. "Yes." Ankhamon stepped back and moved back to his throne to sit on it. "I have proof of everything I said," he said, smiling. Things were not adding up.

"But the disease reappeared due to the crew member Amenhotep," Hatathor said.

"That is what we were told publicly. The truth is far more bitter. I was the one who took the interview of several girls involved in the mission, before the disease symptoms appeared in Amenhotep. They told me that some died during the flight back to Lyra. It means the plague was spreading. But Hathor continued her flight —she should have stopped somewhere. I lost my family because of these two, Hathor and Ehsis. Because of their mistake, my sons contracted the disease. Only my daughter survived. My home is still in Sutekh now. I could not bear the pain of this loss, so I spoke out, and Ptah tried to make a deal with me," Ankhamon said miserably. "Can you show me what evidence you have?" Hatathor asked.

"I hacked the data of HSS long ago. I know what shit they tell others and what is the truth. But what will you give me in return?" Ankhamon inquired, looking into his eyes. Hatathor was silent.

"I even know when Seth died," Ankhamon played another card.

"What!" Hatathor could not believe what he had heard. He had him this time. "You owe me if you can

321

tell me the truth," Hatathor said, sounding desperate. Ankhamon moved his hand to give a sign to follow him.

Hatathor followed. They went to another room full of data items, like newspapers and files. Ankhamon took out a data disk and placed it on the computer. He spent some time doing data mining, and then he executed some commands.

"Look here. This is the list of the crew members of the mission to Keb. Most of the men died because of mysterious diseases, even when they were on Keb. Look at the time of their death. Seth, your father, died late at night. The location of his death was near the pyramid. Usir died eight hours after that, in triage. This is all in data. The women lied that Seth, your father, died in helping Usir, and they fell into the pit. There is something they were hiding, my friend," Ankhamon explained. "The disease didn't reappear when they landed on Lyra. They carried the virus with them and brought it to our Lyra. It spread out because of the son of Hathor. Look at the data. The birth of Heru is even after Usir. This is quite mysterious. How come we were not told about this? All this time, Ehsis and Hathor told us that the queen's son died on Keb. But in fact, he died when they were returning to Lyra. It means she brought the plague to our land. She did all this intentionally. She is not worthy of being called a queen." Ankhamon stopped.

Hatathor's mind was spinning. He had been told that his father, Seth, died while saving Usir. The two were killed in an accident on the spot. Why was he misinformed all this time? Why were his mother and grandparents misinformed?

"Ankhamon, are you sure this is the HSS-related crew?" he asked again.

"Yes. Yes. I knew they were lying, but I could not make it public because I was also a citizen. But I am telling you because you are the son of Seth," Ankhamon said in a miserable tone. Hatathor lost the ground under his feet. So many lies since his childhood. He was cursing himself for not contacting Ankhamon before. "What a curse Hathor and Ehsis are!" Hatathor exclaimed in a fury.

"Now you know the truth. What will you give me?" Ankhamon said.

Hatathor thought. "I will do whatever you say. I no longer support Hathor," he said.

"Brother Hatathor, together we will make this country strong again. We will unite the nation again. But make me the king," Ankhamon laid out his demand. Hatathor was stumped. "We have another major problem," Hatathor said.

"What problem?" Ankhamon asked, slightly disappointed.

"Ehsis and Hathor are planning to send the human to Keb to bring back more curses!" he announced.

"They should not do such stupid things. Already we are short of men due to the mistake of these two women," the man said worriedly.

"My priority is to save Lyra. I will destroy the HSS.

Nobody can stop me now," Hatathor said. Ankhamon smiled mischievously.

"Beware, child. The queen can murder anyone. She is above the law!" Ankhamon warned.

Hatathor nodded. "I may come back," he said, and left abruptly. He came out of Tekhenu, went inside the chopper, and started the engine. The words of Ankhamon were resounding in his head like a cymbal.

He pressed some buttons on the panel, and a box started blinking on the screen, waiting to hear the password. Hatathor pronounced the shibboleth, and a compartment opened. He took out a big briefcase from a hidden compartment and opened it. The briefcase had a secret weapon that he had designed himself. The weapon could be worn as a sleeve. It was still under development phase, and had not been revealed even to the military high command. Hatathor had planned to show it to Hathor and gain her favor to become a full-rank general. He put it on his sleeve, and it detected the user.

"User: Major General Hatathor," the device announced.

*It is working fine*, he thought. Hatathor pressed few buttons and checked the batteries. The chopper took off vertically upwards; he was heading towards the Benben pyramid to ask some crucial questions.

\*\*\*

Hours had passed since the conclusion of the meeting. However, the military command was still dazed and confused by the turn of events. Meanwhile, the Secretary of State and Queen Hathor left the High Council meeting room to deal with other national issues and future challenges. The senior military command was still discussing the matter at hand and its needless secrecy. Some of the personnel openly expressed their displeasure regarding the meeting. In their minds, they believed that if one matter was off-limits, several other issues would also be well above their pay grade. There was a clear divide and trust issues between them and these two women.

Dr. Kityr—the head of the Kingdom Health and Safety department—excused himself, as he was busy in some interplanetary virology conference. The generals were anxious, and were still in their meeting room. Some wanted to discuss further. According to a few serious and old generals, what Hathor and Ehsis were planning was akin to jeopardizing the very fabric of the society. General Lukmas disagreed with this.

"I don't think so. No need for this meeting, as far as I am concerned. Queen Hathor's orders are binding. Our job is not to interfere with her decisions, although we can offer her suggestions. As we can see today, she did not pay heed to our words. If anything, today's meeting has specified our status as merely a peacekeeping force. That is the long and short of it. Besides, I need to clear the facility for launch by this date. I am too busy today for more meetings. See you later," he exclaimed hurriedly, and left.

"We will see you later. Very well then, shall we?"

he said to the others.

General Eli smirked at his attitude. They saw Lukmas leave in his vehicle, disappearing from their sight after a few moments. Now they could start their all-men meeting, as the two most powerful ladies of the kingdom had planned something which could threaten the male population. "Thank you, friends, for staying and discussing further. Major General Hatathor, commander of weaponry design, has also gone out quickly, and he hasn't returned yet. He raised many pertinent concerns. Maybe he will come back soon, but we cannot wait longer," General Dodvan said to the others. The other generals standing also nodded; however, general Hatathor was missing in the ranks. They needed to invite him to the meeting, as he was a key player in this matter.

"You all know that this situation is developing fast. It's prime time to act and do what is right and just. Only for this specific purpose, I called in this second meeting of gentlemen only," he explained.

The opening note was the tip of the iceberg. Every person who was present in the room felt the urge to voice his opinion. For the military high command, the queen and Secretary's attitude was unfair and uncalled for, even though Ehsis had played a major role in most military command decisions and sensitive situations. Her stand on this matter was different.

General Eli, Head of Internal Affairs and Security, shook his head and said, "I cannot believe that I would live to see a day when we listen to such nonsense as what I heard back there. A place known for its un-holiness, diseases, and curses suddenly turned into a tourist spot. Wow, what a plan. Send an earthling back to Earth to bring the antidote." Others nodded in agreement.

"Are we so stupid that a human can make a fool out of us?" another commented. There were some murmurs. "How about we kill the human? We make it look like a suicide in the police station. No human, no travel to Keb!" proposed General Oseria, Commander of Land Forces. All paused for the moment.

"That is one viable option. This way, both queen and Secretary would not suspect anything," Oseria said further. "But remember, if we fail in this attempt, the queen will intensify the human's security, and this would become even more difficult to attempt the second time," he said cautiously. "The queen is too old now. It's better that I convince her she must reconsider her decision. Otherwise, if that human brought us more viruses, I am afraid another problem would arise. Ehsis is not letting her see reason," Oseria said.

"I have a feeling that something is being hidden from us. Why was the information on HSS trips not made public?" General Eli pointed out. The question was hanging in the air.

"How about we all go and talk to Hathor?" one general said.

"Useless! She won't listen to us anymore."

"Then what shall we do?" another question came.

"The clock is ticking. We cannot wait to gather

intelligence data. Just execute the plan which we think is just," General Popious said. All eyes were on him.

"Kill the human. He is the bone of contention!" another suggestion came.

"We are the military...the only military Akhom has. The queen and her Secretary will reconcile with the situation if there is no option left," he said assuredly. "If the Art Heru kingdom tracking unit is installed in thehuman's hand, then we can hunt him down!" The other generals laughed in guttural voices.

"But there are some like Lukmas or Kityr. These people are still supporting every move of Ehsis," came one voice. "That is why they are not here," someone else snapped.

"Remove the queen!" General Popious, Commander of Naval Forces, suggested.

"What?" all others in the room shouted in surprise. The generals looked nervous and thoughtful at the same time. "You mean, rebellion?" someone said.

"Yes! We remove the two women and install Ankhamon as the new king," he said firmly.

"But this is dangerous. A civil war might happen, and some of the battalions will not surrender," one said.

"Fear, my friends—fear, if people came to know that Hathor is bringing another virus to Lyra using the human. Would they accept this act? No, we will inculcate fear in their hearts. Then we will be the saviors. We imprison the queen and Ehsis. The only question is, who will fill the vacuum of power?" Oseria laid out the plan. "Make Ankhamon our new leader," Popious suggested the alternative. "That journalist?" someone confirmed

Everyone looked at each other.

"But he is a cult leader!" one old general said.

Popious commented further: "That is the power of a cult. People are always afraid of them. Ankhamon will do as we advise him, and we will make him our puppet. I do not want to retire too soon," he said, laughing.

"What if Hathor and Ehsis take shelter on some other planet and try to stop us?" one general mentioned his fears. "My friends, for your country and planet, you have to make such decisions," he said firmly. "We will go and talk to Hathor one last time. If she refuses, then we will dethrone her by force under article 321(d) and send her to Keb, along with the human," one laughed and said in a determined manner. "General Lukmas and General Kityr will not support us. What will we do with them?" Osevia asked.

"We will neutralize all threats to the kingdom. Such people are a threat. We will impeccably execute the plan. The plan is to make it look like Brethren attacked and took over the capital. We will play in the background. The supporters of the queen will get a surprise. Those who resist too much will be court-martialed or killed," he explained.

"We should negotiate with Ankhahom on the terms and conditions first," Popious said. Suddenly, General Eli received a message on his device. "Gentlemen, the queen has ordered police to remove Al-Khidr from the police station and to the Benben," he announced. The men looked at each other as if their conversation had been leaked. Popious said, "Act fast, before it's too late!"

# Chapter 22

# The Death Squad

AL-KHIDR and Nefertiti were strolling in the garden along the river Iteru. He was no longer considered a thief, and soon he would return to Earth.

It was a starry night, and sky looked ravishing. Al-Khidr had to wait until the queen and her grand-vizier Ehsis made everything ready. Meanwhile, he was telling Nefertiti what he would do when he got back to Earth.

# CHAPTER 22. THE DEATH SQUAD

"When I go back, I will have to adjust to new normal life. My friends and relatives will ask questions about my sudden disappearance, for sure." Nefertiti was listening with interest.

"I will go to Baghdad and inform Caliph everything that happened here," he said to himself, but then laughed at this madness. "What?" Nefertiti asked.

"What if the Caliph Al-Ma'mun takes me as a lunatic and put me in observation? Nay, this won't work. I have to hide the story of this journey from people who know me. They will not understand unless they experienced it. I guess the only reasonable idea is to keep the information to myself and go about business as usual. All I can say is that I was visiting the Ethiopian region to find some rare herbs for my new medicine experiment, but returned unsuccessful—yeah that should be a wonderful story for them."

Nefertiti laughed. She was thinking about something else. "How long you will take to come back?" Nefertiti asked. "Will you miss me?" Al-Khidr asked.

"Maybe—indeed, yes," she said "You know, ever since you are here, I started liking Earth. In police, most of the time, we are busy and get little chance to go for an outing and movies. But ever since I started talking to you, I feel like it's all a movie. A never-ending story—our story." She looked into Al-Khidr eyes. "Did you like story of Alladin and the Magic Lamp?"

"Yes, but where did he purchase that carpet?" Nefertiti asked.

"Hahaha, that was a magical carpet, not a machine!" Al-Khidr said.

"Hahaha, oh really!" Nefertiti laughed.

"I wish I could take you with me to Earth. I can make a nice tajine for you. My mom taught me how to cook," Al-Khidr said. "Ah, tajine is food? The name itself sounds delicious!" Nefertiti said. "I like you. You are a man of your word. You made a promise to the queen that you will bring the cure. She believed in you and Ehsis, too. You know, when you said that it's a promise like words on stone, I felt like you were telling the whole Lyra...Can you make one more promise? To me only?" Nefertiti said. Today she was damn romantic.

"Yes. What?" Al-Khidr asked in his own style.

"Don't forget me when you are back in your world. I know I am not very beautiful, but I am good at heart," Nefertiti said. "You did so much or me. You believed in me. How can I forget about you?" Then he pointed at his heart and said: "You live here!" Nefertiti hugged him with joy. She had found true love.

Suddenly, Al-Khidr felt pain in his lower left hand. He pulled his hand towards his chest and said in agony, "Argh...so much pain...I ask you if you can help me in getting rid of it."

"Oh, I'm sorry...what happened?" Nefertiti exclaimed. "I wish I can help, but you have to wait till tomorrow morning, as the staff of the tracking unit installation might have gone already," Nefertiti replied with a sorry face.

# CHAPTER 22. THE DEATH SQUAD

Suddenly she remembered something, and she ran towards her vehicle, which was parked at a distance.

"I have a first-aid box in the vehicle. It has an instant pain removing spray. I'll be right back," Nefertiti shouted while running towards her vehicle. Al-Khidr waited for a while, but she didn't return. After a few minutes, the pain went away. Al-Khidr was better now, but still he felt heavy in his mind.

*Nefertiti? Where is she now? She went to her vehicle to bring some painkiller spray, Al-Khidr wondered.* A zapping sound was heard, and a laser shot just past by his shoulder. Someone missed the aim. Al-Khidr realized that someone was shooting at him. He turned and saw the silhouette of two men running towards him and taking aims. Al-Khidr saw some big rocks nearby, and he leapt towards the rocks. Again, the laser shots were fired and a loud boom was heard.

He was saved again. The laser shot hit the rock instead of him. There were no light bulbs, but he could see the shadows; the assassins were moving fast towards him. Why on earth, someone wants to kill me?

One assailant jumped, and he reached directly over the rock, behind which Al-Khidr was hiding. That was the moment! Al-Khidr threw sand into the assassin's eyes, and the latter dropped his gun. Luckily, the gun stuck between the rocks. He was shouting in pain. By this time, another assassin also arrived, and he took aim at Al-Khidr. Al-Khidr was still on the ground, and the wind was blowing towards him. He could not throw sand again. "Oh God, what shall I do? Save me, Lord," he beseeched. A laser shot was heard, and the second assassin was shot dead. It was Nefertiti who was aiming now.

Al-Khidr ran and reached the vehicle. "Where were you?" yelled Al-Khidr.

Nefertiti looked at Al-Khidr and said, "Run, they are not only two!" Nefertiti got into her vehicle and opened the latch from the back. Al-Khidr climbed into the hovering vehicle, which was ascending fast into the air. Some shots were fired from the ground, but they missed Al-Khidr.

"Looks like your life is in danger. They were after you," said Nefertiti, who was gathering her breath to speak. "What did I do? Why did they wanted to kill me?"

"When I went to the car, I received the call from Secretary Ehsis, who instructed me to transfer you to the Benben tonight. The queen wanted me to ensure your safety." "What! What's going on?" Al-Khidr asked nervously. "I don't know." Nefertiti pulled the lever, and her vertically lifted police vehicle got the wings on the sides of it. The vehicle was transformed into a plane. The plane started maneuvering like a bat over the high-rise building and skyscrapers. They were chased by another plane, which was targeting them and firing red laser beams. However, Nefertiti was a formidable foe for them and was diligently maneuvering the craft.

She was moving towards the royal Benben pyramid. The people were watching the chase and firing through windows and the ground below. The pilot of the opponents must have the same military-level skills, as Nefertiti's aircraft received a shot at the engine and it started giving black smoke. Luckily, they were right above the river Iteru. Nefertiti opened the hatch and said to Al-Khidr, "Jump into the river. I'll meet you soon!"

Al-Khidr looked below. For him, it was too high, but he closed his eyes and jumped into the river.

Nefertiti continued to fly the descending and damaged plane just to distract the pursuing assassin's aircraft. The opponents' plane realized that Al-Khidr was not on board, so they stopped following Nefertiti's plane and went after Al-Khidr. Nefertiti shouted, "Damn you, rascals!"

Al-Khidr was inside the river water, and it was reflecting the moonlight. The enemy aircraft had located him, but had difficulty in pinpointing Al-Khidr's position in water. They started firing laser shots on the river and the water started warming up.

Nefertiti took a turn and flew up and went towards the enemy aircraft. Once she reached high enough, she turned off her engine and glided her plane for a head-on-collision with the enemy's plane.

The enemy's plane was firing on Al-Khidr, who took refuge behind a rock inside the waters of Iteru. He had been saved so far, but couldn't hold his breath much longer. The enemy's plane was firing incessantly. They didn't notice Nefertiti's plane right over them, but Nefertiti jumped into the river just before the crash and the two planes blasted into a huge fireball. The two pilots inside the enemy's plane were burned, along with wreckage of their plane. Nefertiti and Al-Khidr had swum out of the waters. As soon as they came out, Al-Khidr moved forward and kissed Nefertiti and both fell on the sand. She and Al-Khidr were lying on the sand, panting and looking at the stars.

"Thank you, you are always like a god-sent angel, beloved Nefertiti," Al-Khidr said while breathing heavily.

"I am doing my duty. But yeah, I would die before they could harm you," she said with tear-filled eyes.

"What a memorable night!"

A twist of fate; a Lyrian in love with a human, who came from twenty-five light years away.

***

It was not late in the night when Hatathor landed his chopper in Lyra Gardens. He walked towards the great Benben pyramid. The words of Ankhamon were reverberating in his mind.

The Royal guards stopped Hatathor at the checkpoint of the Sphinx.

"General, we do not see an appoinment for a meeting at this hour. Besides that, we need permission from the queen to allow you to enter." "It is an urgent matter related to the security of the kingdom," Hatathor said.

"General, let us get permission first," a guard said.

## Chapter 22. The Death Squad

"As I said, we came here on a matter related to national security, neither can it be delayed till morning, nor can we discuss it through voice messaging." "General, we understand your concerns...but we are also doing our duty, and the protocol must be followed," another guard insisted.

Suddenly the sounds of laser shots being fired on Nefertiti's plane could be heard, which made the guards more nervous.

"Would you wait for fulfilment of protocols if I tell you that spies of Honkira have breached our security and are attacking in full scale soon?" The royal-guards started sweating, and finally gave the security clearance to Major General Hatathor.

*** 

Queen Hathor was sitting on her throne. She was wearing a blue dress and had her crown on her head. Hatathor entered the great Benben hall and knelt. Hathor asked, "What's going on? Why did you come here at this hour? Did Honkira attack? I heard laser shots." "No, Mother. Just a regular police chase after some robbers."

"I see," said Hathor, surprised. "Then what is it that you wanted to tell me about these robbers and made you come here?" "Mother, I have a few requests. I hope you listen to me and consider it. I say that again, reconsider your decision, as it will endanger the life of everyone on Lyra. Also, I want full access to HSS data," Hatathor said.

The queen immediately realized where Hatathor was going. "The data is sealed! It cannot be shared with anyone," she said. "Why is it sealed?" Hatathor said in a bitter tone. "Are you in your senses, Maj. General? You know you cannot defy my decisions," Hathor said.

"I want access to the truth. Why you are sending the human to earth even though everyone is advising the opposite to you? Why did you seal the HSS-related data?" Hatathor burst out emotionally.

"I see a hope in his eyes, and I can tell you that being on so many planets and with the wisdom I have, I know this boy is not lying! I have become hopeful that he will bring the cure for the disease," Hathor said.

Hatathor clenched his fist in rage, and he could see his own reflection in the finely polished black granite.

Hatathor said, "Queen of Akhom! I am afraid I can no longer say yes! I sense you are hiding something— some of your dark secrets. Your decision will open a new portal of chaos in Lyra."

Hathor stood up, enraged. She shouted, "Hatathor, do not cross your limit!" Queen Hathor then went close to the stairs of the throne stage and angrily said, "Hatathor I am warning you. Do not act like your father, Seth. I can sense that fear has taken over your sense of understanding."

Hatathor looked at Hathor and couldn't control himself. "Seth! Why you have mentioned my father? What does this have to do with him?"

Hathor lost her temper completely. Ehsis was not there to control her. She growled, "Seth, your father, had poisoned my husband and unleashed a deadly disease on Lyra. Do not force me to do what I did in my rage with him."

Major General Hatathor, now crying with tears dropping from his eyes, said, "No, no, never! You being the mother, the protector, how could you kill my father?" Hathor said, "Yes, I did, and I will do it again and again for the safety of the Kingdom of Akhom. Seth unleased this disease and killed Usir and the men of our team. I cannot forget what he did to me."

Hatathor said, "How could you do this to me? You turned all my devotion into insignificance! For all these galactic cycles we revered you as a mother, and now you are telling us that all what we learned from you was a bunch of lies. Ankhamon was right! You are a deceiver."

Hathor said, "Sometimes, mothers need to tell lies to make life pleasant for our children. We bear the pain while you live happily."

"You have no children, woman! You are barren!" Hatathor shouted.

Hathor couldn't stand it; she was emotionaly lost too, and stepped back and fell on her throne.

"Go away! Go away Hatathor—don't make me do this," Hathor said in painful voice.

"I will not let you send that human to cursed places. You bought the virus to Lyra, not Seth. You lied, woman. I'll murder that human and destroy your HSS. Al-Khidr will go to Earth over my dead body!"

The queen stood again, and she was really mad at this. "Hatathor, enough. My rage will burn all those who stood against me."

There were twelve Sekhmets inside as queen's royal guards, which moved forward to protect the queen. The cats sensed that the situation was getting out of control. They transformed into more beastly forms and started growling at Hatathor. Their fangs came out. One Sekhmet circled the queen, and some approached Hatathor. "Cats, go to hell!"

Hatathor pressed his sleeve-weapon, and a deflector field was created around him, thrusting the cats away. Some Sekhmets hit the walls and died; some were wounded, and some were back, growling at him.

"Enough!" Queen Hathor shouted.

The surviving Sekhmets stopped and looked back at queen.

Hathor lifted her hand and pressed a button on her bracelet. Her crown-weapon activated and sparks started jumping in the horns of her crown. The sparks were ready to be launched.

"Go away, Hatathor. I relieve you from the military. Ehsis was right; I should have listened to her," the queen said again.

The guards stationed at the Sphinx also entered, and they were looking at Hatathor. They had expected that Hatathor might leave, but Hatathor did nothing. His loyalties were over, and he was in a boiling rage. His mind had been switched off as soon as he learned his father was murdered. He thought that this was probably how his father might had been killed—by electrocution. Hatathor took out a weapon from his pocket, which transformed into a bident.

"You are no longer a queen. Your sins are unforgiveable!" Hatathor shouted.

Hathor stepped back and pressed the button of her bracelet, and electric sparks fell on Hatathor. But nothing happened; he was in his protective shield. He roared and threw his bident towards the queen. The bident went into air; many Sekhmets tried to block it, but the bident hit the queen and the force was so powerful that it pushed her, and she fell behind her throne. The bident had pierced through her belly.

Then he turned, killing the Sekhmets and the guards, too, who were firing laser shots at him. Hatathor was still in the defensive shield, so nothing happened to him. Hatathor walked over and broke their necks. As long as his shield was on, he could not use the laser gun or any other weapon.

Hathor was on the floor behind the throne, bleeding and dying. Hathor had removed her mask, gasping for more air. Her wrinkled face was showing her agony even more. Hatathor leapt forward and killed all the cats which were wounded and not dead yet. The queen was behind the throne, and Hatathor did not have a direct view on her. She pressed one more button on her bracelet, and the Benben pyramid converted into one giant alarm. The alarms could be heard all over the city. Hatathor grew panicked. He went behind the throne to pick up his bident.

The queen stopped her breathing, pretending that she was dead. She was just waiting for someone else to come. Hatathor came closer and said to the queen's body, "Pity of you, Mother, your loyal cats failed in protecting you. Your friend Ehsis also failed in protecting you. No one was here to protect you!" Hathor said nothing.

Hatathor left the place as sounds of approaching sirens were growing. When he came out, he could hear the loud alarms of police, ambulances, and military, all rushing towards the Benben. He ran towards the Lyra gardens and lifted off in his chopper. No one noticed him, as now the entire sky was full of flying vehicles and chopper was rushing towards Benben.

***

Al-Khidr and Nefertiti heard the alarm sound as they were talking near the river after the attack.

Nefertiti sat up and said, "What's happening? The alarm sound is coming from the direction of the Benben pyramid."

They ran towards the Benben pyramid. The police, military choppers, spaceships, and city vehicles were all flying towards it.

"It must be very serious!"

When they reached the pyramid, there were already ambulances, police, and military. The place was cordoned off, and people were gathered outside, crying and shouting: "Long live Mother, Mother!"

"What happened?" she shouted.

"Mother is wounded. Someone attacked her!"

"Oh my God!"

Nefertiti moved through the swarm of people and reached the entrance. She showed her ID and entered the sphinx. She stood in shock. It was a gory scene. There was blood all over. She then entered the Great Hall of the pyramid and found that the royal guards' Sekhmets were dead as well. There were many people around the back of the throne.

Nefertiti rushed behind the throne and saw Queen Hathor lying on the floor, with blood oozing out of her belly. Her head was on the lap of Ehsis, and doctors were all around her.

The medical team was moving gadgets over the queen.

"Her life signature is diminishing...We need help," the doctor announced.

Crying, Ehsis asked, "Who did this to you?" Hathor was weak, but audible, and she said to Ehsis while holding her hand: "Save Akhom. Send the human to Earth. Let my wish be fulfilled!"

Ehsis said, "Yes, Hathor. I will do it. You should not worry."

Hathor lifted her hand and gave to Ehsis her signet, which she had already taken off of her finger. "This ring is key!"

"What?" Ehsis asked, but Hathor was too weak to

respond. She closed her eyes and was feeling too weak to talk. "Do something!" Ehsis shouted.

"We started a blood transfusion. But...a lot of her blood was lost..."

The queen opened her eyes, smiled one last time, and her glance was towards the heavens. Her eyes were motionless, and she was not blinking. She breathed out. "No, no, that's not happening." Ehsis cried.

Nefertiti came out of the pyramid. She was crying, and Al-Khidr held Nefertiti in his arms. "Mother is gone! She is dead!"

***

Hatathor was inside his apartment, in a room where the light was off. There was no one at the apartment. He was smoking and just looking outside through the window towards the statue down in the square. His phone, his beeper, his other devices were ringing, beeping. But he was not picking them up. Generals were trying to contact him, but did not want to talk to anyone.

Sometimes he laughed, and sometimes he erupted in crying. He was going through an emotional rollercoaster. The statues in the square were of Usir and Seth, both standing with their backs touching each other. In front of them were several fountains, and the statues were installed the middle of a water pond. Multicolored lights were illuminating the whole place.

"Lies, lies, all lies," Hatathor shouted. "She killed my father, but when she first visited us, she said, 'I came here to kiss you!' " . Hatathor remembered when he was still young, and Hathor came to their place to pay homage to Seth and meet his family. It was a newspaper thing. A lot of journalists were around. All were taking pictures, and he was happy, at the time. Actually, he missed his father, but he never said that.

He stood up and started looking at the pictures of his father, mother, grandparents. All dead. They smiled back at him.

Hatathor smiled too, but then erupted again in crying. "I am sorry, Seth. I saluted your murders! But I repent to you. I killed Hathor. I will kill all those who killed you. I will not spare Ehsis, either. But is it enough? Just killing her would not give much pain." Hatathor was talking in a frenzy to himself. "I will kill her after making her fail. I will see the genuine pain on her face when I kill the human; I'll make her suffer." After all, they had killed Seth and pretended they were innocent.

"Murderous women! I will wipe their name out. I will destroy all they have created. I will explode HSS—no one can stop me now!" Hatathor stopped crying. He had found the purpose of his life.

# Chapter 23

# The Key

IT was morning in Misraim city, and there was no
hustle and bustle that day—the city was under curfew.
The queen was murdered, and the fear was that such
an attack could be launched again. Police and rangers
were patrolling in the city. The mode was somber and
future was uncertain.

According to the law, as a secretary of state, Ehsis
was the administrator of the kingdom until the emergency ended and she was sworn in as queen. The emergency declared could last months, as investigations

might take time. There was no information available on the assailants. Police were in the process of gathering information on the attackers. All evidence was gathered, and a period of national morning was announced. But because of security reasons, the burial was delayed until the matter was cleared up.

Ehsis summoned the officers of KIU (Kingdom Intelligence Unit) officials to her office. The current and former generals were sitting on both sides of a table, and Ehsis was leading the meeting. She said, "General Eli—as Head of Internal Affairs and Security, what information do you have?" "Madam Secretary, there are no surveillance recordings inside the Benben. The attackers took the camera recordings with them. Inside the Benben pyramid, there were also no cameras, as the queen considered it a breach of her privacy. So, we do not have any information on who orchestrated this massacre in a planned manner; also, they left no survivors," Eli said.

"How many do you think there were?" Ehsis asked.

"Our forensic teams are examining the evidence. But there was a lot that happened inside the throne room. There were signs of burning, and the queen's belly was cut with a very sharp weapon. The blood samples which we gathered so far are all either of Sekhmets or of the late queen. We don't have any other sample. This was done with very high-level skills, in which the attacker or attackers were not wounded."

"It's a pity that our security system failed and someone among you will be responsible," she said painfully, and looked at generals. "This is not how a most advanced kingdom of galaxies operates! I want all information on communications made during this time. Gather the signatures sent to other planets, especially to those sent to Honkira," Ehsis ordered.

"Madam Secretary, it's done already. The diplomats who wanted to meet you to express their concerns include Honkira as well. I do not think that they did this. They felt sorry for the late queen."

"Is this done by the Brethren?" Ehsis asked.

"Madam Secretary, no significant movement on Tekhenu was reported," a general informed.

"You will be fired, generals, if you do not give meaningful intelligence within a few days," she said sternly to all generals. "I want results and tasks completed on time. All dismissed except Gen. Eli and Gen. Lukmas."

When all left, Ehsis said to Eli, "One thing more: I haven't seen Major General Hatathor yet. I don't want to be annoyed by his presence here. But I need a brief report on his whereabouts yesterday—I hope you understand what I mean," Ehsis instructed him, and then asked him to leave. Now, only Lukmas was in her office. Ehsis said to Lukmas, "General Lukmas, I want to give some specific tasks to you. It was the will of Queen Hathor to send the human to Earth as soon as possible. I want you to go now to the HSS facility and check everything. I'll be visiting in few hours. I want to keep this plan top secret." "Madam Secretary, I want to assure you we are doing all what we can do. The facility is cleaned, and the power supply was restored last month. The queen had asked me to work on it at top secret level. I summoned some trustworthy staff from the Galactic Exploration Unit, and they checked the status of the equipment. Some of the equipment is defunct, so we did some replacements and updates. However, the access to Hall of Stars is denied. The queen told us we should wait until she comes over there," Lukmas said.

"I see. Our Queen Hathor was a visionary and had great foresightedness. I will visit today to check myself," Ehsis said. "No military or police officer is allowed to enter the HSS facility without my permission," Ehsis said further. When the general left, Ehsis ordered her staff, "Call Nefertiti and the human here."

***

"Hatathor!...he is such a stupid person. He has complicated the whole situation. He left no choice for us. He always liked to do something either hidden or extra in his rage," General Dodvan said.

"Generals, I still don't understand why Hatathor killed her," another general added his view.

"Luckily, I arrived at Benben before Kityr and Lukmas and took out the camera recordings. Had they been seen by anyone else, Hatathor would be hunted by all security forces of the kingdom," General Popious said.

The generals were meeting in their den and arguing with each other on a next plan of action. "Here, you will see all."

Popious inserted the recorder into the device, and the security video was played. All watched with an element of surprise. "There must a reason why Hatathor went to this extreme. He did it personally by going there." All nodded in agreement.

"We have an emergency situation here. We cannot allow power to be transferred to Ehsis. She already had suspicions about Hatathor. I am afraid that our names would be exposed too, in case Ehsis senses something and interrogates Hatathor. Do you understand?" General Eli said. "This could have been a perfect clandestine operation, but sadly, Hatathor is such a pain in the ass," Popious added. "Besides that, four of our men were killed by police. Two were killed near the river, and two others died in a plane crash. Apparently, four men failed! Police saved the alien-human and killed our men. If Ehsis discovers their identities, then what will happen? I can imagine your hanging corpses at the obelisk square," Oseria said in a sarcastic tone.

"Sir, Master Ankhamon is live on video call now," one trustworthy lieutenant announced.

All eyes were on the screen to see Master Ankhamon, after a long time.

"Aakhu Neter un (blessings of God be on you), Generals. Greetings from Ankhamon to you all!"

"Blessings of God will soon come to you, Ankhamon—would you like to be the king of Akhom?"

Ankhamon laughed and said, "Generals, if you think

that for the survival of our kingdom, I could do anything, then I am happy to be the king. But you have to do it as soon as possible. Ehsis is a famous huntress," Ankhamon said with a mischievous smile. He knew that the coup leaders now had no other option left. Ankhamon closed the video call and smiled.

I will use them as my puppets, Ankhamon thought to himself.

***

Nefertiti and Al-Khidr reached a highly secured bunker in which Ehsis was staying. It was no different from a regular office, but had many displays around her desk. Ehsis was thinking deeply in her office. She was sweating, perplexed, and she was moving the red ruby signet on her finger that was given to her by the queen. Al-Khidr and Nefertiti entered the room, and Nefertiti greeted Ehsis.

"I came to know that last night, you were attacked and chased by an aircraft before the queen was murdered?" Ehsis asked.

"Yes, Madam Secretary," Nefertiti said. "They were actually after Al-Khidr," she said while looking at Al-Khidr.

"I see," Ehsis said. "I now realize that we need to send Al-Khidr as soon as possible. This is what Hathor advised. There are internal forces which are stopping her." Ehsis looked at Al-Khidr and Nefertiti and said, "I must tell you what has happened on Keb before you leave our planet. It is your choice that you loved to help us. I am glad that you preferred to save a dwindling species—I mean, us."

There were tears in her eyes. "Hathor and I tried our best to make our society intact and come to terms with the disease. However, our efforts are breaking apart. There is sense of displeasure in our army, and soon there could be a full-scale coup here. It is better that you go and never return," Ehsis said to Al-Khidr.

Nefertiti looked flabbergasted and anxious. She kept silent, and glanced at Al-Khidr with tearful eyes, waiting for his reply.

"No! I promised to the late queen. I will fulfil my promise. I now know there is life beyond our planet, and my goal is to help the life, not to destroy it. You may be different inside, but you look like us. I cannot step back now...the sphere I discovered in the pyramid was kept hidden for ages. I got it by the will of God, only because he wanted me to come to your planet," Al-Khidr said.

Ehsis and Nefertiti looked at each other.

"Very well. I see your determination," Ehsis said, and opened her desk drawer and took out a brief-case. She put it on her lap, and Al-Khidr and Nefertiti couldn't see what was inside. Ehsis took out something and place it on the top of the desk. The thing started rolling and then become static. It was the jump-sphere—the artifact from the Giza Pyramid.

Al-Khidr looked at sphere and at Ehsis.

"I wanted to check whether you are just whimsical, or determined!" Ehsis said. "This device cannot be left unattended," Ehsis added, and as she was looking at the sphere, she continued explaining: "Yes, it is the same sphere which brought you here. As soon as Hathor realized you arrived on Lyra with the sphere, she ordered me to secure the device and take it out from the police station."

She then turned the briefcase and showed them the rest. There, five jump-spheres were meticulously placed in secured positions in the briefcase. "These were the most important thing for us."

Al-Khidr and Nefertiti looked at each other.

"Keb was a beautiful planet. We wanted to stay there longer, but God's will was different. We made pyramids and monuments and carved out our galactic journey on the stones. When you go back, you will see Keb through our eyes, as eyes cannot see what mind doesn't know!" Ehsis said. "I am very happy, Madam Secretary, that you have faith in my words. My promise, though, is mere words which are spoken, but they are etched on the stone. I will fulfil my promise!" Al-Khidr said.

"The thing you got from pyramid was made by us. You were brought to us because we programmed it. We left it on Earth. Two of our diligent crew members were sick, and we hoped that they may recover and come back. So, we gave them two spheres. Looks like you got one of them and activated it with Amris."
"Amris?" Al-Khidr said.

"Yes, it must be a piece of Amris which was left with the sphere to reactivate this device, Maft-Shespt—

the jump sphere...This is the name of this device in Lyrian language. Charged with exotic matter, it can move you from one plane of stars to another. The fabric of time and space will be breached by activating this device, but it's a very special procedure. Most of the scientists who had designed it died from the disease long ago. Hathor and I know only the activation procedure and protocols, as I was trained at HSS. Since it's dangerous to have such a device, it was a top secret project, and Hathor decided as queen to seal all records and close the Hall of Stars."

Al-Khidr was repeating the words: "Maft-Shespt...Maft-Shespt..."

Ehsis paused for a while.

"There is a danger as well. A slight disturbance can lead to different results. The sphere creates a non-linear trajectory in space and time. A slight disturbance may bring you to an inhospitable or an unbearable planet. You may die if this happens, as not all planets have air which we and humans can breathe. I hope you get enough from me to reconsider everything," Ehsis said further.

"I have given a promise to a queen. I will fulfil it," Al-Khidr said.

Nefertiti held the hand of Al-Khidr and looked at him admirably. "There is a compartment in the sphere. Can you see this hole?" Ehsis showed Al-Khidr a small hole in the sphere. "If you put a needle in it, a compartment will appear. We need only five to six leaves to test against the virus. You take the leaves, roll them up and put them in this compartment. They will be safe as long as the sphere is not charged again. So, you have to protect it. To start the sphere back, you need to put the piece of Amris in it. I have placed an Amris piece inside," Ehsis advised further.

Then Ehsis took out a needle from her drawer and pressed it into the hole in the sphere. The sphere gave a clicking sound, and then she held the lower part into her hands and moved the top of sphere. The sphere opened from top like a scarab beetle's wings. She moved the covers and they opened more, giving them access to the internal compartment.

"It has place enough to contain the leaves," she said. Al-Khidr learned more secrets of the sphere.

Ehsis ordered a helicopter to be ready to transport Nefertiti, Al-Khidr, and herself to the Hept Sehetch Sheta facility. As the chopper went up into air, Nefertiti and Al-Khidr started looking through the window. After a while, the chopper was flying over the HSS facility. It was all cloudy, but Al-Khidr took little time to recognize it. It was the same place he had arrived less than ten days ago, when he first entered the planet Lyra. The entrance to the docking station for the sphere was on the side of mountains, high above in the clouds.

"This is the place. The sphere took me there," he excitedly said to Nefertiti, who also looked at the place and glanced back at Ehsis. They both nodded head in affirmation.

"Yes. This is Hept Sehetch Sheta—the organization to learn the stars' secrets. This highly secured area was once used by our teams of space explorations," Ehsis informed both.

Al-Khidr excitedly started looking back outside. He could see more of the HSS facility. There was also a pyramid in the middle of the mountains, hidden from sight. They landed on top of a mountain, and after descending some stairs, they were inside an enormous facility. They moved to the main building. General Lukmas, Head of Space Operations, was there to greet Secretary Ehsis.

The hall was brightly lit, and everything looked futuristic by human standards. Many scientists were there, and all were dressed in white coats. They were working on different stations and machines.

"We are checking all services, madam. These scientists here are my most trusted staff now working at Galactic Exploration Unit. For the last few days they were deputed here, solely to make the facility functional again." Lukmas announced. "Good job, everyone. The Kingdom of Akhom is proud of your services. I was also one of you—a scientist here. I am very glad that you are doing this urgent work." Ehsis appreciated the scientists and moved on.

They walked and entered another long, tilted, grand corridor, which led them to a hall. The hall had a door of metal, and it was huge. There was something written in Lyrian over the door. Al-Khidr was surprised to read the title.  It was written in the same script and style, as was written on the jump-sphere.  It read: "As above, so below."  The walls surrounding the hall had images of different galaxies, carved by artists with aesthetic sense.  "Madam, there is one problem.  We don't have the access to this hall."

"This door will lead us to Usekh-t Sehetch—the Hall of Stars," Ehsis said, and she was looking at the door.  She was going through a flashback of memories until she came back to the present, and heard Lukmas, who was saying: "The door is sealed with royal decree, and the security lock is installed on it.  We are not allowing to unlock it unless Madam Secretary allows a cryptologist to do so," General Lukmas said.

"The security lock?  I order you to open it.  Show it to the master cryptologist," Ehsis ordered, while still lost in memories.  After a few minutes, some staff arrived with bags.  They went to the door and examined the lock.  Then opened their bags, and Al-Khidr noticed they were full of buttons of all kinds.

"It is not a normal numerical key code.  It looks like a device; some sort of gadget.  We are afraid that it could trigger a weapon," the head of cryptologists said.  "I understand," Ehsis said.

She knew well what lay behind that door, and why Hathor had ordered it to be locked in this manner. Before HSS was closed, this was one of the most important control rooms.

Ehsis moved forward and looked at the lock.  It looked like a rhombus-shaped opening, and she thought about what the key to this door could be. Ehsis had to think fast, before it was too late. There must be a key to this door. Hathor had mentioned no key code before, as far as her memory went. "Oh God. I wish Hathor was alive."

In rage, she clenched her fist and punched the palm of her other hand.

"Ouch!" There was a little blood oozing out."

Nefertiti and Al-Khidr came forward to help her. A military officer rushed for a first-aid box.

"What happened, Madam?" Nefertiti asked. "Oh, this ring which Hathor gave me! Its gem is sharp." Why was Hathor wearing it? Ehsis thought. Then suddenly, it came to her mind. Is this the key? Ehsis examined the ring closely. From the size, it looked like a normal stone. She asked for help from the cryptologist.

The team arrived and examined the ring. There was a code printed on it at yocto-scale level. "We can see some sort of code printed on the gem," they said. Ehsis now knew what she was looking for was right in her hand. She took the ring back and wore it, then she made a fist and pushed the gem on ring into the lock, and it was a perfect fit. Ehsis gave a little turn to her fist; the lock gave some beeping sounds, and the door was unlocked. A voice said: "Access granted to Queen Hathor."

\*\*\*

"Ankhamon gave his consent, but he does not want

to topple the government using the brethren. He wanted the coup to be orchestrated by us," Popious said, repeating what Ankhamon said in his own subtle style. The generals were back in their discussion inside the control room and were discussing the options. "What shall we do now? Ehsis is asking me about Hatathor. We are contacting him, and he is not answering. He didn't attend the meeting this morning with Ehsis. She is suspicious of him. If police or someone else from the military captured him and interrogated him, then he could give out our names," Eli informed the rest. "Ankhamon is a shrewd guy. After all, he was a journalist and a notorious hacker. He will not do anything by himself. He wanted us to create a conducive landscape for his kingship," Dodvan was thoughtfully commenting.

A message arrived at Eli's phone. He read it while all were talking. Eli said to others: "I got the news that Hatathor's chopper is heading towards HSS. Also, an hour earlier, the signature of the chopper assigned to Ehsis was detected by the intelligence unit. Her chopper has already landed at HSS."

Hearing this, Popious said, "It means both Ehsis and Hatathor are now at HSS. We have a favorable coincidence here. The best is that we kill now both Ehsis and Hatathor at HSS and claim that Hatathor had killed Ehsis and the queen. This video is enough for us. We then easily install Ankhamon as new administrator, and the public will accept it easily. Just don't make him king, though!" Popious articulated his thoughts on this matter. "I will mobilize all land forces! Dodvan, you declare military emergency at all border and air space. I will go personally to HSS to wipe out both Ehsis and Hatathor," General Oseria suggested.

"I will go to Tekhenu to bring Ankhamon officially back to the city," Popious said. All agreed on this proposal.

# Chapter 24

# The Hall of Stars

ONCE the door opened, a team of military engineers and scientists went inside. They started disinfecting and cleaning the place. They took half an hour to clean it and check the power supply and functionality of all the equipment. Vega was already set, and the sky was clear. After thousands of years, Ehsis had stepped into this room. Everywhere she looked, she saw people around. Her mind was playing games.

The hall was a facility with many devices and panels. The technology was old, by current Lyrian standards, but still functional. For Al-Khidr, it was way too advanced. "We were trained in this place ages ago," Ehsis said. "I used to sit there. We spent hours working here, contacting other teams on different planets—light years away, working on their missions. That was a time!"

"The disease from earth shook our confidence. We thought we knew everything. But God gave us a new challenge!" Al-Khidr and Nefertiti were listening with interest and silence.

Along the walls, there were many stations and panels. Scientists were sitting there. There were three levels of working stations. Ehsis looked at Al-Khidr and Nefertiti and said, "We shall start now."

Ehsis then went to a key station and pressed some buttons until the panels started blinking, the entire station came to life, and all the scientists present clapped in joy.

Ehsis turned towards Gen Lukmas, his military personnel, and the scientists from Galactic Exploration Unit and addressed them. "General Lukmas, head of Space Operations, diligent military staff, and esteemed scientists! Thank you very much! You did a wonderful job. It is with your incessant help and effort that we can start this ancient machine again. I am proud of you all.

"It was the vision of our late Queen Hathor—the Mother, as you called her—to see this facility functional. You guys have done a wonderful job of replacing the faulty instrumentation with new ones, the old computers with latest Hesb-t systems, and checking everything. I am thankful to you all, and will soon announce the upgrades in salaries and allowances. Long live Akhom."

All the scientists were happy. Lukmas said, "Madam Secretary, thank you for your kind words. Indeed, we liked this work, and thank you having confidence in our team of scientists."

Ehsis turned and said to Al-Khidr, "Now, I will show you space as we view it." She entered some data into the system and pressed the button. She turned and said to Nefertiti and Al-Khidr, "Look behind you!"

They both turned and saw the holographic images of the stars and planets formed over the hexagon that emerged from the floor. Al-Khidr noticed that one side of the hexagon was around the length of six human arms. It was one giant orrery. The hologram of vast galaxies, stars, and planets started rotating and moving in their orbits and spirals. The orrery was created from the database of knowledge which was collected over the years to understand the universe. Al-Khidr was looking at all with awe. The constellations were moving in it like the ghosts. Then Ehsis said to Al-Khidr, "This is Lyra, and here is star Vega. If you descend from star Vega, you will reach your planet— Keb." "Al-Eard!" Al-Khidr exclaimed.

Ehsis said for the image that appeared in hologram. The orrery hologram was showing the calculated trajectory of the wormhole. It was from Lyra to Earth, like a spiraling pathway.

# CHAPTER 24. THE HALL OF STARS

"Of course, you will need the sphere!" Ehsis said to Nefertiti, "Give me Maft-Shespt—the sphere."

Nefertiti took one out from the briefcase, which Ehsis gave her earlier to hold and take care of, and handed it over to her. Ehsis looked at the sphere and then pushed it into a hemisphere socket, which appeared from the machine where she was standing. The socket clamped the sphere and started rotating with high speed. The hologram also followed the rotation and started rotating and changing, and finally, the target was locked on planet Earth. Two tunnels were created from Lyra's spiral down in star layers to Earth, and another was going from Earth back to Lyra. The two tunnels were spiraling, but following different trajectories.

"I programmed the sphere. It will take you to Keb, and will bring you back as well—God willing," Ehsis said to Al-Khidr. "Start the radiation protection sequence," Ehsis ordered the scientists.

Scientists moved forward, asking Al-Khidr to stand in the vertical pod. Al-Khidr did that, and the pod was closed. Then he saw some beams of lights moving over him. He could see Nefertiti, Ehsis, and many scientists around through the window. At first, he felt the pod was getting hot. He started sweating and felt very nervous about it, but then the whole pod was filled up with some smoky gas. He could breathe, but couldn't look outside now.

"The Radiation protection sequence is now completed," the device announced, and the pod opened.

Al-Khidr came out, but collapsed on the floor. Nefertiti and one other scientist helped him to walk, and he sat on a chair. When Al-Khidr came back to his senses, Ehsis said, "The sphere is ready to bring you back."

"You must come back!" Nefertiti said with sobbing eyes. Al-Khidr nodded his head.

***

Ehsis, Nefertiti and scientists were now inside the hall, and the door was locked from inside.

Ehsis said, "We are short on time. Come with me, we will go to the hall of stars."

Ehsis ran till the end of the hall and she opened another door using the queen's key again.

This was the hall of stars. As they passed through the door, the wonder and awe struck them. They were in a huge hall with tapered walls, and stars and galaxies were carved over them. There was only one panel after the door. The floor of the hall was elevated up to knee level and looked like the black granite. Right over the floor hung a metallic ring, which was held there by struts and chains.

Ehsis went to the only panel in the hall and pressed the button. The apex roof started moving, and transferred into eight triangles and opened up. The metallic ring was below the apex.

In the middle of the black floor was an elevated station, at which Ehsis asked Al-Khidr to stand.

367

# Chapter 24.  The Hall of Stars

"The Tepta Sehetch — a tunnel that I showed you in the hologram will now be created above you, and will lead you to Earth. On my mark, you will hold the jump-sphere with the hole side towards the sky."

Al-Khidr nodded his head. He was right under the metallic ring. Ehsis pressed another button, and electric sparks formed on the ring, which first interacted with the pyramid walls and then shot up towards the sky.

He looked up, and saw a tunnel was formed and was going up in the sky, as far as his sight went. Its walls were like fire and steam, rising towards the sky. The light was falling onto his face like lighting, and the whole room was brightened.

"Al-Nafaque bain Al-Nujoom (a tunnel between the stars)!" Al-Khidr uttered in Arabic.

Ehsis came forward and said: "Al-Khidr, you hold the sphere in both hands and an exotic black matter will charge the sphere. We call the black matter Kam-t Nenui. But beware try not to move until the sphere is fully charged. You will know it when all seven symbols become red. Once red you will be lifted towards the sky and will go inside the tunnel".

She showed the same mysterious markings on the sphere carved around the central cavity of the sphere, for whose secret Al-Khidr had traveled from one city to another. Ehsis said, "The tunnel is a breach created in space and time fabric, and it will close soon. We have less time. We need to fill up the sphere with enough black matter so that you go as well as you return. You will now hold the sphere in your hands and keep it above your head. You must return back to Lyra; otherwise, the sphere will start radiating back and can kill you."

Al-Khidr raised the sphere above his head with the hole facing the sky.

Ehsis, Nefertiti, and the remaining scientists were looking at Al-Khidr.

"I love you, Al-Khidr!" Nefertiti said with sobbing eyes. "I will come back, God willing! He will make my promise a truth," Al-Khidr said. Al-Khidr looked around one last time. There were poignant feelings on everyone's face. Then Ehsis said, "May God help us all" and pressed a button.

A burst of intense light formed as an inverted, conical pyramid, which was issuing from the same metallic ring, but now the lower part of the ring, rotated and channeled a stream of black liquid, which was going into the cavity of the sphere, but not spilling out.

A voice echoed in the hall: "Charging sequence initiated. Trajectory locked. Tunnel will close in seven cycles."

Al-Khidr did not know what was going on. His whole body was shaking, and he was sweating. His face and body were shimmering under the light coming from the charging ring. The light was causing something to move inside the sphere. It sounded and shook like it was boiling, but Al-Khidr had no feeling of heat. One of the sphere markings had become red, showing that charging had started. Now he could not move;

otherwise, something terrible could happen. Ehsis received a call from her personal intelligence officer.

"Madam Secretary, an armed convoy of the Brethren of Consciousness has been reported. They are heading towards the Capitol in a military convoy." "What? What the heck they are doing?" Ehsis said to herself. However people in the hall didn't realize the intensity of situation. Ehsis went out of the hall of stars, and General Lukmas called Ehsis as well.

"Madam Secretary, I am afraid that we need to abandon our visit of HSS. Many generals are not picking up their phones. If Ankhamon is moving towards the city in a military convoy, then it's a mutiny!"

"No, general, I had a hunch that something was brewing. I think Hathor found out, and they killed her." "Madam Secretary, I insist you go to some other secure location. Three spaceships are ready here for your escape, as per emergency protocol of the kingdom." Suddenly, laser shots were heard. Nefertiti and the scientists looked at Ehsis. Nefertiti said, "Madam, you look anxious." Ehsis said nothing. She did not want to create panic.

Lukmas called back Ehsis, "Major General Hatathor arrived with arms; he is moving towards the HSS." "Is he alone, or are there more generals with him?"

"We do not know fully, Madam!" Ehsis said to Lukmas, "Give my command to your staff there that stop Hatathor at all costs and neutralize any threats. Decimate the rebels." "But Madam—it's not safe for you to remain here," Lukmas insisted again.

"I have to. I know some are after this place. I am locking myself in the hall until I send the human to Earth," Ehsis said in a determined way. Suddenly, laser shots were heard all around the facility. The hooting was intense, and screams could be heard.

Ehsis received a message: "Madam, Hatathor has gone mad. I don't know why. I say you lock the door."

With a minute, another message arrived: "Madam, my forces cannot stop Hatathor. He has some sort of protective shield. He has entered the facility, and he is heading towards the hall of stars...I cannot come now...heavy fighting going on...I...am stopping rebels outside from entering," Lukmas said in another voice message. Ehsis looked at all and said, "Hatathor wants to destroy this place. Close the first door!" Ehsis roared, and ran out of the hall of stars.

***

Nefertiti ran to the door of the first hall, and with help of other; they closed it. It was a big and solid door, but of special material. A voice in the hall echoed: "The first cycle had competed."

The door of the first hall was locked, and there were only fifteen scientists and ten military staff inside the hall. Only Ehsis and Nefertiti had the guns. The scientists were totally unprepared for this situation.

Ehsis ordered, "You all, take cover!"

There was intense firing going on surrounding the hall of stars and sounds of cries and fires could be heard. "Madam, the force that arrived, they are the rebels dressed in military uniform. They are firing on us and on Hatathor, as well. I advise you before I get killed that you escape through the level three exit door. The door is on your left in the hall, and it will lead you to the tunnel underground and then to a cave in the mountain, which has an opening to abyss. It's not noticeable from top. Three spaceships are ready there. I already informed the pilots. The spaceships have a cloning capability. You can escape now," Lukmas' voice-message said.

"Oh God, what's happening? Is it a full-scale military coup?" Ehsis said to herself. Suddenly, the door was banged loudly. Someone was trying to open it. A new sound could be heard, coming directly from the door, as if something was being placed near the door. Tick-tick-tick. "It is a bomb placed right behind the door," one man shouted.

"Take shelter and take necessary precautions," Ehsis ordered.

Nefertiti and Ehsis were ready to fire as the bomb blasted the door. But the door was not opened.

A voice in the hall echoed: "The second cycle has competed." Then there were two sounds emerging simultaneously.

Tick-tick-tick...Tick-tick-tick... A bunch of ignition devices were installed; the door exploded this time. Hatathor was now inside, and he was inside the hemispherical protective energy shield. Ehsis and others were surprised to see his shield.

"Traitor!" Ehsis shouted. "Murderous bitch!" Hatathor

shouted. "Your era of lies and deception is over!" Hatathor was holding the head of a personal guard of Ehsis. He threw the head, which landed and rolled at her feet.

"I didn't murder anyone!" Ehsis shouted back.

"You forgot my father, Seth! You'll pay for your sins now," Hatathor growled.

"You are as stupid as your father was!" she shouted back. "I will kill you, bitch!" he growled again.

A voice echoed in the hall: "The third cycle has completed." "Don't fight, Hatathor, surrender!" Nefertiti said.

Suddenly, there were electromagnetic field surges, and Hatathor's protective shield vanished. His sleeve-device had some problem. Nefertiti fired at Hatathor, but he took cover behind the walls inside the first hall. Ehsis, Nefertiti and the royal guards were shooting, and scientists had taken the cover. Hatathor saw the orrery hologram, but he had no time to see closely on what Ehsis was doing.

The entire hall of stars was glowing with intense lights from charging sequences and laser shots. Al-Khidr was alone in Usekh-t Sehetch and listening to the laser shots, but could not move due to the charging sequence. The marking on the sphere had just turned on the fourth marking. It meant he still had to wait. A voice echoed in the hall: "The fourth cycle has completed."

During this havoc, Hatathor's foot hit Ehsis' briefcase, and it opened. A jump-sphere rolled up to Major

General Hatathor. He looked at the sphere, and the first thing that came to his mind was that it was a weapon. Hatathor put the sphere in his pocket to investigate it later.

Nefertiti noted that Hatathor had put a sphere in his pocket. "I should have kept the briefcase with me," she said to herself.

Ehsis was firing, but then her gun stopped functioning and she ran towards the second door at the end of the hall. Hatathor wanted to kill Ehsis, so he fired at her, but missed the shot. Hatathor thought Ehsis was running from her to save herself. He ran after her. "Close the door of the hall of stars!" Ehsis shouted.

Ehsis and some scientists entered the hall of stars, and they started pushing the door to close it. Nefertiti was outside and firing at Hatathor to stop him, but he took cover and managed to reach the door after descending the stairs. Nefertiti ran up the stairs to take direct aim. Hatathor pushed to open the door as Ehsis and some scientists were trying to close it to stop Hatathor to enter the hall. But it was huge, and Hatathor was no match for them. They fell on the floor.

As soon as Hatathor came into the hall, he was awestruck for a moment. He saw Al-Khidr for the first time, and the wormhole in the magnificent hall of stars, but he had not seen the wormhole before, so he was clueless about the formation. As he stared at the wormhole, Nefertiti got a sufficient chance to take one more aim from outside. She fired at Hatathor. Apparently, she missed Hatathor, as he moved from his position, but she could hear his laser gun drop. Hatathor become furious and moved towards the two scientists, killed them, and threw their bodies like a ball. Other scientists ran out of the hall to save themselves. Ehsis was watching in horror and stepping back. Nefertiti ran into the hall, and her gun stopped working. Al-Khidr became afraid that the maniac Hatathor would harm Nefertiti.

"Nefertiti!" Al-Khidr shouted in deep, fearful voice.

Ehsis ran around the granite floor to protect herself. She fell, and her foot was sprained. She was now in agony and could not move fast. Nefertiti ran towards Ehsis to save her. She took aim at Hatathor, but her gun was still not working. She kept the gun in her hands, even though it was not working, just in case she could use it like a hammer. Hatathor climbed onto the black floor and moved towards Ehsis, but noticed that Al-Khidr was much closer than Ehsis. He shouted at her, "Cursed, bitch, I will not let you live. But first. I will butcher this human in front of your eyes and then explode this whole cursed place!" The voice echoed, "The fifth cycle has completed."

Hatathor, who was now on the granite floor, took out his weapon, which transformed into a bident. He was in front of Al-Khidr, but at a distance of twenty feet. Al Khidr knew Hatathor would throw his bident at him, but he could not move. "Don't do this, please!" Ehsis said, crying.

# CHAPTER 24. THE HALL OF STARS

Nefertiti was shocked. She didn't know what to do, but she climbed the granite floor. Hatathor aimed at Al-Khidr and threw his bident. The bident was approaching Al-Khidr as Nefertiti and the others all shouted in fear. The death of Al-Khidr was imminent.

Nefertiti threw her gun, which hit the bident and deviated its path; it deflected a little and hit the sphere. Within seconds, the spilled exotic matter expanded and took the shape of a balloon like an infinity symbol, engulfing both Al-Khidr and Hatathor inside. It was static for a fraction of a second, like all frozen in time. A three-dimensional shockwave formed which threw both Nefertiti and Ehsis away.

The balloon swallowed both, and they went into the wormhole. When Ehsis and Nefertiti opened their eyes, Al-Khidr was not at the station. The entire hall was echoing with a warning: "Charging cycle interrupted!" "Al-Khidr, only God can save you now!" Ehsis said. Nefertiti couldn't believe it; she was exhausted, and collapsed on floor, unconscious. Ehsis looked around. Hatathor was also not there.

# Appendices

# Appendix A

# The Author's Note

Medieval Arab historians have mentioned that casing stones on the pyramids used to have images and cryptic writings written over them. Some Medieval Arabs and Coptic Christians could read those and they interpreted that it is written that the pyramids were made when the zodiac of cancer was tilted towards the north pole star of Sweeping Eagle (star Vega). This refers to the age of cancer. The zodiac of cancer was called stars of water by ancient Egyptians. The zodiacal age is determined on 20 March when the spring equinox occurs and the celestial equator intersects with the elliptic plane. We are nowadays going through the age of Pisces. An age lasts around 2,160 years. As there are 12 zodiac signs, therefore, for all ages of zodiac to occur 25,920 years are required. The last age of cancer occurred around the date around 7,500 BC. Before that it was in the year 33,420 BC when the age of cancer occurs. Interestingly, according to modern astronomy softwares, at the spring equinox of 33,420 BC with the dawn of an age of cancer, the star Vega is the brightest star near the north pole. Another information comes from the enigmatic zodiac, which was placed at the roof of the temple of Hathor, Dendera, Egypt. One cannot draw a complete view of the sky with precise information about the appearance of zodiac signs unless generations had recorded this information throughout 25,920 years. The traditional view of Egyptologists is that the Temple of Hathor at Dendera was constructed during Greco-Roman period. However, evidence contrary to this assumption is present in the temple itself. The zodiac cannot be made in the near past of 7,500 BC but must have been made at least on and before 33,420 BC in the age of cancer.

In the zodiac of Dendera, the zodiac signs are placed in a spiral with the innermost sign of the zodiac of cancer. Late John Anthony West said in one interview that Egyptian civilization is dated back to 34,000 year: "There is a chronological tablet, a fragmentary chronological papyrus, where the Egyptians talk about these long reigns of divine beings who first ruled Egypt, the gods. It goes on to describe another long period when Egypt was ruled by the Followers, or the Companions, of Horus, and the years are given. Put that all together and the Egyptians are telling us that their civilization began somewhere about 34,000 or 36,000 years ago. The tablets themselves are a bit destroyed, so you can't be very sure".

Some images carved on the walls of Dendera's crypt show that those stone slabs were installed as secret knowledge and must have been brought there from some other place, as different stones are used on the crypt's walls.

The star Vega in north and occurrence of zodiacal age of cancer had happened four times in the past: (i) around 7,500 BC, (ii) 33420 BC and (iii) 59,340 BC and (iv) 85,260 BC. This last date of 85,260 BC was suggested by writings over the casing stones as local astronomers estimated it as 72,000 before Jesus and this is the closest occurence I received through software Stellarium. This bring us to four complete cycles of 12 constellations of zodiac starting from 7,500 BC. The fifteenth century Arab historian Abu-Muhasin Taghri 1470 AD wrote: First the great Haram (pyramid) was constructed and over it the star positions were carved along with magical incantations... After that the western Haram (pyramid) was constructed and over the casing-stones images of instruments and weapons were painted. Afterwards, the Eastern Haram (pyramid) was constructed.

This reference shows that the zodiac of Dendera could be part of the Great Pyramid's outer casing before it was made hidden from public eyes by the priest of the Temple. At the centre of the zodiac, the sign of Anubis or dog is not referring to any known constellation, but it refers to the statue of Sphinx. The Sphinx was the name given by Greeks referring to the statue of a character mentioned in Greek mythology.

We know the Sphinx is aligned towards the East and it has a hole in its head. Most likely the hole is made for the observer to stand on the head of Sphinx and align his view with East and observe the age of the zodiac on the eve of spring equinox.

Egyptians themselves told us through the Dream Stele that Sphinx was buried in the ground and discovered by Pharaoh Thutmose after seeing the spot in his dream. Arab historian Al-Saffadi (died 1317 AD) has written in book Nadhat-ul-Al-Malik wal-Malook about Sphinx: And in front of the Pyramid there is a colossal statue which is called Bahwah (check-post or signpost). It was eroded by the Great Flood, but its head is still there till now and people now call it Abul-Houl (Father of Terror). Al-Masoudi 957 AH wrote in Akhbar Zaman: Suarid son of Felimon was the ruler over Egypt around 300 years before the Great Flood. He saw in a dream that cataclysm occurs at Earth and stars fell on the Earth.

In Giza, the pyramid of Khufu is in the north and the Pyramid of Menkaure is in the south. Sometimes when we read the medieval Arabic historians' books, we ignore the passages which describe these northern and southern pyramids. According to Suyuti, the name of the king who constructed the pyramids was Suarid son of Selhuoque son of Shiryaque. According to Al-Saffadi, the king Shonteer son of Selhuoque had ordered the construction of Pyramids before a great flood. According to Al-Masoudi in Akhbar-uz-Zaman: "Coptics narrated that on one of the pyramids an im-

age of a naked woman with horns was painted . . . .
Also, on another pyramid a yellow (white) naked man
with horns was painted."

Al-Maqrizi reported in Al-Mawaiz wal-Itebaar bi-
Zikr al-Khatat that Coptics wrote in their books: "The
northern spiritual pyramid (possibly pyramid of Kufu
or the great pyramid of Giza) depicted on it a young
naked man with yellow (white) skin tone and fangs in
his mouth. The southern spiritual pyramid (possibly
Pyramid of Menkaure) there depicted on it a naked
young woman with fangs in her mouth. And the colored spiritual pyramid (possibly Pyramid of Khafre)
has an old man image who was holding an incense
burner".

According to Ibn Nuqtah in book Al-Ifadatah wal
Itebaar: "Note that the casing stones on the Great
pyramid and Pyramid of Menkaure were white. However, the Pyramid of Khafre has red stones layer."

According to the book Kamaz- al-Darra by Al-
Dawadi the pre-flood priests interpreted two calamities
that would befall on Earth. Their time was given in
astrological ways like: "As soon as the zodiac of Leo
ended and zodiac of cancer starts a degree, a great
calamity would befall on Earth and that will be when
sun and moon enter the zodiac of Aries. . . . . after
some years of that event, another calamity would occur when a blast of fire would fall on Earth, which
very few will survive". This probably refers to a great
flood and the solar flare event in which the Egyptian
city of Tannis (Djanet also called Sn el-Hagar) was

destroyed. Tannis was discovered in 1939 by a French archaeologist named Pierre Montet. These references are interesting as more and more evidence is coming which now challenge the traditional views purported in the field of Egyptology.

According to Arab historians Al-Masudi (died 956 AD), Al-Hasan Al-Saffadi (died 1317 AD), Al-Maqr?z? (died 1442 AD), and Al-Suyuti (died 1505 AD), the pyramids had casing stones. In the year 1303 AD, an earthquake caused the falling of the casing stones which were used in the construction of roads and bridges. Thus, the true facade of pyramids and the inscriptions engraved on their walls were lost in time. There is no significant scientific evidence that a great flood occurred around 2000 or 3000 BC.

# About the Author

Nassim Odin holds PhD degree in Aerospace Engineering and he teaches engineering. He likes to read about the pyramids and ancient civilizations.
https://www.nassimodin.com

## The Sphere of Destiny
### — book blurb —

Al-Khidr, a medieval alchemist, is awestruck when he discovers a mysterious metallic sphere inside a pyramid. His curiosity catapults him through space and time to an alien planet called Lyra, where he learns that aliens consider Earth a cursed planet, and the pyramids on Earth were built by them. The queen wants to send the human back to Earth to bring a cure to the Mutmut disease. But a rebellion breaks out! With danger looming, a short time frame, and his life on the line, Al-Khidr has to do what he thinks is right and just. Find out more about his journey in this adrenaline-rushing book, the first in a sci-fi trilogy!

The Sphere Trilogy

Following QR code will lead you to the Sphere Trilogy page at
Amazon store.